HEROIC LOVE

Powerful, simple, tender, these four short novels—plus a short story—are the work of a fine American author. Edward Loomis's first novel, *End of a War*, was hailed enthusiastically by John Dos Passos, Wallace Stegner, Granville Hicks, and many others. Now, in these long tales of the West and of the war, he proves that he is that most welcome of writers: a first-rate storyteller who can be enjoyed by a wide audience.

The title story and "Mustangs" take place *today* in a town on the California-Nevada border, where civilization meets the desert mountains and raw nature. "Heroic Love" tells of a young rancher torn between love for an older man and that man's young wife. "Mustangs," set against a background of wild-horse hunts, is the story of a rebellious, free-spirited man trying to break loose from the shackles of the modern age.

The last three stories deal with World War II in a way that no other American has written about it. "Wounds" tells of an infantryman in Holland who finds that his standards of happiness and peace have altered drastically in combat. "Friendship" is about two comrades, a tough Jewish sergeant from Chicago and a young Southern private, and what the younger man learns from the older in the last days of the German war. "A Marriage" concerns two American soldiers and a German girl, bound together in affection and revenge.

These beautiful tales will be prized by those who want what readers have wanted through the ages: to be moved—by the moving experiences of other human beings.

B Y

Edward Loomis

HEROIC LOVE (1960)
THE CHARCOAL HORSE (1959)
END OF A WAR (1958)

HEROIC LOVE

HEROIC LOVE

Edward Loomis

Alfred·A·Knopf   *New York*

1 9 6 0

L. C. catalog card number: 60–9989

© Edward Loomis, 1960

The title story "Heroic Love" © Edward Loomis and
Nicholas Ray, 1960
"A Marriage" © HMH Publishing Company, Inc., 1960

THIS IS A BORZOI BOOK,
PUBLISHED BY ALFRED A. KNOPF, INC.

FIRST EDITION

"A Marriage" originally appeared in *Playboy* under the title of
"The Bargain."

❧ To Ruth ❧

CONTENTS

CONTENTS

PART I ❧ *The West*

HEROIC LOVE

I N A SMALL TOWN, a hero is a civic responsibility, for everyone to participate in, for everyone to enjoy. A hero receives attention because he belongs to the people in whose esteem his heroism lives, and this means that a hero has a hard life; this means that a hero will often be troubled by friendly people, and this will introduce the career of Orville Ledyard, once the hero of our town and now one of our most distinguished citizens.

The name of our town is Albo, and it is the county seat of a big county in eastern California; an old town for a western town, in a desert valley first seen by Americans when the great scout Jedediah Smith passed through on his way to the Humboldt River. There are two kinds of ruins. The first kind is abandoned ranches; the water which once kept them green now flows in an aqueduct to Los Angeles. It is cold water, which flows down from the Sierra Nevada range; in season, we are allowed to take fish from it before it reaches the reservoirs to the south. The other kind of ruins is invisible now; our big cottonwoods have roots which here and there coil among the ruins of the Albo Fort, which was built here by John C. Frémont more than a hundred years ago. The adobe has crumbled away, the pine logs have rotted.

But when Orville Ledyard was a hero, there were many ranches, and many cattle climbing to the mountains during the summer, and Albo was smaller than it is now by some thousand-odd souls. That was before the Great Depression, when Albo was a little back-country cattle and mining town of some fifteen hundred people; when the road to Los Angeles was still washboard gravel; when most of the travel through town moved on the narrow-gauge railroad that ran from Reno to Los Angeles; when I was younger, and less charitable, and more ready for adventure; when I was practicing law in two rooms above Jacob Alexander's Barber Shop; and when, in spite of twelve churches (not counting the Roman Catholic church for Mexicans and renegade Piutes), I had managed to get and hold a mistress, the young wife of a competitor—altogether, a time which seems long ago, the halcyon days of youth.

Albo then was not too far removed from the frontier, in time or in spirit, and its virtues were therefore frontier virtues, its heroes necessarily of the type who are happy in wild places. A hero in such a place at such a time would have to be a man of action, that is my point; and so Orville Ledyard was a man of action.

But of a rare type! True, he performed one remarkable act of disinterested physical heroism; it was written up in our paper, and even won a mention in the Carson City paper; I will tell you about it. And, beyond that, he was the kind of man who could be expected to perform such exploits; among other things, he was a cowboy. In that long-ago time when I first knew Orville Ledyard, there were cowboys in the valley, and of these cowboys Orville, then just twenty-one years of age, was acknowledged the best. He had been born an only child on a cattle ranch in Nevada, just over the line toward Gold Point, and raised there until he was twelve years old, when his father had bought another ranch just north of Albo; and there Orville was living alone when I first knew him, his mother and father having died of influenza when he was sixteen.

Single-handedly Orville had managed the ranch, and kept a good white-faced herd when that was not often done in that country. He was a California cowboy, a dally-roper whose saddle had to have a huge horn. He rode a center-fire saddle and occasionally used the spade bit, thus accepting without question the customs of his own country. But he was a good roper and a beautiful rider, who had started at the age of fifteen winning every roping event and both bucking-horse events in the September rodeos at Albo.

And he was a hunter. He knew the slopes and high valleys where deer wandered in the Sierra, and he knew the distant meadows of the Piute Mountains, where in stately arrogance and ease the bucks grew to such great age that sometimes the horns fell from their narrow skulls. Each year he trapped mustangs on the high plains of Nevada.

A good cowboy, a tough young man. Small wonder that when he acted bravely one cool night he became an accepted hero; the people of the town had been waiting for him to act so, to fix his image for us as the supple Achilles of our dust and sorrows. It was Orville, a boy of twenty-one, who crept into the darkness of the back rooms of Mason's Hardware Store in search of a Chinese cook of indeterminate age who had shot three people with a stolen revolver and thrown a meat cleaver at a Negro dishwasher. Orville acted while older men stood by wondering.

We were a small town then, so that I could not miss hearing the shooting. It was ten o'clock of a cool April night when I arrived in front of Mason's store, where a crowd of men and boys had gathered; and it was from this group, this twitching multitude, that Orville was detaching himself as I arrived. It was the right crowd for the occasion, a mean crowd, a trifling crowd, but with just enough good men in it to make Orville's isolation an honor to him. A homely legend was gathering itself in that windy street, an ominous but somehow handsome little scene deficient in light, like those darkness-filled photographs of the Civil War which have made Brady famous. I could sense that a thing was about to happen which would be remembered for a long time in our town.

"Old China boy's in the back rooms of Mason's!" someone shouted to me. "Already shot three and cleavered one!"

Orville stood clear of the others. He was wearing a heavy black serge suit, his only one, reserved for church and for his weekly visits to town, and a light tan Stetson of huge brim, so that as he stood there in the dusty road, in the uncertain light, he made a fine and striking figure. He stood with hands on hips, unmoving, as lights pattered across him.

"Where's the marshal?" I asked one of the men in the crowd, and was told that the marshal had gone to Tonopah after a Piute who had escaped from our jail. I knew that the county sheriff was not in town, and thus I knew that there was no authority for Orville to found his action on, and none of the moral support that sometimes comes with responsibility.

He was deliberate, but quick. He removed his coat, folded it, and set it on the ground at his feet; then he pulled his boots off and set them beside the coat; and then he started walking toward the front of Mason's store as the crowd grew quiet. In a ragged, gasping silence he paused at the door long

enough to unlock it; long enough for me to hear several people say that he would be all right until he started into the
back rooms; and then he disappeared into the darkness that
gaped behind the open door. He closed the door behind him.
I knew that he wanted no light behind him as he moved in,
and this was technical knowledge which comforted me; but
I knew also that I was seeing something seen by other men in
other lands before me—the gritty little fact that makes a core
for legends. Now, remembering, I think of Ulysses with his
charred stake poised above the huge, animal-like eye; of
Beowulf swimming downward into the mere.

Next came silence, which lasted a long time; long enough
for me to achieve a feeling of guilt for my idleness; long
enough for a few others in the crowd to do the same, and
show it by scuffing their boots unhappily, like saddened boys,
in the dust of the street. Now and then someone whispered;
but the crowd would have no noise. Fierce angry stares im-
paled the whisperers, and I began to sense a devotional quality in the assembly, the kind of emotional heat that comes
with worship.

Thus, noise from within the hardware store caused the release of intricate pressures in the crowd. There was a thick
and wavering sigh. The noise from the crowd stopped—it
had been mere noise, a racket—and the crowd moved forward a little until the leaders, aware of what might happen,
shamefacedly stopped. I felt unhappy then, and I could sense
that others felt so.

And then Orville appeared at the door he had entered, half
carrying, half dragging the small figure of a man—the Chinaman, his queue disordered. Instantly the crowd raced forward, and someone shouted something at the Chinaman;
someone else called, clearly: "Lynch the Chink son-of-a-
bitch!"

Only two or three such cries, as I remember; not more, because most of the men in the crowd were waiting to take instruction from Orville; but those cries of rage completed the occasion. They represented human wickedness there in the dusty street, in the cool air, and thus they provided Orville with something to bear against. He represented human goodness in the midst of action—what is called heroism, in fact; and now the cries of rage gave his quality a chance to be seen.

He raised his left hand; his right was holding the Chinaman by the shoulder. He held his left hand steady and spoke sharply.

"Stand back!" he said. "Stand back!"

Slowly the crowd caught its movement in its own entanglements. The leaders stopped, and then the crowd stopped.

"That's better," Orville said. "Now, listen here. I'm going to tell it just the once. This man is going to get his trial! Anyone bothers this man before he has his trial will have to reckon with me. Right now, here, I stand for law and order, gentlemen!"

That was the end of the scene. Orville regained his coat and boots, which were brought to him by admiring boys, and then took the Chinaman to the town jail and stayed there with him until the crowd broke up. Altogether, a good job of work for a young man, and certainly enough to make a hero out of him, at least in our town. People met on the streets and told one another the story, agreeing that it was a lucky thing for the town's future to have Orville in it. When, after the trial some three months later, the Chinaman was taken away to be executed, Orville's deed was gratefully remembered, and it was agreed that his young presence refined the town's moral tone.

So much for rude action. Now it is my duty to claim that

Orville was a man of mind; a true statement, it is, and I will
stand by it. He was fortunate in his education, which was
good for him in a way that few educations can be good these
days, for it helped make him a better man. His father, a Mis-
sourian, taught him Latin and a love of reading, and his
mother encouraged him. He studied hard at his schools and
performed well, but the private lessons in his home and much
reading had the greatest effect in forming his mind. By the
time he was sixteen, he told me once, he had already read
Gibbon, Macaulay, and Hume. These works must have
helped him learn that gravity of manner which later won
him such favor with the town's ladies. He read Shakespeare,
of course, and of fiction he read the standard authors of the
nineteenth century, Dickens, Scott, Thackeray, and a few
of the humorists. Long afterward he could still laugh at
Surtees. And naturally he read widely in the normal Latin
authors. He could chant Virgil indefinitely, and knew Per-
sius; he quoted Tacitus, whom he admired as the strongest
writer of the Silver Age, and once he recited for me the
closing passage of the *Agricola,* causing himself to be near
tears at the end.

A rare type, as I have said. But neither his skill as a cowboy
nor his learning would have astounded me if he had not so
harmoniously possessed them. He was no double man; his
was a single nature, an honest progression of acts accomplished with the precision due them. His work gave him hard
hands, with calluses polished into the palms by the hard
lariat ropes he used. His work kept him outside during the
day, darkening his face and hardening his body, so that in appearance, during the day, he looked the medium-sized young
cowboy that he was; just as by night, when he sat bent heavily upon books, he looked the young student in the first daze
of learning. But he was something more than cowboy or

student or any mere succession of these restricting states: he was that rarity, a lucky man, born to health and vigor, born with the gifts of mind, and trained young to respect his sense of what was right; which was a good, reasonably strong sense, about as sturdy as a young man has a right to expect.

As he told me once, after the incident of the Chinaman, "When a man knows he should do something, then it's worth his soul not to do it, and that's all there is to it. And so I try to do the things I know I should do."

And his respect for the right, in part an inheritance from his parents, in part a victory won from his studies, gave a most pleasing outline to his capabilities. He had a country face, one of those Texas or Arizona faces, ruddy and clean-lined, with chapped lips and sunburnt cheekbones, so that it took some imagination to comprehend his quality, but I was able to do it. It was natural that I should recognize his quality as soon as I discovered his range. Well I remember my surprise at finding a cowboy who read Tacitus—at finding such a man in such a dusty, sweaty, cattle-stinking place.

And I remember well that in Orville Ledyard as he was when I first knew him, I recognized a genuine, if limited, possibility of American greatness. A homely figure, he was; a rustic, even antic gait, and a rough conversation, but as fine a prospect as any I ever met with. Americans are optimists; I'm American, and so why not believe that Orville's gifts would prosper? He caused me to think of our great men; not of the New Englanders, of course, but of the Virginians and Kentuckians, of the wry long-headed men from Ohio and Illinois, doughty men of fine spirit; and of other great men, for Orville's grace was not provincial.

He had such fine brown eyes, our Orville of the heroic period! Ingenuous eyes, but radiant with guile; he meant no harm, he even meant well, but he comprehended most of our failings; he confronted his world, that motley world—of desert, mountains, cattle, and a dusty town, and of the sonorities of Silver Age Latin flooding his mind in the cold desert nights—with the clear intention of taking what he needed, what was best for him to take. It was, then, a measure of his innocence, of his honesty, that he was also prepared to heed his sense of what was right; drawn tense between intelligence and innocence he had his being in those happy days.

It was no surprise that he should have decided, some time before I knew him, to take up the law, for that was the profession above all others available to him which seemed to offer a ground for heroic achievement. So it has been, in America; and certainly I sometimes regarded Orville as a boy who might become president. Even at twenty-one he had a good share of the lofty port and presence needed for the task. Like Tom Sawyer in that melancholy epigram, he was a boy who could go far if he escaped hanging. Of course Orville was already past the college age as he made his preparations. He was saving money earned by the ranch, and that was a slow and difficult process, but he was not at all fainthearted, and he had encouragement from my worthy competitor in Albo and my senior, Cassius Martin.

That was a man named for the Last of the Romans, and well named, for he was a severe, high-scrupled man, and Cassius could well meet Orville and instruct him, for Cassius controlled an elegant Latinity and a fine speaking voice. He was an impressive man, and kind in his way, respected and well liked in our town.

But the fact that Orville came to the law, came late, and through the kindness of Cassius Martin, through advice which confirmed a generalized paternalism, a fact which was in no real sense an accident, did finally involve the accidental, and in a most banal fashion: through the wife of Cassius, a handsome girl named Rose, some twenty years younger than Cassius. She was a decent girl, I believe. I respect her even now, and at that long-ago time I sometimes thought I loved her, and was intermittently sure of it during the more than two years when she served as my mistress.

For she was indeed my mistress. With her I had dishonored most of the dark corners of Cassius's house, and his bed as well; been happy in night-time rambles, and gone singing home on many cold dark mornings. A warm-natured girl she was, ever froward, ever constant in her favors to me; and so the unhappy accident which she meant for Orville Ledyard was truly startling, and remains so in memory. I had a privileged position, as you can see. I had access to Orville as well as to Cassius, and I knew Rose. I could view that little cluster of human beings, the middle-aged man, the young wife, and the young man, as none of them could view the others, for no one was watching me. I was there, at the heart of the tempest, like that vacuum, that emptied air, which is the center of a hurricane. And of course what I saw was that Orville had fallen in love with Rose and desired her, and that Rose, my own Rose whom I sometimes loved, responded as any woman might respond to a man like Orville; and I did not miss the great fact in this tempest, which was that Orville could not bring himself to betray his benefactor.

What other decision could such a man make? Better for him perhaps, as things turned out, and better for most heroes in the same unhappy fix, if he had made some coarse assault and argued with his conscience later. Suppose he had taken her from me and held her awhile; could Cassius have been the poorer? But then Orville did not know that he would have to take poor Rose from me, and so he felt anguish whenever Cassius spoke to him kindly, and almost visibly quivered sometimes when Rose was near.

The situation had developed quite naturally from Orville's great deed accomplished upon the Chinaman. At that time he was reading with Cassius in Latin literature and in the law, as a preparation for his entry into college, which was scheduled for sometime a year or so later. As it happened, he had been coming from one of his sessions with Cassius on the night the Chinaman ran wild. At the same time, or epoch, in our lives, Rose had already been my mistress for almost a year and a half, and we were both reasonably happy, though hardly very calm, in our arrangements. We were the kind of lovers who speak rather more often of making love than of being in it. We came together with a friendly but never gentle heat.

As to the secret of our arrangement, I would say that it was the normal secret of such arrangements. Rose was tired of her husband, Cassius; tired of his absorption in his work, in his Latin, in his wide and cheerful reading; and unhappy without knowing the reason for it because she had no child. A new man could please her merely by being new. I, of course, was struggling along young and unattached, with normal instincts and only normal powers of control. In those days any opportunity could be my undoing, and Rose was a pretty girl who was willing to be an opportunity. Thus we were quite normal about our perfidy; we were dark with it in the places where anybody would in time be dark, stained in the will and sensibility.

Finally, to complete this image, I believe that Orville by this time already admired Rose. There was no compelling reason why he should not. She was a good-looking dark-haired woman—not the prettiest in town, and certainly no rarity even there, but satisfactory. She was, in appearance, about equally suited to a church choir in a small town and to city hotels, and this says something about her. She had the kind of authority that enables a woman to be at ease with waiters, and to show anger without losing poise; the kind of authority that often goes with a trimmed and careful hardness of character; and so she was a little hard, in her intelligent way. She was a town girl who had once been a country girl and who could become a city girl with ease. Handsome but firm, that was her type. Her special attraction of face was a delicacy of bone at cheek and temple, so that her skin was marvelously smooth at those places.

In figure she had another kind of authority. She had a full but somehow disciplined and athletic body, and that body in its movements could have a sinewy elegance—but only when she wished it to, when she had a cause to press. She could do what she liked with that little rump, that rising breast.

And Rose had, I must confess, a faintly wanton look. A man staring at her might well believe she promised potent delights. It was only a matter, for me, of completing a circle of emotional logic to guess the impression she must have made on Orville when later, in addition to showing herself to him, she allowed him to understand that she loved him, that he could have for himself those charms which so dismayed him. How his heart must have thumped for her then—and his neck reddened! It saddens me to think about his sufferings afterward.

Thus, being smitten early, perhaps at the instance of a light fit of flirting on the part of Rose, but not showing it, Orville was especially vulnerable when Rose began a determined attack. This is a guess, of course, but, if true, it would explain the suddenness of the kindling when finally that kindling happened; a kindling which came, I know, largely by Rose's choosing and, most unhappily, by my original folly.

For it was I, of course, who told Rose about Orville's act of heroism. Some two or three nights after it, Cassius being

out of town on an errand to Carson City, I arrived at the
back door of the Martin house and was admitted warmly, by
Rose, to the house and to the favors I had come seeking.
Later, while we lay quietly in the big fourposter bed upstairs, it seemed amusing to tell Rose about Orville's bravery.

It was a big frame house, painted white, with tall narrow
windows, steep roofs, and scrollwork at the eaves; a fact
about the house was that it could have that absurd scrollwork and still retain its look of right-angled severity. There
was a porch on the east face of the house, and on the porch a
small glass-topped table, a swing, and two rocking chairs—a
Middle Western house, it was, of the kind you can still see in
places like Topeka and Des Moines; on summer evenings
there will be a man in shirt sleeves in the front yard, watering
the lawn.

In such a house I felt like a stranger, a far-wanderer. It was
a good sober house, with a dozen rooms in it, but the rooms
had gone hollow on that husbandless night. Any little sound
could have a booming echo in that emptiness; small sounds
grew big a little while after they happened. There was a
wind, and it did things to shutters, and to the big cottonwoods outside, which were just coming green again; and
there was about half a moon, which gave us a silver light for
our pleasures, and gave to Rose's face, where it lay on the
pillow, a glaze of light which almost made her look pure. I
remember watching her face in that somber chilly light as I
talked, and thinking that the face must be cold because of the
coldness of the light; and so I reached out and touched her
cheek and temple, and found the skin oily and hot to my
touch, as if with lust, or love.

But I talked on, until I was ready to touch her again, this
time for my pleasure, and gave her a full accounting of Orville's new-won greatness; but when I touched her, she

turned away, claiming fatigue. When I tried again later, she claimed sleepiness, saying in a dim voice that she had been unable to rest the night before and the night before that. Thus she delivered an intimation of a meaning, and the meaning was not lost on me. She did not do it again for a long time, but I understood then, and more clearly later, what had happened.

That night I lost her, such was the fact, though the event of loss did not for some time show itself. As Walter Scott might have said, I lost her heart—her poor dislocated heart, so swelling with love. Some part of her stained soul I kept, and have with me still, in honorable memory of our lechery, but her I lost, the woman to give pleasure and comfort I lost that night, through my own folly, to the image of a young man which I had so corrected for her yearnings that she could not resist it.

Altogether, I see now, it makes a bill of some size and consequence against Rose; and yet she was not quite that kind of girl. I had given her eyes with which to see Orville, whom before she had never really noticed because he was only a cowboy who came sometimes to take up Cassius's time with his desire for education; and so she saw him, and confirmed the image I had given her. Favor her with credit, I say. She was impressed by a man; she did not love an emptiness.

How Cassius ever missed her new inclination I could not then understand. True, she did not send me away or lock her doors against me—chiefly, I believe, because she feared retaliation—and her commitment to me may have kept her spirits and behavior filled out to a properly decent outline; but to my eye she seemed openly in love with Orville, and unable to avoid showing it when he was near.

I remember one night a week or so after my telling Orville's story to Rose. I had gone to the Martin house to find

Rose and arrange a meeting for later in the week; ostensibly
I had come for conversation with Cassius about law and politics. I found Orville there, in the room which Cassius had
taught Rose to call the parlor, with Rose and Cassius both
present. Cassius and Orville each had a book—a Latin text, I
forget the author—and it was clear that this was not a regular thing. Cassius was a little put out, ill at ease. Orville was
red in the face, and somehow both uncomfortable and intensely happy.

It was one of those arrangements of people which a new-
comer can sometimes read like a newspaper headline.

"Rose thinks she can learn Latin by listening to us," Cassius
said harshly. "You see she's here. And yet I can no more get
her interested in the Latin grammar . . ." Cassius let his sen-
tence go and shook his head.

"I think hearing the Latin may give me an interest," Rose
said. "It's a new idea of mine. I like to hear men's voices."

Orville said nothing at all, but I knew that he understood
very well what Rose had come seeking. And so I was in no
position to stay long; it was apparent that Rose would not be
ready to make arrangements for meeting me. I left, and it is
worth noting how I felt on that occasion; it is revealing, of
course, and in a way flattering to me. I was, naturally, unhappy to have proof that Rose had—in her intentions, anyway—forsaken me. I felt as any young man would feel then.
The platitude about it would include, as terms, both sorrow
and anger. Also I was lustful; that which I could not have,
seemed gorgeous to me. So much is natural; what is hardly
natural is this: that I worried about my successful rival, that
I feared he might damage his noble prospects. This feeling as
I remember it can still please me, for it implies an image of
myself which has certain graceful extensions; but, more important, this feeling has meaning with respect to Orville. Not

every man would concern me so. You are to understand that
Orville was a man who caused his friends to conceive unusual
responsibilities.

Rose, of course, had a different view of Orville as a responsibility. She had let him know the state of her feelings,
she had shown her love, and now she was waiting to be taken.
I believe she understood her responsibility to Orville to include one duty, that she be available, and no more. At the
same time, she did not exclude me, partly because she was
afraid that I might act jealously, and partly because she was
cautious, so that she was unwilling to give up present comforts to future possibilities. Rose at all times dealt in facts,
and so she slept with me now and then while she waited for
Orville to make up his mind.

She waited in vain, however. Orville would not betray
Cassius, though he suffered greatly, and thus a most difficult
and unhappy relation came to exist, a relation which I could
see in all its fullness. Rose suffered sometimes from anger,
and low spirits, and disgust, and could not avoid showing
these emotions as she gave herself away in the beds we shared,
and in the hay of a neighbor's barn. She was no longer completely mine, and sometimes I could sense what emotion or
thought was dispossessing me.

Orville, after a time, got in the habit of visiting me at my
office; thus I could see his unhappy state. He grew pale, in
spite of his outdoor work. He lost weight, and otherwise
languished, and, so Cassius told me, he lost interest in his
Latin and his law, enough so that Cassius had become concerned.

One afternoon at the Courthouse, Cassius asked me to see
if I could find out what was bothering Orville.

"It's a good boy and a fine mind," Cassius said in his
straightforward fashion. "I wouldn't want to see him throw

himself away. Look into it, will you? In my position it's a little hard . . ."

It was not long before Orville was speaking to me in long parables, extended hypothetical examples, about the nature of Love, and about its causes, consequences, and cures; and so, it seemed to me, the difficult and unhappy relation reached its first climax there in my office. It is hardly strange that I was embarrassed and unhappy. That I responded coarsely, with references to Burton's *Anatomy of Melancholy*, with its shrewd and intricate remedies for Heroical Love! I spoke to Orville about the remedy of cucumber and hellebore, taken internally; and about the remedy of Much Venerie; and about that final remedy called Giving in; and forced the unhappy young man to laugh with me, because I knew he would never admit that he was the sufferer who lingered unhappily and staggered from Love's darts behind that false front of hypothesis.

And so it went. I could read in Rose's behavior and in Orville's conversation the progress of the affair. I could know the progressive intensity of the private conversations which Rose arranged, which caused Rose such bewilderment, which caused in Orville so much white-lipped suffering.

Of this stage of affairs it is hardly necessary to speak at length. It is true, perhaps, that Orville might not have been so badly hurt had he been more experienced with women, but he was as he was. He had known a girl or two at rodeo time, I suppose; not more; not enough to acquire knowledge, and nowhere near enough to enable him to cope with a determined lust like that of Rose, and the kind of love which Rose could find in lust. Orville, at this stage, was defenseless, unable to avoid suffering. His great gifts were as nothing to him, though, as he once confessed to me, he had taken to reading Plutarch's *Morals*, in English translation, in an attempt to find relief. Quite simply, Orville was confronted with impossibilities. He could not remain himself and betray his friend Cassius; and he was moving in an atmosphere of suffering which might soon dissolve him.

On one memorable night I saw Orville in the deeps of this harrowing love. There had been stories that he had not been taking care of his stock as he should. Neighbors had heard the milk cows bellowing late at night, for example, and one of his bulls had been roaming loose for three days. The stories came to me after a time, and it seemed wise one night to pay Orville a visit to see how he was faring. I had hopes of learning something; and I learned.

I found him drunk on the big bed in which he had been begotten, in which he had been born, in which he slept now, since his parents' death. A big plain bed of dark-stained walnut, it was, an heirloom from Missouri; it had a white cotton coverlet. He was fully dressed, down to his boots. His big Stetson was propped over his face in such a way as to cover his face, and he was very drunk, besotted, in fact, consciousness almost gone. When I reached him, he was gasping. It had been a great effort for him to speak loud enough to call me into the house.

Naturally, I was at a loss for a time, and finally found no better plan than to make coffee. This I did, over his protests, and he came around enough to talk to me, very plainly this time, without any hypotheses, without false fronts of any kind, though without using names; and this was, I believe, the turning point of his unhappy relation with my poor Rose. It seemed so at the time. Looked at from the present, from this dim and much-corroded eminence in time, it seems clearly so. It was the last hours of the original Orville.

He asked me right away whether I knew a way to achieve sleep when a man is sick for love. Such were his words, and they made me uneasy in that high-ceilinged room. It was such a room as dignified Kansas farmers and their wives would have for sleeping and loving, in a house that might have been transplanted from the Middle West: hardly the place to speak about a man who was sick for love! And it was plain that Orville was a good housekeeper. The house was clean, and smelled clean, as white frame Gothic houses should smell. His mother's curtains hung in the windows, and this was a touching sight which caused me to remember Orville's innocence and made me sad. Plainly, Orville was maintaining his mother's ways, in honor of her memory.

But at that moment Orville was alarmed by love. "The first thing I need is a cure for insomnia," he said. "Would you believe it? I've not slept for three days now, except for an hour I got yesterday afternoon under the pines in the yard. True. One hour of sleep in three days. What's a man to do?"

I felt guilty about the coffee I had made him drink, and said so. I was struggling with Orville's plight. I was trying to believe in it.

"Coffee won't wake me, and won't put me to sleep. I won't sleep tonight either, I know it." Then he explained his troubles, in detail, with a half-drunken eloquence which I admired; but saying the usual things, of course, the normal line through ancient sentences.

"—I've seen bulls in this fix, plenty of 'em. They'll groan, and beller, and wear a ditch alongside a fence, and grow poor, grow mighty poor while they're doing it—even grow sad, sometimes, I think! I've seen 'em sad—they have ways of showing sorrow. But I've never had much feeling for 'em, somehow. I guess I've been wanting in sympathy, and it hurts my feelings to learn that. I've lost weight. Fifteen pounds it is now. And I've lost my color, and most of my strength, seems like. I haven't cared for Latin in over a month now, and I'd never have believed that that could happen to me. How in the world am I ever going to get any sleep?"

A little of this went a long way with me, and I began to believe in his plight. I felt a duty. The duty came down on me like a nightfall, and so I said the things I was able to say, the immemorial and immemorially ineffective propositions.

"Why bother so about a woman?" I asked him; and he shook his head to indicate that it was not in his power to change his yearnings.

"Why does the bull bother?" he said. "She told me she loves me. She breathes fast when she tells me, and she keeps the lights low. Once she even began to sweat a little, over the right temple. She did it, I swear, and, oh, it was fetching! Why can't you believe that? Didn't it ever happen to you?"

Then I asked him why he did not simply give in and take her, and then do what he could afterward. "She's just a woman!" I said, while I felt much more than I spoke. "Take her. She's been asking for it! And remember, she'll hate you if you don't, mark my words, and she'll make you suffer for it. Why let a woman tear you apart? Why let a mere woman bother you?"

"Everything bothers me," he said then, with dignity, "or matters some way. I guess that's it. And of course I can't bring myself to hurt a friend. Can't do that. That's where the trouble lies. That's where, I'm afraid."

After a time I repeated myself, hoping that mere weight of words might have an effect; but then I gave up and left him, after first helping him to find the other bottle of whisky he had brought home with him. The next morning the milk cows bellowed again, far into the morning, and once again at night, so that the neighbors became almost angry with Orville; and it went so for almost a week, getting worse each

day, until the neighbors began to speak of getting the town
marshal out to speak to Orville. Throughout this period I
was in troubled mind, and it was my conviction that something was about to happen.

What could a man do who was placed as Orville was
placed, confronted so tangibly with formidable impossibilities? Poor Orville, he was truly caught. But it is true, alas,
that any man will act, finally, when so pressed, and thus discover change—as Orville acted and discovered change. So
it is that changes happen, I suppose; and who is to say that a
man who suffers should not be allowed to find his way out of
suffering? It would go hard with me to forbid the lost to try
to find themselves.

What Orville did, however, was a surprise to me, and to
others, though it was signaled by an event which seemed a
happy one. On a Sunday morning a week or ten days after
my talk with him Orville appeared bright and early at his
barn to tend to his milk cows, on time at this chore for the
first time in several weeks. He whistled and sang, so the story
went, and the neighbors felt called upon to spread the good
word as quickly as possible, so that I heard it that morning at
my breakfast in the town restaurant. It was not until later,
however, that the reasons for Orville's cheerfulness came
out, and then there was some question about Orville's right
to be cheerful. It developed after a time, and through the
subtle digestive powers of town gossip, that Orville had a
little disgraced himself on the Saturday night preceding his
happy Sunday morning; disgraced himself with a certain Elvira Almayer, in a haymow that belonged to Elvira's father,
but, after the fashion of young men, gone home happy afterward.

At the time I was amused and not quite convinced. A little
later, however, I had reason to lose my amusement, as it be-

came clear to me what course Orville had at last taken out of his troubles. For I believed that I had suggested that course to Orville, half jokingly but precisely; at least, I hurt myself with that allegation. To be brief, it became clear within the space of a month or six weeks after the affair of Elvira that Orville had had recourse to the most violent of Burton's remedies. He had plunged himself into Much Venerie; he had become a successful lover of young girls in our town, even of a few virgins, and in fact he had become for his contemporaries an amatory hero. Perhaps you can understand how easy it was for him: he was good enough looking, by town standards; he was a good cowboy, respected for his exploits with horses, ropes, wild cattle; he was an accepted hero, the conqueror of the Chinaman; and, most important, he was a man of intelligence and great energy who needed only the exercise to learn device and stratagem in the wars of love.

As far as I know, the only piece of equipment he bought was a buggy, and it is a gauge of our town's civilization in the twenties that Orville could still be fashionable in one. He was both fashionable and rakish. He had a little bay mare that he broke to the harness, and he kept her in fine condition. His harness had a fine glow to its leather, and a satisfyingly mild tinkling to its hardware. The buggy itself was a gleaming thing.

Gleaming but, after a time, also infamous. There had always been a faint swagger of lordliness to Orville's ways; he walked high, and sometimes made sharp fun of fools. It was possible for him to receive a public favor with complete indifference if he disliked the giver, and he could court trouble and show temper, but all this seemed right and proper, or at least permissible, in him as he had been. Not with his buggy, however. With his buggy he became a little hard to take. What had been acceptable as fine intellectual qualities or

high spirits in Orville's walks through town became something else when Orville was whipping his mare down the
main street; when he pulled up arrogantly to ask a girl to ride
with him. It was not long before the girls of the town understood what the buggy meant to them. It became known that
a girl's honor rode, for better or worse, right beside her when
she accepted a ride in that buggy.

It seems childish now, all that parade; but Orville had
style. He could pop that buggy whip in a way to make small
boys weep with envy and make their elder brothers turn
away unhappily. He could make his mare pace, canter, and
walk at the most imperceptible commands. He had buggy
and mare quite at his mercy. Some of the most pleasing
images I carry now in memory are from the days of Orville's
buggy, and are images of it. I remember the swanky,
leather-and-horse smell of his arrival at an Elks' picnic with a
pretty blonde girl whose family had just moved to town. I
remember him in his cowboy uniform, seeing him leave a
black-haired girl, the daughter of the town's only dentist,
in the buggy behind the bucking chutes at the rodeo in the
fall; leave her, make his way through the corrals, get down
on a horse and come out in a fine ride on a wild bucker to
win first prize for the day; and then gravely walk back to
the buggy and drive out of the rodeo grounds, headed in the
direction of Jackson's Grove.

That sort of thing; you can see how it might go. There
was never any question about Orville's achievements, whatever they might be! He had a firm way of doing a job that
helped people remember who had done it. Girls who had
once enjoyed his favor rarely complained about him afterward. Most of them admitted freely that they still considered
Orville a "good friend"; sometimes a girl even smiled when
she said this, and then it was possible to guess with some jus-

tification that Orville had made a midnight call recently. In the space of six or seven months after the beginning of Orville's campaign it was generally agreed—among the young men, who knew a little, among the girls, who knew more, and among the expert gossips, who knew everything that really mattered—that Orville had conquered and otherwise had his will of eleven different girls, all young, all pretty, none of them of the easily vulnerable, too warmhearted kind. Naturally, it was alleged that some of these were virgins, and that two or three were pregnant as a result of Orville's labors.

Burton's remedy with a vengeance! It is worth mentioning that Orville admitted to me once, when we were both coming out of the county library, that he had indeed been thinking of Burton when he undertook his scheme. "It was do something or die of it," he said. "By God, it was. And so I did something. I'll keep on doing it until I don't need it, and do it right."

It then occurred to me to ask whether he thought it was paying too much for the whistle—something clumsy of that sort, at any rate, and Orville did not much respect it. "To take a dozen women to get away from one, that doesn't sound very economical to me," I said. "I'm not trying to tell you what to do, Orville!"

He answered me very soberly. "I made my choice," he said. "I haven't bothered any married women, and so now I'll do what I set out to do, and do everything that's supposed to be done. If a job's worth doing, it's worth doing well, isn't it?"

A comic revenge upon an unkind world, it was, and now and then I so regarded it; but, like any revenge, bound to have consequences. Given the situation, I knew what they would be, and it was a cause of pain that I was able to see my forebodings embodied, day by day, in a thickening chronicle of facts. It was enough to make a moralist out of me—and did, in fact, after a time, when I had leisure to inspect the facts which had risen before me.

First of all, there were quarrels, unavoidably, with maddened fathers and with unlucky suitors. Orville avoided none of these. It became known very quickly that Orville was more than willing to fight anybody over the love of any young girl. It was plain in the bloodstained and battered look of his face and hands on too many occasions that he would compete with any father, with any lover. And since Orville was tough enough to win most of his fights, and stubborn enough to deny the fruits of victory when he lost, so that he returned again and again to places where he had been beaten, he caused many young men and many fathers to despair. But despair makes hate, and it was not long before Orville was well hated—a consequence I could not look at with any comfort.

Next, there were indeed two pregnancies which Orville could have caused. It was rumored that Orville sold cattle to pay for the services of doctors in faraway cities; certainly his herd was diminishing noticeably. It began to be thought in the town that Orville was hardhearted, or that he wore an armor against virtuous thoughts, and this too caused hatred. I knew, of course, that Orville was in a way indulging a too great love of virtue in his scheme of conquests, that he was attempting to avoid hurting his friend Cassius; but this was meek, small knowledge even in me as I confronted Orville's consequences; and no one else in the world knew it, so that it was quite without any helpful consequences of its own.

And then there was the matter of Orville's heroism, which was, for the town, chiefly a fact which existed in the collective mind of the town. I was there; it was possible for me to see the comic workings of the town's mind as that mind asked itself unpleasant questions. Was Orville's new effort a heroic effort? Was it quite the thing to be expected of a recognized hero? Was it quite the proper thing to follow the conquest of the Chinaman? Slowly the answers got themselves made. Slowly the town's mind came round to a decision. Strangely, in spite of the enmities which Orville had by that time built up, the decision was a gentle and fair one, and I was forced to share in it. The decision was disappointment —in Orville himself, in what he had made of himself, in the way he had gone on from his great triumph; and the disappointment came with feelings of sadness.

A strange kind of justice! It was not long before I understood that Orville acquiesced in the town's decision; and his own disappointment appeared first as a kind of intellectual hesitation. He became a little hard to talk to.

Finally, of course, there was the reaction of Rose, my Rose and Cassius's Rose. This I had foreseen; it gave me a muted pleasure to see how accurately. Rose very quickly came around to hating Orville. At about the time Orville was attempting his third conquest—of a girl Rose knew, a soprano in the Methodist church choir which Rose frequented as a contralto—Rose required Cassius to forbid Orville the house. She announced her grounds clearly: that Orville was a disgrace, a ruined young man, not fit for decent company. She was very firm. Cassius was so upset that he came to me with the story and asked me to arrange with Orville for law-and-Latin meetings in my office. This I did, but of course in a little while word of the arrangement reached Rose. I could then tell from Cassius's face that she was making him smart for it. And of course I had direct ways of discovering Rose's feelings.

Naturally, she did not speak to me about Orville, for Rose
was never brazen, but she became suddenly warmer to me as
she became cooler to Orville. That was an intense time in my
life. We became less friendly and more passionate, and thus I
was able to learn something about the nature of lust, about
the nature of love. We had such fierce and sweaty struggles
as no man could forget, and it disturbs me yet that I could
sense in Rose's fury a desire to cuckold poor Orville in some
final way. Sometimes, nowadays, I wonder how I knew that
savage little fact which beat away there at the heart of our
lust; but I knew. One knows. It takes only a warning to
waken perception, and I had had plenty of warnings from
Rose. It was often my idea of her that she could be comfortable with a revenge.

Thus, for the time being, Rose; but it was Cassius who suffered more painfully than anyone else in town because of
Orville's wild lecheries. His sorrow, I suppose, was the most
grievous consequence of Orville's actions, and it exposed
ranges of feeling in him which I could never have guessed at.
During one of the law-and-Latin meetings in my office, I
remember, Cassius appeared almost half an hour early,
clearly in order to speak to me; he began speaking immediately after he arrived. Standing there in my office—which
was also my living room when I was off duty—he was a tall
heavy figure in his black suit, bald, with a tough middle-aged
face and a deep, chest-resounding voice. All in all, not the
kind of man I would expect to confess despair.

"There's something I want to do," he said. "But I don't
know what it is. I can't seem to find it. The town is getting
aroused, man. Look at my poor Rose, how she carries on!
By God, something will have to be done, that's all there is to
it. We'll have to find something and do it."

I said I agreed, but that I was bewildered, and that it might be foolish to talk to Orville. "You can't talk to a tom-cat," I said. "Any more than to a wildcat."

"It's that he's such a fine boy!" Cassius said. "It's the best and smartest boy that ever I knew, and I love him like a son. Can't you see how it makes me feel to see him fall so far short of himself? God damn those willing little girls!"

He was in a rage; he was also near to tears, and so he stood before me a fine image of anger contending with sorrow. So might Orestes once have stood after hearing about Aegisthus, so Hamlet before the ghost; and it was a quality he had there in my office, in that dim and shrouded place, that he seemed almost an image of uncorrupted youth; and thus I learned something about him. I learned that he had not yet given in to time and the world. He remained, in some deep part of him, the virtuous young man he had once been, remained even a little naïve, and this was a comfort to me. His head had grown bald, his voice rough with whisky and cigars, but some essential part of his goodness had resisted change. Extravagant language, almost, for discussing a man who could not even keep his wife away from young men, but true language; that was the way I found him.

"I'm going to be drunk," he said. "I swear to God I'm going to be drunk for the first time since the war. I can't stand it, I tell you."

For a while I was afraid that he might not conduct himself properly during the meeting with Orville; but of course he did conduct himself properly, at great cost, with great pain, but with dignity and politeness, and with that assurance that can come only to a good man in difficult chances. I came to admire him that night, and it was a discovery. Surprise and wonder happened to me—to a mind made clear by shock; and a little later there were consequences.

It was a small consequence, however, that I was able to make from it; a costly one to me but really helpful to no one else. A week or so later I gave up Rose, or began to. I had to discover what I already knew, that Rose was not easily got rid of, but I began my attempt, and took my beating, and had a kind of success after a time.

Before that success, however, and after a campaign of some ten or eleven months, Orville gave up his career as a lover of young girls. He sold his buggy and the buggy's harness; the mare went back under the saddle; and the news of these events spread rapidly, traveling in stories which often involved laughter. Once again Orville resumed his old habit of coming to town only once a week, for his law-and-Latin meeting with Cassius. He was polite to the girls he knew, but formal—he treated them like cousins from faraway towns.

Naturally, there was a sensation in the town, as there always must be when a rake reforms. At first there was distrust. Young men and a few fathers were heard to say that Orville was planning some monstrous new seduction. The name of the choir leader of the Baptist church, a married woman, was mentioned, and for a week this woman's cheeks were flushed with the scandal. After distrust came a period of mourning, for there were some, both women and men, who had admired Orville's style. These saw in Orville's withdrawal something like the death of youth, and I heard rumors of sentimental tears.

And then came acceptance. There began to be general agreement that Orville had returned to himself. His exploit with the Chinaman was recalled. People who had not spoken to him for months made a point of seeking him out, and it was not long before the town had once again arranged a place for Orville as the town hero.

Orville himself was visibly unhappy; properly unhappy as

it seemed to the town, and thus the reconciliation reached a
formal close.

"The plain truth is," Orville told me once when I went
out to his ranch to see him, "that I just don't care any more.
I suffer from ennui. I don't feel bad, you understand, but
I'm awful tired of girls."

It was another strange occasion at Orville's ranch. I had
found him, in the evening, asleep in a hammock strung up between two of his pines. "My trouble now is that I can't stay
awake," he told me a little while after I waked him. "I've
been sleeping all day after sleeping all night, and I feel pretty
sleepy now. I get up to milk the cows, that's about all. Sometimes I don't move an eyelid for hours."

It was a shock for me, I can tell you. I knew very well
what ennui was, for I had lived some bad days in it, but I
could hardly bring myself to believe that Orville could ever
fall into it. He had had such energy and such calm; I remembered that serene liberation of his energies in one task after
another which had for so long been his distinguishing fea-
ture.

"I know what ennui is," I said, "and I'm sorry to hear that
you do."

I stood there in front of the tidy white frame house and
wondered at the pace of change. It was a smallish house, half
hidden but not obscured by the dark pines; its kind are still to
be found, by thousands, under cottonwoods or pines or ma-
ples, throughout the farmlands of the Middle West, standing
upright and firm as places for families and children, with the
wheat going away on all sides in a massive, gleaming light. A
steep white house; and ancient boxes and peeling, cracked old
trunks stood in the high narrow darkness of the attic; this
Orville had told me; and it was likely that old love letters
moldered and grew yellow in forgotten corners of those

trunks and boxes—in dusty pent-up air which might still be
fragrant with rose petals treasured up in Mason jars.

The past was in that house, and it was a gracious past. As I
watched the house, I thought about such things as ice-cream
socials held in the grounds of a church, with the men deco-
rously taking care of the freezers, and the children hovering
near and uttering shrill fierce cries; of picnics memorialized
in sun-smeared snapshots, with the women wearing sweeping hats with brims like sails that wavered in wind and grazed
the long dark hair of the women who wore them; and of
family reunions, those stately celebrations of passing time
and of death growing into families—happening always in the
best picnic grove in the county, under cottonwoods likely,
with buggies and horses at the edge of the grove, with the
children straying, getting lost, and the parents gravely
mourning the dead.

Orville's house was a house for old-fashioned people, and
it was a shock for me to consider that; for Orville in his way
was old-fashioned, a true son to his dead parents. He belonged to that house, and knew the allegiances which it im-
posed, and I could see these facts as qualities grained into his
whole character, the course of his whole life; and yet he was
at the same time a famous seducer, and now suffered from
painful sophistications of a disease which his ancestors could
never have known. He was suffering from ennui, no old-
fashioned disease for his kind of people, by his own confes-
sion, and by the plain evidence of his loose, dulled relaxation
into the gentle swinging motion of the hammock, as if the
hammock imitated the swaying of his dazed and sleepy mind.

His will suffered, that was the fact of it, and a kind of horror came to me as I considered what Orville's ancestors
would have had to say about such suffering, because it was
likely that Orville would now say the same things to him-

self. Those ancestors would have called him lazy and said no more, and their contempt would have fallen on him. It did not help me that I knew Orville was not lazy; it did not make me happy to see a disease of the will.

"I feel empty," Orville said. "I lie here in this hammock and I feel light as a feather. Comes up a little wind, why, it just ripples me a little and goes right on by. I lie here and forget where I am. I sleep and sleep and never dream at all. Is that what you know about ennui?"

It was close enough to what I knew. I grew uncomfortable, and left soon, Orville having told me, called to me from his hammock as I departed, that he joked but was not amused by his joking.

"It's no laughing matter!" he called. "Never mind the things I say!"

I learned a few days later from Cassius that Orville had still not quite come up to himself in his Latin, but Cassius was not much concerned about that. He was happy to have Orville back. He pronounced a triumph over the willing little girls.

"Women have a place," he said. "Now let 'em remember what it is!"

I saw Orville, after that, each time he came to my office for his meetings with Cassius, and I was able to observe some little changes in him. Little but not unimportant: new kinds of knowledge had touched his character here and there, and marked him. Where once he had happened before my eyes with a kind of purity, kindled from one moment to the next, he now came blurred a little, a little spotted. Any man is a number of faces, of masks, but once Orville's masks had formed an imposing continuity which had often left me dazed, which had always made me happy, sure that I watched a better man; but no more. The innocence was gone, and something else was gone with it: Orville now was a stained man like any other.

"Once I wanted to be a hero," he told me one night. "A kind of town hero, but not only that—you know what I mean. Now I think I'd be happy just to have my strength back. Why, do you know, there was a time when I wanted to be president, and when I knew I could be a good senator if I wanted to."

I guessed that Orville would not remain in his state of lethargy; I could not believe that ennui would hold him for long; but it held him. After a time I felt that consent was involved in Orville's miseries, that he had agreed to ennui, and I came to the idea that he was waiting for something to happen. There was a strange quality to Orville's idleness. I knew the idle surface, which the wind rippled, and I had a sense of empty depths, abysmal silences; but I also had a sense, confirmed in ways I never understood, of hidden, close-kept eagerness. Eager anticipation was there. That part of Orville which was most alive was waiting for something to happen, and I was frightened to notice, alongside that waiting, a cold willingness to accept what might come.

I believed that Orville was vulnerable then as never before; for who can tell what might come? In the interest of the right, in hopes of escaping an offense against a friend, Orville had chosen to commit a lesser wrong—or what had seemed a lesser wrong, and now, presumably, there were weeping girls in the town of Albo. The question which held me then, and holds me now, is what their weeping did to Orville.

"I'm short of confidence just now," he told me at one of our conferences. "It's hard for me to believe that I know what I'm doing. Did you hear that Mary Ellen Board has left town? Last week. Left her home and family. A thing I don't like is that she told me she'd do that if I quit her. Now I wonder how she'll be in Los Angeles. You see? I'm losing my confidence."

Something had happened to Orville's powers of judgment, that was clear. His sense of the right had become a little confused.

"So I just lie in my hammock waiting," he said. "I have a feeling for time now. It's like something I eat, something that becomes a part of me. A funny thing is that it doesn't have any weight at all. But I know it's there, and I'm a glutton of it. I wonder what will happen next."

Small wonder that I was saddened.

"I've taken to watching sunrises and sunsets from my hammock," Orville said. "They remind me that there's plenty of time outside me still."

He had a lively fancy, Orville, and he used it to amuse me, but I was only a little amused. I was busy trying to escape Rose; a hard job, and an unpleasant one because it was impossible for me to explain my real motives to her. How could I tell her that I no longer wished to betray her husband? But I was trying. One of my devices was to call on Cassius in the evenings, as in the past when I had come to make arrangements with Rose, but on these occasions I stayed with Cassius and talked to him. And so it happened that when Cassius admitted me one night, with a fine big smile on his face, and showed me into the parlor, Rose and Orville were sitting there: a duplicate to that scene I remembered from the past, when I had so clearly witnessed Rose showing her love to Orville. Cassius was happy. He was eager, like a boy, and he could hardly wait to get me into the library with him so that he could whisper his bright new secret to me. "I got her to let him come back in the house—yesterday it was! I've been at her and at her ever since Orville reformed, but

she just wouldn't have it. I swear to God there's nothing like
a woman up in arms about a moral question, nothing in the
world! And she's still got her dander up, and no mistake. My
poor Rose is not the one to let a feud die out without making
the other party suffer for it. But I told Orville what the story
was, and now he's on his best behavior, and I believe it'll
work out. By Joe, I knew I had a right to have confidence in
that boy!" There was more such talk as Cassius poured the
bourbon, and the talk left me a little dazed. Cassius offered
me a cigar, and as I lighted it, he said triumphantly: "By the
living God, it's something to reclaim a fine boy from lechery! I'm almost willing to be drunk for joy!"

When we returned to the parlor, I found a tableau which
reassured me. Rose sat bolt upright on a straight-backed
chair, with her knitting in her lap; she was silent, and it was
possible to sense in the atmosphere of the room that she had
been silent since we had left it, or nearly so; and she was
showing anger, mainly by a vicious way she had of clicking
her knitting needles together. Orville was uncomfortable,
plainly, but not so uncomfortable as I might have liked.
There was something sour, a little sick, in that scene, and it
seemed to me then that it came straight from Orville's condition of qualified poise. Had he been as before, red-necked
and boyish and fumbling in his speech, I could have been
happy; but as he sat there in the parlor, saying nothing except to questions from Cassius, and looking at the pattern in
the old carpet, he reminded me of the Orville who had
whipped his fine mare down the main street in the traces of a
gleaming buggy.

I was alarmed. I had every reason to be afraid, and I knew
the kind of trouble that might come; but nothing happened
that night, nor during the days that followed, and my fears
were lulled. I was busy with my efforts to shake off Rose,

and it happened that some two or three weeks after Orville's reconciliation with Rose's house I was finally able to win from Rose a statement that she would let me go. It did not come in such a plain form as that, of course. It amounted only to this, that she would not mind if we canceled an appointment we had made long since to celebrate in a neighbor's hay our second anniversary. That was all. It was enough, and I was free.

For perhaps a week I was in no mood for anything but celebrations, and so I rioted in my folly, getting drunk twice, and going once to Carson City for two nights and a day of gambling. As I have said, I had come to respect Cassius, and at that time in my life it was cause for joy when I could show that kind of respect, even when I was obliged to show it in deep privacy. When I returned from Carson City, still feeling free, and feeling also mildly irresponsible because I had lost most of my money, it seemed a natural thing to visit Orville and to attempt cheering him up.

Thus, when I found Orville in no need of cheering up, found him busy and active over books when I visited him in the evening, with no hammock strung up between the pines, I was in just that state of foolishness which enabled me to rejoice with him in his deliverance from ennui. I asked him whether he was still a glutton of time; and he told me that he was not.

"I don't have to be, any longer," he told me. "Something has happened to time. It's slowed up, somehow, hardly moving any more. To tell the truth, I've forgotten all about it. I don't even look at the sunrises and sunsets any more!"

We had such foolery for perhaps an hour before I went home, and that night I slept a foolish sleep.

The next day I met Cassius at the Courthouse in the normal way—we both had business there—but to no normal end.

That was a rarity, a true meeting; an accident in which two people arrive in understanding at the same place, or happening, without having time to put up defensive masks.

When I first saw him, Cassius was standing at the top of the front steps to the Courthouse. He was leaning into the shadow of one of the wooden pillars.

I spoke to him, but he only nodded, and for a moment I suffered a brief flare-up of fear, thinking that I had been discovered at last in my crimes against him. But then I noticed that he was not really seeing me.

"I'm sorry," he said after a moment. "I didn't sleep well last night."

His face was no good for hiding emotion. It was possible for me to pierce the shade in which he held his head. I was able to know something about Cassius that I had never expected to know: he was suffering from suspicion, and it hurt him. He was not a man to be much bothered by suspicion in the normal order of his life, but now, plainly, there had been an interruption of the normal order of his life. In a clear moment we had our meeting, and what he knew, I guessed; I guessed what had happened while I lurched miserably from folly to folly. Rose and Orville: the bad thing, the almost inconceivable thing, now made to seem an almost inevitable thing; Rose and Orville, at long last, and in spite of Orville's efforts . . .

I became a little dizzy as I stood in front of the shadow which held Cassius. I was in bright sunshine, pouring down on me, as I remembered the sudden ease of my last parting from Rose, as when the last stitch in an old cut pulls out at last, causing no twinge of pain; as I remembered the relaxation of Orville's ennui; as I confronted Cassius's suspicion. "Cassius will have been warned against Orville by Orville's own doings," I thought, "and because he loves Orville he'll understand him as he'd never understand me or Rose or me and Rose together."

I did a strange thing then, which I believe was no mere weakness. I closed my eyes, and blinked, and wept a little, there in broad daylight. I was wearing a hat, and I bent my head down, so that I was no obvious public spectacle, but I believe that Cassius noticed what was happening. He was the kind of man who did not miss such things; a generous heart will wince at others' tears. He began talking, in spite of his own burgeoning sorrow, and in a moment I had recovered myself. He continued talking long enough for me to mop my brow—and eyes—with my handkerchief before he departed.

"Rose is waiting for me," he said gravely. "If anyone asks for me, tell them that I will be in my office later this afternoon." Then he left me, heading home. He walked with his back straight in the black coat, an old-fashioned gentleman of the middle years, going away from me.

It was a searing moment. To its intensities I attribute my actions for the rest of the day, and my failures; for that was a day black with failure. From that day I learned that some kinds of failure are wicked and obscene, a lesson which the years have reinforced.

Naturally, I went from the Courthouse to Orville, finding him at work on a gate near his barn, and I wasted no time in coming to the point. I was angry, and my anger felt sanctified because I nursed it in the name of another man, of Cassius. I had some of the coldness which all agents have, and a good deal of that serenity which comes with dedication. I felt free to say anything, because I was not speaking for myself.

Orville was cheerful, glad to see me, and energetic about that gladness, so that I could know he had had some of his certainties recently refreshed. He could afford to be kind to me because he felt secure, and thus I was able to shock him quite easily.

"God damn it, Orville," I said, "I want you to turn loose of Rose Martin, and just as quick as you can do it."

That must have been the first time Orville had ever been kept from action by mere words. Certainly I could see that he wanted to act: in an instant he was ready to fight, and I briefly regretted the switch-blade knife I had not thought to carry with me that morning. But in that same instant when he became ready to fight, even to try killing me, something else happened to him that made fighting, or any action, impossible to him. What, precisely, I don't expect to know, but I suspect that it was a feeling of chill, of coldness driven into bone; that feeling of dismay which sometimes comes with unwelcome knowledge. He did not move, and for a long time did not speak. I had him at my mercy.

"I don't understand why you did it, Orville," I said, and it pleased me that he flinched while I did not. "Any man is liable to a little unexpected rutting now and then, and you've had your share of that. But you knew what was at stake with Rose. God damn it, man, Cassius is your friend!"

Something changed in his face, and I had the feeling that he was remembering. His face sickened, and he grew pale. I have seen the same expression on the faces of men who are on the point of drinking too much whisky.

"And you struggled for so long, Orville, and paid so high, to stay away from her. Good Lord, have you forgotten the twelve or eleven girls, and the two or three virgins, and the two pregnancies? To throw it all away at last!"

"Sit down," Orville said then. He sank to the ground and rested his back against the fence, and there was something in this movement, something of spirit gone slack, of dullness returning, which unmanned me. There was my victory, slumped on dusty earth, propped against a board fence, and it was more victory than I had bargained for. At about this moment, when I was already beginning to suffer, I was reminded of my own false position, as by the workings of a god of justice. There in that hot light I learned another lesson, that hypocrisy can be most virulently painful. It is a sickness, like any other; but its fever and chills warp the mind, not the body, and make the soul giddy.

"Christ help us all," I said. "I'm sorry, Orville." I sat down beside him. After a while he began to talk.

"I keep forgetting myself," he said. "As if I were a child, and I were my own toy, left somewhere under a bush." At that moment his words seemed just; he had the look, in the way his body slumped against the board fence, of a wrecked toy, a battered doll; he was not a small man, but now he looked small. Plainly, he had forgotten himself in the pain which had found him, and now he was merely present against the board fence, not in any way active there. He looked the way human bodies look when they are hurt—in the newspaper photographs this would be the white blur of a man's shirt alongside the wreckage of a car, or the jagged light and dark of a woman's ripped dress beside the same wreckage.

His awareness of himself was gone—of the way he touched or owned or loved the little world he knew. There was a faintly dazed look about his eyes, and it was impossible for me to see in him the old heroic idea I had had of him. He looked sad and confused, and I remembered the face of a welterweight boxer I had once seen; just so the boxer's face had been, the brain clouded by blows, the clouds showing in the blurred look of the face. The thought came to me that for Orville, too, it was beginning to be hard to recognize in himself the old heroic idea.

And then he began to come back a little. I sensed a con-

siderable effort, and I knew he was struggling. He did not
change his position, except to straighten one leg, but there
was a difference in his appearance. It came to me after a time
that he was no longer relaxed against the board fence, that
now he was holding himself, drawing slack muscles tight.
Some part of his dignity returned. Intelligence was at work
almost visibly in him, compelling his attention to the fact that
he must live and move. "I spend a lot of time these days looking under bushes for that toy," he said. "Not quite what I'd
expected to be doing at this age. I guess I told you once how
I thought I could make a president, and knew I could be a
senator. That's the way I used to think. A senator or a Su-
preme Court judge, that was about the bottom of my plans;
what I'd settle for if I had an accident—say, if I went blind.
I used to think about the library I'd have. There'd be leather-
covered chairs, and my lawbooks bound in calfskin. You can
see what I had in mind. Cato or Brutus in an American
lawyer's library, and the country waiting for what I had to
say. Well, I could still think that way, I guess. I do, in fact,
some of the time, because I have a notion of what I could
do." He spoke calmly, gently, as if to a child; as if to himself. When he paused, he shook his head.

"So much for that," he said. He pulled his hat down over
his eyes and straightened his body; he had all his dignity back
by now, and he looked more like the Orville I had known.
In a clear voice he made a little speech: "I didn't love her.
After about the fifth girl from town I stopped loving her.
And I didn't want her. There's plenty better looking in
town, and a few I know that have a better action, if it comes
to that. True. All that's true. And of course she doesn't have
anything to say. She only likes the sound of Latin, or the
men's voices saying it.

"But she hated me. That, or seemed to. How could I tell

the difference, with a woman I hardly knew? She said she hated me: the first time I went back to her house, while you and Cassius were in the library. 'I hate you, Orville Ledyard,' she said. 'I hate you with a pure cold hate, and I'll make you feel it.' Can you imagine that? It didn't help my feelings any, I can tell you.

"Nobody likes to be hated. I never have, I've always tried to stay away from that. Well, I showed myself that I could do without her love, but I never yet learned how to get along with a woman's hate, and that's about where the trouble started, because I knew I had a remedy. You know what remedy—I've never yet seen it fail. You see, I'd learned a few things from the girls in town, and learned a few things about myself, so I knew I didn't have to let her hate me. *Knew* it!

"And then there was the problem aspect to it. I guess I never tried before to get a woman who hated me. And I was bored, remember. I had that ennui—it is a fact that I suffered from it. I'd been waiting for something to happen when she told me that she hated me, and that seemed like what I'd been waiting for. Something happened, anyway.

"What I'm remembering now, what I've been remembering since you came, is that as soon as she started giving in, and even while she was about it—and don't think *that* isn't a game she knows the ins and outs of—I was regretting it all. She didn't really hate me, of course. That was just her come-on. She's not really very ignorant about the way these things work. So that I had a hold of her, but was thinking about Cassius. I was thinking that I never liked another man half so well, saving my own father, and Cassius has been like a father to me. It makes a story, doesn't it?"

Immediately I asked him why he did not instantly quit her,

leave her, drop her, cut her dead, and for a moment I felt I had the answer to my woes. But he would not do it. It was not in his bargain with her to act in that fashion.

"It's up to her," he said. "I'm going to try to keep the faith with her, if with no one else."

And that was the way I had to leave it. For a time I considered telling him about my connection with Rose, in hopes of causing him to feel disgust with her, so that he would leave her; but I could not bring myself to it. It was not possible to me, and I left Orville with a feeling that I perhaps loved that poor tormented girl more than any man living could love her.

Not the best state of feeling for one who wished to negotiate with her. When I left Orville, I had made up my mind to speak to Rose, and to ask her to give Orville up, to yield him up to the simpler life he had known before she had caught him.

And so I made arrangements. I sent a boy to Cassius's office with a request for a book—a lawbook, of course, because I wanted the illusion of solemn business—and when the boy returned with the book I knew that Cassius was safely away from home. The boy told me, in addition, that there were two clients waiting patiently in Cassius's outer office. Then I walked to the Martin house and knocked at the front door. I was a friend of the family, but I would soon be alone with the wife.

Rose was at home. She admitted me with a smile, and it was not long before I knew that she was glad to see me. She wanted someone to talk to, that was part of it; there were some things she could discuss only with me, and this fact was a bond. Also, I think, in some way she still loved me, and my sense of this was as warm in the room as Rose herself, as the woman who stood pale and faintly provoked before me. I discovered then that I still loved her, and thus we achieved a frightening kind of tension even before we spoke.

I was for some time unable to speak. It is not easy to return to a once-loved woman. The fact of love is there in her person, and it is only history that hurts; and history can be forgotten for a little while.

She took me to the parlor and gave me lemonade. She drank tea from a little silver pot, and smiled steadily at me.

"It's so good to have you back," she said, raising her hand as if to prevent protests. "For lemonade, for talk. You understand. Sometimes this is a very lonely house." She was wearing a house dress of some lightweight but dark-colored material—something near a brown; and for a moment, while she succeeded in looking lonely, the dress seemed to be her body, and her body had a thick, impending presence which seemed very close to me; heavy of thigh, shoulder, hip. She became more alive than she had been, in an instant, troubling old desire, but somehow forcing me away; caused me to sense within her body the life which held her there, but, when she smiled, caused me to sense mortality as if I were breathing it like air. That was a life so intensely living that it made me think of death, and so I stood stock-still and was almost afraid until the moment passed.

She no longer bothered to look lonely. Her dark eyes, glistening at me, controlled the woman she had chosen to become, and she was suddenly austere and slender, an elegant figure posing for me in an isolation which from moment to moment she spun out of her own being. She was drenched in distance, by her own choosing, and far away in light; restless sunlight crisscrossed the room from the windows. She looked handsome at that moment, after the fashion of women in furs on a well-darkened winter street. Pretty women look so when they are remote from the men who watch them. "I won't even ask you to explain why you came back," she said.

That room was haunted for me. There were heavy drapes over the narrow windows, drapes tall enough to hide a man, and once I had hidden myself in them while Cassius, on an unexpected errand, looked for a paper in the next room. Ghosts were there in that parlor; they were the lovers we had been, where we had kissed, where I had made comic pursuits of her, where she had been waiting for me on the sofa one winter afternoon, naked and radiant, with a red paper rose in her hair to remind me of happy summer days. It was hard for me to speak; I was thinking unhappily of Cassius.

"I have business, Rose," I said uncomfortably. "There's something I want to talk to you about."

"I understood that you came to talk," she said. "For a visit. That's natural enough."

She was cool, and I was not. I had the feeling that she was enjoying herself. It came into my mind as a kind of revelation that I must be careful about speaking out to her, and must be careful about mentioning Orville's name, for I had discovered somehow, in the way she held herself, in the way she controlled her voice, that she was waiting for me, primed in those matters which most concerned me.

"I came to see how you are," I said, "how you're getting on."

"My health is good," she said. "I had a cold last week, but it's all gone now. I have a little headache in the afternoons, but it usually goes away with tea."

"I'm glad. You deserve good health, Rose. But I wasn't so much worried about your health. I'm concerned about *you*, Rose." It was a wretched start, likely to end itself before I could begin to control it, but it had an effect which I could observe. Rose colored a little. I think she allowed her face to color, but then she must have wished me to understand something by it. I believe she wanted me to know that I could still affect her, that she was not unmoved by my presence there in that haunted room. She may even have intended me to remember the red paper rose.

"I worry about you, Rose. I haven't seen much of you lately."

At this she moved her lips in a way she had, turning the corners down, and closing her eyes at the same time. This meant anger, but only a mild anger, which in the past she had used only to give piquancy to her features. Now I was not sure. I was confused, unable to think of anything to say. After a long and well-calculated moment she spoke, this time firmly, with a kind of prim violence.

"You want to know if I've been faithful to you, isn't that it?"

"That's not it, Rose!"

"Well, I haven't been, and I don't mean to be in the future, and that's that. Would you like to go home now?"

She rose from her chair, clutching her saucer in one hand and her teacup in the other. She seemed angry and unhappy, and she appeared to be suggesting that she was charmingly bewildered. She allowed herself the scowl of a little girl; she blinked back tears.

"That doesn't mean that I don't still love you," she said.

She began to weep, and in a little while it seemed right for me to console her. I touched her hair, above the right ear, where she had been working on a new curl, and spoke softly to her. She wept for a time against the lapels of my coat, but only long enough to make a minor reconciliation, when it came, seem natural. We were familiar with each other; the feeling must have been like that of a silver wedding anniversary.

"You're so mean," she said. "You make me hate you."

"I'm not," I said. "But then I can't let you tyrannize."

"Oh, you! You haven't changed a bit!"

Such talk passed enough time for us so that we could safely, with emotions under control, go on to more interesting and more important matters. Characteristically, it was Rose who made the transition.

"I'd be so glad to have you back," she said. "Really I would! I can't come in this room without thinking about you."

"Forsaking all others?" I asked. "Would I be the only one?"

"The only one."

"And no diversions? No games?"

"Just you. Just old you, the way we've always been."

I knew I would reject her. In my mind as I spoke to her was the idea, jacketed in thick feeling, that my health as a man, and even my sanity, depended on freedom from her; and on a freedom achieved, not on a dismissal given. It is hard now to understand the intensity of that idea and those feelings, but I can still bring them back, have them again in memory, and they are like a nausea. Thus, as I penetrated Rose's proposal to take me back, with its clear implication that she would then let Orville go, I found dizzying hazards in my way. Oddly, for me, I had an opportunity to be a hero of sorts, and knew it: a hero of the self-sacrificing variety, yielding up the best and strongest part of myself to the interests of others.

A reflection I avoid these days has to do with the shuddering violence of my withdrawal from that heroism, that self-sacrifice. I made no loud sounds, but the violence was there, all of it inside, and the more painful for being so ruthlessly contained. Even at the time I was smitten, baffled, by the fact

that I was in a position to avoid heroism—that so high duty
—in the name of honest morality.

To myself I said: "I can't betray Cassius again. I can't betray Cassius again"; while to Rose I said: "I'm sorry, my dear,
but I'm afraid it's impossible."

She was not surprised or even angry, so it seemed, and
she asked for no explanations, so that I was left unpropped
in my stanchly moral state; but she was prepared. She had
the alternatives neatly worked out. In that power politics of
the emotions which we were so intensely playing, she moved
precisely within the cruel limits of her knowledge. Like Met-
ternich, she knew all the boundaries, all the internal combina-
tions, all the pretenders, and, like him, she knew what she
wanted.

"I knew you wouldn't," she said. "Of course you understand that you won't have any claims on me? From this instant. I don't mean to be unfriendly, but I want you to understand. I must do what I can for my little troubles, by myself
—tea for the headache, the smell of coffee for my sinuses. I
so want you to understand. Do you understand?"

She watched me closely, and for the occasion she wore the
most sober of her masks: that one reserved for the times
when she wished to show attention to a man who impressed
her. Her eyes showed concern, her mouth, wonder; and it
will be with me to the end of my life that somehow, by some
artifice twisted into the set of her shoulders and her head, she
contrived to show love.

"We do understand?" she said.

"We understand," I said, "though I'll be damned if I like
it, Rose. Why can't you—"

"Tut," she said. "You must remember that I'm a married
lady."

Thus my failure with Rose, a more grievous failure than

my failure with Orville, and one which had almost immediate consequences.

The very next day, which was an unusually cold day in late April, with a clear brilliant sun, Cassius, my friend and colleague Cassius Martin, drove Orville Ledyard from the streets of Albo with a buggy whip; drove him from one end of the main street to the other, out of town, and half a mile along the road to Orville's ranch; drove him in no usual way, it is true, but drove him nonetheless. The abused husband took revenge. Half the town came out to gape and watch.

Just how the timing of these events happened will remain a mystery to me, I am sure. It is possible that Rose, angry with me and with Orville, and wishing a revenge upon us and upon Cassius as well, may simply have told Cassius that Orville had most villainously and skillfully seduced her, using arts learned in his conquests of the town girls, against her will but beyond her powers of resistance; something like that, some clumsy lie effectively garnished with tears and deep, horribly racking sobs. This is possible, not likely.

Or it may have been that Rose, without ever speaking, showed her guilt; left its traces in the way she talked at the dinner table, and polished the silver, and washed the dishes; in the way she cleaned house, and in the way she put on her nightgown—in any of those places and moments of the married life which can be a ground for perception. She could have suffered from a guilty conscience without being able to speak of it; she could have been longing, unhappily, for peace, for an emotional calm. Again, this is possible, not likely. Rose in those days was a lively, happy woman. I cannot believe that she wanted change badly enough to work for it.

It is my notion that the relationship of Rose and Orville,

being not quite so coldhearted as my relation with Rose, and never so fully under the control of self-interest, never so vulnerable to the censorship of strong vanities, was simply more visible than my relationship with Rose had been. It was more there; it had a more virulent and pungent existence. Like a day at the circus, it had an air of spontaneity, an almost visible exuberance, and it may be that in the Martin house it was both visible and palpable. Poor Cassius may have felt it in his fingertips, in raised hair at the back of his neck, and there seen it like a ghost walking the halls. In any event, he found out about it, and took action. Having been fooled once, and for a long time, he was not fooled again. It may be that there is a power which sees to it that decent husbands are not fooled over and over again.

And so we had that memorable day, an astonishing day in Albo, one which few people there to have it and know it will ever forget. It was like a pageant invented to instruct and amuse the people, and it had a quality as of pageant, or show, in the contrived sadness of its close.

It began in the lobby of the Courthouse at about ten in the morning. There Cassius called a boy in from the porch and told him to go out to the Ledyard ranch for Orville and ask him to come into town, to Cassius's office, by noon. Cassius made no secret of it. He gave the boy a quarter, and the boy scampered. So much I saw, and no more, and Cassius did not speak to me, but what I saw was enough to put me on guard, and I took care to be near Cassius's office that noon, in a place where I could see what happened. I was afraid. There had been trouble, there could be more.

But when Orville arrived, Cassius greeted him mildly from the door of his office and went out to shake hands after Orville got down from his horse; the horse was the bay mare that once had pulled the gleaming buggy. To the point of shaking hands, the scene could have been nothing more than a meeting between friends. After they shook hands, it changed, for Cassius then asked Orville, in a clear voice, a little louder than I could quite believe: "Well, son, I called you in to ask you if you've been sleeping with my wife. That's all. Nothing more than that. How about it?"

There was a silence. After such questions, such silences come easy to anyone in range, and by this time, I noticed, there were two or three people stopped within range of Cassius's voice; stopped very sharply, their heads set perplexedly like the heads of deer caught in strong light after dark, with just that quality of mute, animal-like wonder in their eyes.

"Think it over, son," Cassius said. "You know I wouldn't ask you a thing like that if I didn't mean something by it."

Orville did not move. He stood there in stained blue shirt and blue levis and boots, his face dark under his big hat. His head was bent forward; I could not see the expression of his face. After a time he spoke, very softly, as if he were afraid to be heard.

"I can't deny it," he said. "I'd lie if it'd do any good."

"I know you would, son. I know how it is. But I guess I can't bring myself to like it much. Excuse me, will you?"

Orville nodded his head, very slightly, and otherwise did not move while Cassius entered his office and came back quickly with a buggy whip in his hand. Both were oblivious to the slowly gathering crowd.

"I guess you know what this is," Cassius said. "I brought it down from the old barn this morning. Been there since before the war, I guess."

"I know what it is," Orville said. "I used to have one myself."

"I'd expected to whip you out of town with it, son—or try to. Now I don't know. I think maybe I'll just walk along beside you with it." He lifted the whip and tried it in air, as if he were testing a fly rod; the old leather creaked, but the whip swished in the dull silent air and startled some of the watchers, of which there were now twenty or twenty-five. Then, without putting the whip down, Cassius took the reins of Orville's mare and tied them up over the saddle horn, turned the mare by catching the bridle, and then whacked her on the rump. "Git up, there!" he said. "Git on home now!" In a softer voice he said to Orville: "You understand, don't you, son? This is kind of hard on an old man like me. I feel old today, and sad. Your mare will just go on home, I reckon."

"I reckon," Orville said.

"Do you have anything more to say?"

Slowly Orville shook his head. "If I do, I can't think of it right now," he said.

"Then I'd like to say I feel pretty bad! I like to see a man come up to himself—but I guess we can say good-by to all that. I guess I can say, too, that I've loved you, boy. I guess you never noticed that. Or maybe you did, and felt a little foolish about it because you didn't understand it. You're young, you've got all your hard life ahead of you. I guess that's it. Look here. This old whip is beginning to crack along the weave. Come along, son." Cassius took Orville's arm and turned him. Together they walked out into the street, toward the crowd that had gathered, as many as forty or fifty men, women, and children by this time, and that broke and scattered before their progress. Side by side they walked north, toward the edge of town, toward the road that led to the Ledyard ranch, leaving me, and in some genuine way leaving the town. I could know further, watching them, that what was leaving, what was being carried away in that tide-like drift toward open country, would not return though

I wished it; though others wished it, and with power.

The sight of the two men together, the big square man in the black coat and the slender strong figure of the young cowboy in his uniform of washed-out blue clothes and boots and hat, is one which will stay with me; it is the kind of image that comes back, like a nightmare, with the turning seasons. Love, of that kind, and discovered in that way, on a dusty street in a little town, is a burden that a watcher must afterwards bear; and so I have borne it. I was there. In front of the Courthouse, Cassius dropped the whip and bowed his head a little, and the sad procession continued on its way. One of the boys of the town got the whip as a souvenir. Another got Cassius's gold pocket watch, given away by Cassius as he made his return to his office.

"Keep it as a souvenir, boy," Cassius said, "of the time I whipped a good man out of town—or sell it if you like. Time's nothing to me! I'll have a good deal more of it than I'll ever be able to use, anyway."

That is almost the end of the story. There is little more. Orville from that time began to suffer; it could not be otherwise. He had been an authentic hero, an example to boys, and he was, in his heroism, a part of the town's knowledge. His fall could not be a normal fall, from middling virtue to middling shame. The town—and by the town I mean almost all the people in it, as well as that abstract sense of justice which often moves in such places—saw to it that Orville's fall registered on him as an authentic fall, and there can be no doubt that this was instructive for the youth of the town, and a potent warning. All the usual things were done, all the normal slights were brought out for him. He was unable to walk down the main street of town without laughter from small boys. He was not safe in bar or drugstore, and none of the girls in town were permitted to speak to him. He was challenged to fights, and men sometimes spat when he passed by.

The town saw to it that Orville felt disgraced, that is the fact of it, and saw to it, in a little while, that Orville departed, after selling his ranch and all his furniture, so that he could meditate elsewhere on life and virtue. And that was cruel, for Orville knew our town and knew no other; but it was not forbidden him to return, and in time he did return.

Meanwhile he went off to law school, in San Francisco, as he had planned for so long. He had the money from the sale of the ranch, and he hoped to make it last him through his six years of study. For four years I did not see him; and then one bright blue winter day in San Francisco, where I had gone to spend a few days of Christmas near an ocean, I met him upstairs in the Ferry Building. He was changed in appearance; he already had the look, that pale and somewhat sullied look, of the dedicated, long-term student; he was thin, and no longer looked strong, but he seemed healthy. I found him standing unhappily in front of that immense relief map of California which in those days was one of the wonders of the city. He was looking across the miniature Sierra Nevada at the little green button which was Albo, where it gleamed on a brown-paper valley.

Quickly he recognized me when I spoke to him. He explained that he was in the first year of law school, and that he often came homesick down to the Ferry Building to look at the papier-mâché mountains and the painted lakes and streams. He was embarrassed. He admitted that he was doing well in law school. When he left me, I had a sense of a departing student, of a hungry young man now a little old to be still in college; and it took thought for me to remember the heroic Orville Ledyard of old days.

And then twelve years more in Albo passed as in a dream. Cassius died, and Rose went away, to live in Los Angeles with an aunt, so it was said. Girls I had known as fresh and happy faces in Orville's buggy became mothers of children, other men's children, who, as the years passed, were often tall arrogant boys anxious to enter high school or leave it, and pretty girls obsessed with lipstick, rouge, and clothes. I grew older, and more angry.

Orville returned, finally, sixteen years after he had left. He came back in a car, a Pontiac, with his belongings in the back seat and the trunk. He was still a bachelor. He brought with him from his travels many boxes of books, clothes, and a dog; it was a mild-looking, sad little bloodhound.

In Albo he took up the practice of law, having already had some seven or eight years of experience in Bakersfield and Modesto, and he did reasonably well from the start; he was a competent lawyer, for Albo, and he made a decent living. After two years he was able to buy the ruins of his family's ranch—the water rights having been sold some years before to the City of Los Angeles by one of the interim owners. He drilled a well, and restored the house, and began to live there again. Two of the old pines remained, though both were pretty well blistered and scaled by heat and drouth; the barn and all the fences and corrals had been stolen, board by board, many years before.

There were few people in the town who even remembered his early days, and most of those who remembered thought it a kindness to forget. Orville was accepted quickly by the commercial and social leaders in the town, which by this time was an up-to-date tourist center with flashing white motels and restaurants which are mentioned favorably in tourist guidebooks. He was given a sufficient number of chances to decline dinner invitations. He became a distinguished citizen, and when he had a little trouble with a girl from the high school, it was easy for his new friends to make an arrangement which kept the girl quiet; she was happy to accept a cashier's job in a Long Beach restaurant. Two years after his return he was made a member of the Kiwanis Club.

Thus, in middle-class ways, he has come to his fifties. He drinks too much, but he is quiet about it; he never makes a spectacle of himself. In the fall he hunts ducks and geese on the little ponds in the valley and along the aqueduct; and each year he makes a ceremonial deer hunt, with cronies, into the Piute Mountains.

He is still a reader. By now he has a sprawling erudition of immense scope, on such matters as the histories of Motley and Carlyle, the comic works of Surtees, the novels of Walter Scott. He is one of those isolated, village readers; his erudition is carelessly managed, easily forgotten, full of dark little errors; he has read no Latin for thirty years, but he is accepted as a man of great knowledge, and he owns more than two thousand books. Every three or four years he is asked to make the speech at the high-school graduation.

He has, I suppose, found ease and comfort by his escape into the type of the country lawyer. It is a place to be, loose-fitting and undemanding, and it requires of the men who populate it only that they be content to stay in it; it is a respectable man of middle years, conservative in politics, who hunts a little, who likes to read, and prefers the historians of the last century; a common type. You will find it all over this country, more or less tending to the law in little sun-washed courthouses, entering and idly leaving politics; fishing, or talking of it, in the forests of Maine, listening to dogs bay coon in the piney woods of North Carolina, talking wheat in those villages of the Middle West which are so imperfectly shaded by the grain elevators—everywhere, in fact, where it is possible for men to lose themselves.

It is not a bad type. There is often a fine haunted look about the eyes, as with Orville, and this can indicate a deep capacity for sympathy. It can also improve a man's looks, and even make him handsome. So Orville is a handsome man, and visitors to the Courthouse are always taken to see him when he is pleading a case; he is a credit to the town, and to the town's climate. His hair is white; he is regarded with indulgent favor by the wives of his friends, and the boys of the town, if they know him at all, respect him in a qualified, half-derisive way because he is a fine wing shot.

As for me, I do not see him often; we have drifted apart. Possibly we remind each other too strongly of the past, possibly we never had much in common; but we are no longer able to rise to a conversation. We are polite. I think when he reaches sixty we may come around to amusing ourselves with stories of the good old days, but until then I will be content to watch the present. Like Cassius in those last years before he died, I too have more time than I can find a decent use for.

MUSTANGS

❦

❦ ❦ ❦ ❦ ❦
❦ ❦ ❦ ❦ ❦

MR. CLYDE MUNN closed his book and stood up, nodded his head, and the class was over. Truman Hopp, his only Indian, bent forward to tie a shoelace. The other boys stood up, talked, shambled toward the door, and the girls stood up; each girl touched her hair. Everybody was laughing. It was a Friday, school was out, and there was no homework because this was the last week of the term.

The room was warm, and held that mist of habitation which schoolrooms share with other crowded places. Odors of sweat and brilliantine infused the mist: the boys jostled each other, one ran a comb through his hair. A blonde girl passed near the desk, walking with her head high, leaving for a moment a dim smell of perfume behind her. She carried a lipstick, and Mr. Munn guessed that she would decorate herself once more before she left the school building; it was a long walk home, and boys might happen by.

Then the room was empty and Mr. Munn left it quickly, hurrying. His books and notes were in his briefcase; he had nothing more to do; he was free to hurry. Three times he said hello to students going the opposite way. Once he waved to a lady teacher, a Miss Carey who taught plane geometry and algebra, but he kept moving and avoided talk. When he got to his car, he felt his excitement begin to swell in him; the rear wheels whipped gravel into the car's underpinning as he backed out of his parking place.

On the driveway leading out of the school grounds he drove in shade cast by cottonwoods, and then passed into sunlight as he reached the street. It was a limpid, faintly yellow light; in it the mountains showed their outlines clear, and there were two kinds of mountains. There was the Sierra on his left, and the Sierra was sharp black peaks. There were the brown desert mountains on his right, called the Piute Mountains, and these were tall and empty hills. He was glad to have mountains so near.

"Good weather, good weather," he said, as he drove past bars, barbershops, and sporting-goods stores.

At home in the small apartment, he went directly to the bedroom and pulled his tie off. "I've got to hurry," he said aloud. "I've only got ten minutes to get out to Sam's place!" Rapidly he stripped off his shirt and pants and kicked his shoes toward the closet; his coat was already scattered on the bed. He clapped his hands; it was a gesture of simple joy. While he lifted a black cotton work shirt and heavy denim levis from a hook in the closet, he said: "Going mustanging. What luck! Won't I be a sight, though!"

Five minutes later he was traveling north on the highway out of town, approaching the first of the ranches. On both sides of the road were alfalfa fields and pastures neatly fenced. Some of the alfalfa fields were already cut; in another a baler clattered. The irrigation ditches were glossy with tall grass. From time to time he passed a white frame house hidden under trees, and though there were not many

such houses, they changed the scene, and Clyde was aware
of change: Albo was behind him with its motels and sporting-
goods stores and gasoline stations and stucco façades. Albo
was California, an old place renewed by the automobile.
Tourists came to Albo for the mountains, for the fishing,
for the hunting, and the people of Albo took care of them;
everybody except the Indians prospered, and the town grew.
Now that it was prosperous, it had a city glitter, and Clyde
was glad to have it behind him.

He was pleased with the green fields, with the cattle,
and with the white houses, pleased and quietly excited, so
that he was smiling as he turned in at the lane which led to
the Ambrose ranch. He slowed down for the cattle guard
and drove slowly past the main house. Near the corrals and
barn he stopped in front of a small frame cottage.

He was in the shade of a cottonwood, a warm brown shade
with a breeze blowing through it. A bird flickered in the
branches of the tree as Clyde got out and stretched; he sighed
a little, and looked upward for the bird, and saw a brown
wing flutter. For a moment he stood quietly. Anticipation
stirred in him as tangibly as the bird moved in the tree: he
was happy, he was at peace, he was ready to go.

Then there was a shout, and his friend Sam Leathers came
out of the side door to the barn. He was carrying a coiled
rope. "Going mustanging!" he called. Quickly he built a loop
in his rope, whipped it twice just above his head, and then
snapped it to the ground.

"That's the way to take 'em!" he called.

He was a middle-sized man with slender bent legs that
walked clumsily. His movements with the rope were jerky,
abrupt, but graceful, and the rope vibrated precisely in his
hands. He hurried along, re-coiling the rope; he was smiling,

he was excited, he was talking rapidly. The trip was under way.

"We got to hurry, Clyde," he said. "I just finished working. We got to hurry like you never hurried before! We got to be out of here in twenty minutes! We got to catch horses and load 'em and go, Clyde! We've got a long way to go! Did you bring the groceries?"

"They're in the car."

"Good, good, good, good! Come on, hurry, boy. Catch that red horse of mine in the corral and wrangle our ponies on him while I start loading the truck. Hurry on, now, boy!"

Clyde smacked his hands together. "I'm on my way!" he said. He caught the red sorrel horse with no trouble, saddled him with no trouble, and led him to the pasture gate. There were noises from the direction of the truck; Sam was singing cheerfully and aimlessly. Clyde felt a sudden access of pleasure as he prepared to mount; the back of his shirt was hot with sun, and his body felt flexible and strong.

Then the horse moved, before he had reached the off stirrup, before he had time to forget the trip and think about the horse, before he was ready to defend himself. Suddenly the horse was bucking: the horse's back rose against the saddle, humped and hard, like a boulder shifting; the horse jumped, came down hard, and jumped again, so that Clyde was almost off before he was completely on. Frantically he stretched his right foot for the stirrup, wildly strained at the reins. He had time to think: the thought of falling presented itself as an embarrassment. Then his right foot found the stirrup, and he felt the horse's head rise. Not thinking any more, he wheeled the horse right, then left. "Hut, you son of a bitch!" he said, and now he felt better than ever. Sensing someone near, he turned his head and saw Sam at the corral gate. For a moment there was a grim serious look about Sam's eyes and mouth, which gave way quickly to a smile when he saw that all was well.

"I'm going!" Clyde said. "I'm on my way!"

After that, the preparations went swiftly. The horses, one of Sam's and one of Clyde's, were caught, saddled, and loaded in the back of Sam's truck. The groceries went in the cab of the truck, with the ropes and grain and bed rolls. By the time they were finished, Sam's wife, Bonna June, had come out of the cottage with the baby on her hip. She was a heavy-bodied dark girl with strong regular features, much younger than Sam; she was smiling indulgently as she walked up to the truck. "Do you want some coffee before you go?" she asked. "Hello, Clyde. I've got some made, Sam. . . ."

"Girl, you know we don't have time for coffee," Sam said. "Don't you know we've got to make it over there before dark so we can prospect around? Come here now and say good-by, so we can rim out of here! We're in a terrible hurry, girl!"

A little shyly, but complacently, she came to the driver's side and leaned forward to be kissed. As the truck pulled away, she waved after them and then looked down at the child's head. There was a heavy pleasure in her face as she examined the blurred features.

"The baby's looking fine," Clyde said as they turned onto the highway.

"Ain't she a dandy? She weighed fifteen pounds yesterday on the scales in the big house. Bonnie goes up there every day to weigh her and talk to Mrs. Ambrose."

A mile north they turned east on the main highway through the Piute Mountains to Nevada. Sam talked, not so rapidly now that he had to drive, and fitfully, while Clyde watched the country come toward him, pass, and change.

It was a clean dry intelligible country: its history showed in its wrinkles, rises, and steps, and its history spread for miles each way in the yellow light. Clyde watched it and thought about the sorrel horse who had bucked with him; it seemed appropriate to remember such an incident at such a time. The horse had bucked hard, but Clyde had held him, doing well what had to be done; and the deed was proper to the place and time, for horses were part of the country, or part of the life of the country, for the few who cared to make them so. Now, watching the mountains, Clyde knew that he wished to be among that few, and he felt happy with the wish as it grew firm.

"It ought to be a damn fine trip!" Clyde said.

The road turned north and ran parallel to the range. At intervals of four or five miles they passed ranches, each built around one of the streams which greened the desert with water from the mountains. Each ranch, like all the ranches in this country, was a cluster of cottonwoods surrounded by alfalfa fields; no ranch was greener than any other. When there were no more ranches to be seen, they were in the approaches to Piute Pass, and they began to see trees. There were a few joshuas on the lower slopes; above them were junipers. Currents of cool air blew down from the mountains. Once Clyde turned to look back at the Sierra, and thought of speaking to Sam about the beauty of it, but he did not speak because he knew what Sam had to say about the Sierra. Sam disliked the Sierra because it was poor stock country: to Sam it was as simple as that, and it never took him long to say so.

Near the top of the pass the truck heated, and they stopped to let it cool; after that, they did not stop again. The truck ground down the east side of the pass in low gear, and the horses stumbled now and then because the new position was awkward. For a few miles they traveled through a juniper forest and could see little beyond it, but as they neared the bottom of the pass they entered a country of swales and hillocks, and from the tops of the hillocks they could see the mountains of Nevada, range after dim range like an ocean seen through mist.

Sam talked a little about these mountains, and about the valleys which lay between them, and shook his head, saying they were too dry for a small rancher; and then spoke of the ranch they were traveling toward. It was not a ranch at all, but range, sixty miles from one end to the other, most of it leased from the government with only a few thousand acres owned, but all controlled from Bakersfield; there was room on it for miners and mustangs as well as cattle. Clyde listened respectfully. He had never been where they were going, but he liked the thought of uplands grazed by mustangs. His excitement, burned out a little against the mountains they had traveled through, began to come on again.

They entered a country of old volcanoes, settled now into cones of maroon ash and ridges of black lava; and in the middle of it turned south and came to a valley. It was like the Wilson Valley, in which Albo lay, but drier, more empty, and had a brighter glaze; called Fishbone Valley because of the fossils to be found in it from a time when the valley and all about it had been covered by the sea, by a broad bay of the Pacific.

They were traveling a side road now, but it was a good road; it ran straight as an echo into the valley before them. Here and there were clusters of trees which were ranches; the clusters of trees rose clearly defined against the empty light, and there were six clusters in all. They seemed close together, but they were in fact miles apart, scattered about the valley upon the streams which flowed east from the mountains.

They passed the ranches, the green trees and the alfalfa fields, and turned east again toward a new kind of country, leaving the good road. The truck rattled toward a gray upland with mountains rising from the far margins of it. Once they passed a windmill; twice they passed unpainted cabins. And though the cabins were new, with glass in the windows, and doors which fitted, and tarpaper well fixed to the roofs, they were abandoned cabins; they had that look upon them. Weeds grew in the yards, the desert was returning. Beside one of the cabins was a hay rake, the wheels out of line with the axle, the seat gone, many of the tines gone. Almost lost in the tall sage around the cabins were fence posts and a few strands of barbed wire. Sam shook his head as they passed the cabins, and muttered.

"This country's too dry for a poor man," he said.

But as Sam talked on, Clyde could not help thinking that perhaps there were other homesteads, in other valleys, which might support life. "Sometimes I think about homesteading, Sam," he said. "I like to think about it when I get tired of Albo."

"But not here," Sam said. "She's just too awful dry around here. I've seen it, boy."

Then the road entered a wash, and they began to climb steadily. As they neared their destination, Sam talked rapidly. "She's quite a wash," he said. "Look where the water's chewed it out. Old Dick Tatum told me they had a real flood down through here one spring not long ago. He found a calf floating in it, he said. All that water, and doing nobody any good! We're in old Dick's range now, Clyde, all his for thirty miles this way and sixty the other. Well, he runs it, anyway —he says he's got an interest. There's his fence now. That'll be his horse pasture, I reckon."

The wash broadened as they came out onto the upland.

On both sides of the road the land swept away for miles, rising to mountains with trees on them. They arrived suddenly at their destination, with the light thickening toward evening; their destination was a group of small gray buildings and a windmill set off to the right of the road.

The lane was ruts in hard earth. There was a corral, which had a loading chute; the road dipped to a little stream flowing quietly. They crossed the stream and entered high brush, so that they could not see the buildings until they were almost upon them, and then the buildings lay in a soft evening shadow. There was a gate, which Clyde opened. Slowly Sam drove into the lot and pulled up beside the windmill.

For a moment the place appeared lifeless, and Clyde saw instantly how small and gray and mean the buildings were; nothing like the white buildings of the valley ranches and the ranches near the town of Albo, and Clyde was a little surprised. There were two cabins, a row of sheds, more corrals. A dog barked, and Clyde turned his head to see a man standing in the door of one of the cabins.

ii

Dick Tatum was a short heavy man with a hard little belly above his belt. His teeth were crooked, whisky-colored; a haze of beard thickened and blurred the line of his jaws. When he took off his hat inside the cabin, he showed a bald head, and was not an impressive man. He moved slowly and clumsily about the stove. Great pauses lurched through his talk, but he never quite ceased talking. Neither of his guests had much to say.

Clyde sat on a green kitchen chair and watched. The horses had been grained, watered, and released upon a bale of Dick's hay; the groceries and bed rolls had been brought in, and

Dick had persuaded them to give up the scouting. He had insisted that scouting was unnecessary. He was obviously hungry, and, Clyde thought, bored at the prospect of running mustangs. Now he was talking about other things, and most of his talk was directed at Sam.

"The fillaree's that high down there," he said, moving one hand vaguely two or three feet above the floor. "I never see such feed, Sam. Yeoh, them steers are rolling in it, it's tickling their old bellies, Sam—I was down there last week and saw it myself. Old man Marshall was down there, Sam, just looking. I saw Cecil Bunting last week up in Tonopah. . . ."

Ranches were mentioned; some were for sale and could be had for as little as twenty or thirty thousand dollars. They were back-country ranches that only Dick knew about, that interested him, that he might someday think of buying; but they did not sound like pleasant places. Clyde cherished always the thought of the house and two lots which he owned in an Illinois city, an inheritance from his father worth in all perhaps twenty-five thousand dollars, and lately he had thought of the house and lots chiefly as means toward installing himself in a pleasant Western place. He could buy such a place if he chose, and this was a fact he treasured. But now, listening to Dick, Clyde could not think of himself as living in a place sanctioned or even known about by Dick, for Dick was devious and almost sullen in his talk, and his only interest seemed to be a commercial interest. He seemed to want only money or ways of making money.

Names ran mysteriously in and out of his talk, and Clyde could not follow him. Anecdotes were begun, forgotten, resumed again at the wrong places. Hints of feeling appeared, of anger, of irritation, of contempt, but were not explained. Laughter jumped suddenly and slyly out of the monologue. Sam seemed to understand the hints and stories, and joined the laughter at the proper moments, nodding his head to show agreement, but Clyde was left alone in bewilderment.

His enthusiasm for running mustangs was almost gone. He saw in Dick a mean little fat man too busy with frying beef and meaningless stories to bother with the hunt, and he felt Sam moving away from him into Dick's murky world; for Sam was listening politely, apparently with great interest. He sat hunched on a chair, awkward as he always was inside a room, but he held himself like a guest on his best behavior, or like a boy with family near; and not a word about the hunt.

Clyde sighed a little, and made a little laugh to follow the others: he told himself that he might as well not be there. He felt like the new boy in the class, and he remembered unhappily Sam's promises about mustangs. They were noble promises: the big range presided over by Dick Tatum had few cattle on it now because of the recent dry years, perhaps no more than a hundred head, and the wild horses were thriving; Dick would be glad to have them over for a hunt, and would help; there would be action, there would be sport. Sam would find two or three other riders to go with them, and they would have a drive, a sweep of wild horses. . . .

The smell of frying beef began to fill the cabin: thin cuts from a carcass hung in a cellar, muffled in flour and grease now, darkening. The coffee was boiling. Slowly Dick crowded them toward the table and filled plates for them, and Clyde felt warmth at the prospect of food, but the warmth was matched by a chill feeling that the hunt would be a failure, the weekend wasted or made dark by the little man with the bald head and the heavy belly. It was one thing, he told himself, to play games with Sam, to ride good horses, practice roping, and talk; to find pleasure in the company of a cowboy in the evenings and on Sundays, listening to his stories and studying him; but quite another thing to come so far to eat with a stranger in a strange cabin and be dazed by unintelligible talk. Sam was unpleasant when drunk, drunk fairly often, and sometimes cruel to his horses, but he was essentially kind, Clyde was sure, enthusiastic, polite with ladies; and always good company. Dick Tatum looked like none of these, and Clyde was discouraged: he wondered when the others would come, he wondered when he would have a chance to speak with Sam alone.

"Go on, eat, you fellers," Dick said. "There's plenty of beef. I'll have the gravy here in a minute. Help yourself to the coffee. When you reckon those other fellers will come, Sam? Them other mustang hunters?"

"Later," Sam said. "They couldn't get off as early as Clyde and me. Clyde here has got the good kind of job, teaching those kids. They're all worn out by three o'clock, and he's got to let 'em go." Sam smiled, and Clyde was grateful; he recognized an attempt to bring him into the conversation.

Dick swayed back from the stove, rocking awkwardly on the heels of his boots, and looked across the narrow space at Clyde: he had blue chilly eyes, but his face simulated innocence; three times he nodded his head.

"Yeoh," he said. "I never knew many perfessers, now. What do you teach? Arithmetic? I quit school when we came to the arithmetic. I just rimmed on out of there, and that was the first time I left Texas. Here now, Sam, let me give you some gravy. Hold your plate out, Sam."

His monologue continued throughout the meal and did not stop afterward, and after a time Clyde began to understand a little better, to catch meanings, but he did not like the meanings. The cabin became oppressive; it seemed too small. There were three calendars on the walls, and each had a picture of a girl on it: three girls in swimming suits, one with a red-and-white-striped parasol. Two sheepskin coats hung near the stove. With the door closed, the atmosphere was heavy with the smells of grease and sweat and burning cedarwood; the windows were blotched with ancient dust.

The meanings in Dick's talk did nothing to clear the air, and Clyde sank deeper into dejection. It became clear that Dick had few friends, many shadowy enemies; he had praise for no one. There appeared to be a plot against him somewhere to the east, near Goldpoint; men met and talked in a cabin there; the plot had something to do with water rights on the east slope of Gold Mountain. Dick would make a point of leaving clear tracks on that slope within the next two weeks: this much for a warning. Later he might drive his pickup truck through Goldpoint without stopping, and there could be no misunderstandings after that.

Miners had persuaded the county supervisors to put in a road in a canyon to the south, connecting with the main highway in Fishbone Valley; saying that a road would help a new tungsten mine to be developed there; but Dick knew these miners. One had a record from New Mexico: Dick had heard about that one day in Tonopah. Another was a drunk. A third had a wooden leg. It was clear: these men were not miners. Dick had missed a calf near their mine not two weeks before; what were roads for? Next week Dick would ride past their cabins without hurrying.

A family of homesteaders had claimed one of Dick's windmills in Fishbone Valley, but everybody knew about them. The old man was lazy, and drank; and the boys slept with Indian girls.

As for the Indians, it was well known that an Indian butchered a beef any time he had a chance. But by now the Indians had heard about Dick. They could be expected to change their ways.

Clyde grew tired. It required great effort to show approval of stories which dismayed him when he understood them at all. He had never seen a man so tied in suspicion. Not since the war had he seen a man so ready with anger over apparent trifles. It was a great relief when Dick grew sleepy.

By nine o'clock, the other hunters being still absent, Dick persuaded them to go to bed and let the others find their own way in; but he himself continued to talk from his bed. As Clyde fell off to sleep, he could just hear Sam making the required polite answer to a buzz of words from the other room, and Clyde had time to wonder at the extent of Sam's willingness to be agreeable.

Clyde woke the next morning to find things happening. Sam was up, and hurrying; he was busy about the stove. Two men Clyde did not know were standing just outside the opened door, talking to Sam. Dick was sitting on his bed, alternately scratching himself and straightening his cotton socks. Clyde dressed quickly and went out to help. After Sam introduced him to the two men, Scott and Jonas, he went to the woodpile and split kindling for the stove. It was a bright chilly morning. In the corrals the horses stood quietly with their heads in burlap feed bags, and Clyde smiled: that was Sam's work. The hunt might happen after all!

But the preparations went slowly. Dick's plan, hinted at the night before but not revealed, was to load all the horses in Dick's big truck, haul them to a place Dick knew about, unload, and make the chase; anything they caught they could bring back in the other smaller trucks. But Dick was slow: when at last they got under way, it was almost nine o'clock. Sam and Clyde rode with Dick in the big truck; the other two hunters, Will Scott the highway maintenance man and the barber Jonas from Albo, came on behind in their truck. Dick drove crudely; he did not know how to double-clutch. When he shifted gears, the whole truck was racked by the shuddering of gears; and still he talked.

Slowly his plan came clear: there would be a drive to a corral; they would try to take a band of seven or eight mustangs in one big turn. Sam listened attentively, and his early-morning enthusiasm had settled into a deep concentration. Clyde had seen this before. When Sam began to work at the only work he knew well and cared about, work with horses, roping, herding, he tended to disappear into that work; he became what he was doing.

Now he sat carefully in the narrow seat of the truck, looking quietly out at the country they passed. He had large blank blue eyes, and now they bulged a little. A line of strain ran down through his jowls.

Clyde felt once again the pleasure of watching Sam move into action; it was always a fine sight. Clyde felt clumsy, large, unhandy, watching Sam, but he did not mind; it was a pleasure to think about the things Sam could do with his sturdy body. Gloating a little, Clyde contemplated the successes Sam would have. The others would be impressed. Their jaws would sag a little.

They traveled up the highway for perhaps eight miles, the road rising; the peaks at the edge of the upland came nearer with their tree-covered slopes. They turned south near a cluster of buildings which was an abandoned mine, passed a spring with a corral built around it, and entered a winding draw. Twice they passed cattle: long-legged yellow Brahman crosses—cows and calves; a red Durham bull. The old truck, rocking and swaying on the uneven wheel ruts, moved slowly upward.

At the head of the draw they found an abandoned ranch

in a pocket of the upland. A drift fence ran away from them toward the empty house and the corrals; behind the house was one of the mountains. Dick stopped the truck and explained: three miles to the south was a spring where a band of mustangs watered in the mornings; by now they would have a bellyful, and be slow with the weight of water; they could be driven to the drift fence, and turned there to the corrals. The gate to the corrals was open; Dick had seen to that the day before. Vaguely Dick pointed to the south. "On the other side of that little ridge there's a kind of valley," he said. "The spring is at the end of the valley. So we bring 'em up the valley, keeping 'em off the mountain and keeping 'em from coming this way. We take 'em over the little ridge and down into here and bend 'em at the fence."

"Sure, you bet!" Sam said, interrupting. "It's a good layout for a drive! Where do we unload?"

"We can go on a way in the truck," Dick said.

They unloaded a mile away, just out of sight of the valley Dick had promised. Sam and Dick were conferring steadily and seemed in perfect agreement. By the time the horses were out of the truck, a plan had been arranged, and Clyde waited patiently to hear what his share in it would be. He was surprised to find action so near. Grudgingly he acknowledged to himself that he should be grateful to Dick for arranging that action.

When they rode out onto the top of the hill, staying behind the cedars, Clyde saw at the end of the valley a clot of green, which was the spring, and near it irregular patches of rich color, and these patches were wild horses.

He caught his breath. There was a blotch of white under one of the trees at the spring; nearby were the clear light color of bay and the abruptness of black. He could not make out the forms of the horses, but he believed in them. Sam's voice was speaking softly to him, but he did not turn his eyes from the spring.

"Clyde, now, listen to me, boy. Don't make any mistakes. Listen! I only got time to tell it to you once. You see them horses? Old Dick is going to work around 'em and get 'em started. Will Scott and Jonas are going over to the other side, to the mountain, to keep 'em from going out that way. You and I stay on this side, you hear? Get it straight, now—we don't want you messing up the drive, we got a good drive going! This is perfect for a drive! Well, we keep 'em from going this way until they're over the ridge and headed into the drift fence. Then we bend 'em, Clyde. I'll show you your post, and I'll be right near. We got to do it right, boy!"

"Sure, sure," Clyde said. "God damn, look at those ponies! There they *are*, Sam!"

"We got to do it right," Sam said again. "Come on, now."

Clyde looked away from the spring and saw Dick riding off on his old white horse at a stiff trot; he was riding west, he would stay out of sight of the spring. Jonas and Scott were moving off the other way, leaning forward in their saddles, finding a course through trees which would lead them to the mountain.

Clyde reined over to follow Sam. They rode through the trees, through the smell of cedars. The sun was rising, getting warm. A wind blew through the needles of the little cedars, and was resonant in them. The sky was empty, blue. The sound of the horses' hoofs mingled with the sound of twisting leather, and Clyde's rope rubbed against his thigh. He fingered the rope, and felt the live firm fibers of it. Sweat ran down from each armpit, and his heart was thumping.

Sam pulled up and raised his hand. He was riding his big bay; his face was set severely. "Here," he said. "Now, remember this is a drive, Clyde! Keep your rope on the sad-

dle! Don't go fooling with that rope. Take your position behind one of these trees. Keep yourself out of sight, but get
to where you can see those horses when they come. When
it's time, just let 'em see you, and come on behind 'em and
to the side. Don't come out too early, you'll spook 'em back!
Remember what we're trying to do, boy! We can do it if
everybody gets right! I'll be back a way, toward the drift
fence from here—to your left. I'll pick 'em up after you do.
Have you got all that? And remember, if you lose the drive
you can get it back by listening for the other boys hollering. Keep track of the hollering and you'll be all right. I got
to go now."

Abruptly he swung the big bay horse away and was off
through the trees. Tensely Clyde moved out toward the edge
of the trees, taking care to find the tree that would serve him
best; and he found one twisted just low enough to the ground,
its green boughs spreading. Cautiously he moved his black
horse in behind it and looked out: the spring was in sight,
and he felt a strong urge to watch it, but he restrained himself, savoring the feeling even more strongly. Deliberately
he stepped off his horse and tightened his cinches; he ran his
hand over the leather band which held his rope in place.
Everything was ready, everything in place.

Then he remounted and looked out over the landscape;
again drew breath sharply, seeing the horses still circling
the spring, grazing the grass which grew there. He was
nearer to them now. He could just make out the outlines of
the white horse and one of the blacks.

The wind blew up a little and started chills along his back
where the sweat was. He shivered and felt the silence about
him, and for a moment thought there were no sounds but
the sound of the wind in the cedars. Then a cricket stuttered
sharply near him, a steady sound made strange by the silence

it hung in. A bird fluttered in a tree behind him, and he turned his head to look for it, but saw only quivering cedar needles where the bird had been.

Hurriedly he looked again at the wild horses to see that they had not gone away, and again got off to check his cinches. The black horse was restive; perhaps something was wrong; but nothing was wrong, and he remounted more nervous than he had been before.

Time passed; his nervousness disappeared and he became bored. All was quiet at the spring. It was a quiet pastoral scene; until, from behind trees on the slope above the spring, Dick appeared on his white horse. The white horse was walking, picking his way down the slope. For what seemed many minutes the white horse came down the hill while the mustangs at the spring paid no attention, heads bent to the grasses. The black one moved slowly around the others, his movements, from a distance, looking stiff and slow. It seemed no great change when the black horse raised his head, and for a moment Clyde had the nightmarish feeling that perhaps the horses were not mustangs at all, but tame animals who could be caught in the open with a handful of grain.

Then the black horse raised his head higher. Up came the heads of the others. For a few moments a balance between fear and interest shivered in the scene. Clyde's legs quivered against his saddle.

And then the balance was broken, Dick was cantering down the hill, waving one arm, shouting, and the band of mustangs was in motion: chips of color spurting away from the green of the spring, as if blown by a strong wind. They strung out behind the black, first the black, then a bay, another bay, the white, two bays, a buckskin, and at first they were moving slowly, stretching for a start. Their forms appeared around their colors, and Clyde understood that they were much nearer than he had supposed, moving much faster than he had expected. Dust rose behind them. Dick's white horse galloped into the dust and disappeared.

Clyde swallowed, and told himself to keep cool; he must not show himself too soon, he remembered. Briefly the horses passed through trees at the foot of the mountain, until there was a sound of shouting—Scott and Jonas, Clyde thought—and then they reappeared, veering out a little into the valley. They were going faster now, running powerfully. Tentatively Clyde urged his black horse out from behind his tree, and then pulled up; the mustangs were heading up the valley, going fast enough now to make a whiplike line of their motion.

Clyde moved on a little, down the hill, wondering when he should begin to go with them. He remembered Sam's words: "Don't come out too early, you'll spook 'em back!" Suddenly the mustangs veered off again, and were lost in the trees at the foot of the mountain. Clyde said *Now!* and urged the black horse into a gallop down the hill.

Carefully he held the black horse in; there was a long way to go. As he looked out across the valley, he saw Dick on his white horse galloping along with a regular, almost stately ease, and then Dick too was lost in the trees. Once again there was a sound of shouting from the mountain.

Clyde made a good three quarters of a mile at the gallop, angling across the valley and into the trees. There he turned and headed to his left, expecting to come on the drive at any moment. He became aware that he had not seen Sam, and he thought that strange, but he did not pause to look around. After a time he was in a forest, surprisingly tangled, deep, and all was still.

Puzzled, he pulled up and listened. There was nothing to hear except the sounds of forest and mountain. A blue jay

chittered somewhere above him on the mountain. A lizard
watched him from the base of a cedar tree. He looked for
dust, but could see nothing but trees between the branches of
trees, and the floor of the forest thick with brown needles
and soft underfoot; the black horse pawed at the needles with
a soft sound.

He rode on, and after a few steps became convinced that
the drive had failed. It was clear. The mustangs had gone
up the mountain and away; Jonas and Scott had failed. He
pulled up again: surely he would be able to hear the drive if
it were still alive—the men shouting, thudding hoofs. He
slumped down in the saddle and went on at a walk. The
black horse sniffed the resinous air.

Now and then he looked for tracks, but he did not expect
to find any; he guessed that the mustangs had gone up the
mountain somewhere behind him, near the place where they
had entered the trees for the second time. It was too bad.
Sam would be unhappy; it might be hard to persuade him
to undertake another such trip, and Clyde had already decided that another trip was necessary. It would not do, he
told himself, to begin and end his experience of mustangs with
failure. Well, there was time; it would be childish to find de-
feat in one mishap. Sam had always said it was difficult.

Ten minutes later he came out on the little ridge that
formed one side of the pocket where the abandoned ranch
was. He lit a cigarette and went down through the trees,
guessing that he would find the others at the corrals.

What he found, however, was Sam sitting the big bay horse
out in the open, in the middle of the pocket. In the clear
light, man and horse were rounded and quiet as a statue. Sam
was looking down at the brush in front of him.

The high curved belly of a horse lay heaving under
the sage, and Clyde saw it first as a patch of color, of bay;

sweat glittered on it. As he rode closer, he saw what it was. He saw the three tied feet, kicking. He saw the dark of an eye.

"Keep away from him," Sam said quietly. "He's had enough shock already. He's just a colt."

Dazedly, Clyde looked around him. To his right, at the foot of the ridge near the house, he saw another bay colt, this one haltered and tied to a tree. The colt reared, pawed the air, and toppled to his side, falling heavily, still struggling. His hoofs lashed up a blur of dust.

In the corral there was more dust, and within the dust was the buckskin, much bigger than the colts. As Clyde watched, the buckskin reared, struggled, fell.

"Where were you, boy?" Sam asked mildly. "I didn't see you after the drive started. It was a real good drive."

iii

Everything had gone well, it appeared, until Will Scott's bridle broke. The mustangs had swerved past him then, but in the confusion Sam had roped the two bay colts, and Dick the buckskin mare. Now, with the two colts tied in one corral and the buckskin mare in another, the hunters were discussing the hunt.

"It was all right," Dick said. "She just went right along like she should have."

Everyone nodded. Will Scott, a lean little dark-haired man wearing a red plaid hunting cap, nodded vigorously. "I was afraid o' that headstall," he said, "but I sure thought it had another summer in it, yes I did. I was so close to that buckskin mare I could a shouted her down if I'd a tried! She was a good drive, Dick."

"We were right with 'em all the way!" Jonas said. He was

clearly a happy barber as he looked across at Sam respectfully and waited for him to speak.

"I never been on a better drive," Sam said. "She was a
dandy."

Clyde remained silent. He had nothing to say. He had
missed the drive by moving slowly when he should have
moved fast, and now he sensed his separation from the others.
They were polite: they included him in the party but kept
the conversation away from his failure. Nothing they did,
however, could make it possible for him to enter the talk
about the hunt, and he had no doubt of the pleasures of that
talk; the pleasure was on their faces.

Dick, of course, remained calm; he was an old hand, and
showed it. Sam had made it clear on the trip over that Dick
disapproved of mustanging because it was hard on saddle
horses and because he had the old-time stockman's hatred
for mustangs; and Clyde was willing to believe that few
things but money and cattle could interest Dick at any time.

Twice now, since the end of the hunt, Dick had called him
"perfesser," mildly, slyly, but loud enough to be heard.

Jonas and Scott showed their pleasure openly: they would
have stories for their wives. Scott had been raised on a ranch,
but he had been away from it a long time, and had only his
horse and saddle, and now this hunt, to remind him of the
old days; the hunt could be expected to stay in his memory
for a long time. Jonas was an amateur roper who rode in the
parade each year at rodeo time; it would be a long time before the barbershop heard the end of his story.

Sam had moved carefully, holding his fact tight, since the
hunt, and had said little, but Clyde had seen him this way before, after other triumphs, and he understood that Sam was
happy and well pleased. Grimly Clyde assured himself that

he would not hesitate to use that pleasure, that happiness, to persuade Sam to come again. Clyde had decided that it was necessary to come again. He only hoped that the company might be a little different.

Angrily he looked at the little group of men. They were a strange lot, he told himself, to find in a place like this. Sam and Dick belonged; they were cowboys of the true type, clumsy in walking, with battered bodies; they were masters of horses and cattle, and they had proved it. The buckskin mare sulked against the rope not fifteen feet away; still she struggled.

Jonas and Scott were different. Jonas would not have a horse that bucked, and Scott made a living by common labor; the West was changing, the West had changed. Clyde gazed distastefully at Will Scott's red plaid hunting cap: it was an emblem of independence, perhaps, but not to be accepted for that. He looked at Jonas's yellow cowboy boots with the intricate blue patterns running all the way down to the toe; the boots were useful but excessive.

The conversation turned to the captured horses. It was agreed that the bay colts made a nice pair, and Sam let it be known that he planned to break them for children to ride. Dick gave the buckskin mare to Jonas, and the gift seemed natural.

"Old Dick can come out and get one any time he wants, anyway!" Jonas said.

The conversation was slowing down but still active when the sound of a car's motor interrupted it. The car appeared, moving slowly up the rutted road toward the corrals. It was a new car, still shiny under its light coating of dust: a Cadillac. Dick got up and walked slowly down the road to meet it. The car pulled up, and three men got out. Dick shook hands with them and smiled. Casually he walked with them toward the corrals, and Clyde heard him mutter a few words about a little roundup of horses.

Clyde was surprised and a little shocked at the appearance of the men: they seemed the kind to be found in Cadillacs, but he could not understand why they should be here, and he resented their presence instantly. He could feel his face stiffen.

A middle-aged man seemed to be the important one; the others were younger, and seemed uncomfortable. The leader wore a blue nylon sport shirt and gray slacks; over his eyes were elaborate dark glasses. He talked rapidly, and was clearly excited at finding captured mustangs in the corral. Rapidly he spoke to Dick, asking questions; he praised the bay colts and asked who owned them. Once he turned to his friends and asked them if they had ever seen anything like this before, to which they replied uneasily, shaking their heads, and kept their distance from the colts.

Then there were introductions all around, and the hunters explained the hunt, Clyde again abstaining. The name of the middle-aged man was Cathcart; he lived in Fresno, but he was the owner of the Bar Nine Ranch in Fishbone Valley, down for a brief visit from his farming business in the San Joaquin Valley. One of his companions was the pilot of the plane which had brought the party; the other was a secretary.

Clyde had heard of Cathcart; he was an industrialist of vegetables, who owned the Bar Nine Ranch for sport and for income-tax purposes. His plane was talked about in Albo. His name had appeared in Dick's conversations of the night before, and now Clyde began to understand why: Cathcart was worth discussing because he could buy things.

As Clyde watched, standing a little aside because he re-

sented the intrusion of these unlikely people, something
seemed to be happening in the group of men. Dick and Sam
moved aside with Cathcart and spoke softly together; Clyde
could not hear what they were saying. They walked back
and forth past the colts; now and then Sam pointed at one of
the colts and nodded his head, speaking swiftly, until there
were smiles all around. After that, the hunt reached a swift
conclusion.

Clyde was a guest; he did what the others did. There was
a meal of fried beef at Dick's cabin, and more talk of the
hunt; the two bay colts were loaded in Sam's truck, Dick
having agreed to bring the horses to the Ambrose ranch in
his own truck when he came over the next Monday; and by
three o'clock Sam and Clyde were under way again and
Sam was talking wildly about the arrangements Clyde had
watched him make with Cathcart.

"He bought those colts!" Sam said. "Bought 'em, just like
that, and didn't even name a price! We'll make a price after
I get 'em broke for his kids to ride. Mustangs! A pair of
mustang colts! What do you think of that, Clyde? That
shows what you can do with moneyed people, Clyde.
Haven't I told you before?"

Clyde remembered the mustang band running in dust
through the little valley.

"I *know* these moneyed people, Clyde. They don't care
what a thing costs. He's paying me for the colts *and* for the
price of breaking 'em. I've met that class of people before.
That summer I was packing in the Sierras I had moneyed
people with me—real nice people, Clyde! One of 'em tipped
me twenty-five dollars after I'd taken him out for just eight
days. Ah, they're the ones you've got to look for, Clyde. I'll
tell you something, boy. I'm going to find me one of those
people who wants to have a ranch to take his family to—you

know, a little place with a few cows and a few horses—and I'll talk him into letting me run it. I could do that, boy. I might even get an interest if I worked it right. You can do that, Clyde. I've known cowboys that've already done it. That's the way a poor man has got to do it these days, Clyde. That's the way you get a stake started so you can do something. Oh, you watch, Clyde, you watch! And I'll have those colts so gentle a dog could ride 'em!"

Clyde nodded his head to show agreement; it was not necessary to speak. Turning his head, he looked back through the cab window at the misery in the eyes of the colts. They were lying tied to the bed of the truck, their sides heaving.

"I didn't care much for Cathcart," Clyde said a little later. "But I expect he can pay the price."

"He won't even turn his head! And I'll be able to use the money, Clyde. Maybe I'll buy me a quarter horse to train for the cutting contests, and make me some money on him. I can make a cutting horse, Clyde. I've made plenty already in my life, I can do it again. Look there at those cabins and that old hay rake, Clyde—that's what happens to you when you don't have a stake. A poor man's got to look for something besides land these days, let me tell you. Didn't we make a trade with that man!"

Clyde let his thoughts go back, past the entrance of Cathcart, past the presence of Jonas and Scott, to rest with the fine picture of Sam the quick cowboy. It was a true picture, and he liked it, remembering Sam's face at the end of the hunt: pure pleasure was in that face, it was the face of a man who could be what he was doing. Sam lived for fine moments like those moments in the hunt, and he lived high, Clyde thought, for this land produced those moments, and a ready hand could take them. It occurred to Clyde that he could imitate Sam in some ways, without hurting himself or

others, and live high also. He need only choose, and then
reach and take; imitation was easy.

It did no harm now for Sam to talk about money and
moneyed people; he had lived with poverty all his life. In the
barren hills of New Mexico his family had scratched for water and prayed for rain, and now Sam alone was praying for
a different kind of rain, because it was his habit to hope.
Clyde smiled a little, telling himself that one hunt had happened already, and that others would happen later, and that
the hunts were almost enough; the hunts reminded him of
possibilities.

"Maybe we could do it again sometime, Sam," he said.
"We did pretty well today—at least, you did. I'd like to try
it again."

"We'll do it! You goddamn right we'll do it. You bet.
It's real sport, ain't it? Next fall, when you come back. Old
Dick'll be glad to have us. Ain't he a talker, though? He'll
have us back so's he can talk to us. Sure we'll go again. Next
to wild cattle I'll take mustangs any day, Clyde, and that's
a fact."

They were out in the middle of Fishbone Valley now, with
the Piute Mountains before them, dark. Clyde remembered
that he had failed in the hunt, but already that pain was
growing small as he contemplated another hunt; he would
do better then! He relaxed, he let the tide of country roll
past him, peaks, troughs, hollows, and empty light, and grew
calm. He watched a hawk sail off into a point of air which
was the hawk, and then tip itself out of sight; gone suddenly,
changing nothing, gone in distance. Sam talked on. Now and
then one of the colts kicked out with a free foot and rattled
the side of the truck, with a sound like the sound of a
hammer.

iv

Clyde went off to summer school at the great university near San Francisco because classes taken there increased his salary from the Albo High School. In the educational economy of the Albo public schools, classes taken at a university were like money invested; schedules in the principal's office predicted the sure return. Fortunately, Clyde was interested enough in history to enjoy the classes he was told to take; he felt comfortable among the graduate students, and found them pleasant to talk to. It was not a heavy summer.

The valley behind the coast hills was cool when he came to it; he was chilly the first few nights, and slept under blankets. He found a room in an old yellow stucco house that stood in an apricot orchard, and though the orchard was decaying from lack of care, blotched with dead trees, a few of the trees were bearing when he arrived. On the second night he had apricots after supper. There were a dozen big eucalyptus trees around the house, one with an owl in it, and at night he could hear the wind scattering bark fallen from the trees. It was a pleasant place to live, quiet and cool at night for Clyde's studies, washed during the day by a warm and milky light.

Nothing in the summer was so bright as the desert. Most of the good teachers were on vacation; none of Clyde's classes was brilliant. Quietly he listened to the lectures, carefully prepared the required papers. Between classes he drank coffee with friends under a colonnade. Twice a week he played tennis with a student of political science.

It was a mild time. The towns near the university were suburban towns, sustained on money earned in San Francisco, and none of them was handsome. The main streets were merely new; the shop fronts glittered and the restaurants were dull. Clyde avoided the towns, and saw few movies. Three times he went to San Francisco, twice for baseball games which turned out badly, once for a concert; but even in San Francisco the summer made life slow.

But Clyde accepted the summer as a way of passing time for profit, and enjoyed it when he could. He liked teaching because he could usually like his students, and he did not mind studying, but now his thoughts were on the desert, and on the image, assembled gradually in his mind since his arrival in Albo, since his friendship with Sam, of a small ranch or farm, white house, barn, hayfields, and pasture, under a blue mountain; and he was looking forward to mustangs. Sometimes as he sat in his classes he thought about the desert and about the wild horses ranging the high plains of Nevada, and found pleasure in the fact that he could be at home in two worlds. Now and then he got out his rope and practiced with it, roping a kitchen chair. When the time came to return to Albo, feelings of relief and joy accompanied him, and stayed. Even Albo itself seemed pleasant, packed though it was with tourists in for the first round of the Labor Day Rodeo.

The town was full of people. Cars crowded the streets. Many of the townspeople wore cowboy boots and cowboy hats for the occasion. The waitresses in one of the restaurants wore fringed skirts of imitation buckskin, and the bars were packed. It was a mixed-up frolic, a mongrel celebration, but Clyde enjoyed it, and felt at home in it. He had come to this town by accident, because of the job in the high school, but now after a year the town was as much a home to him as any other place. People knew him; his students grinned at him on the streets and bobbed their heads almost respectfully.

Immediately he began to look for Sam Leathers, and he

did not hesitate in choosing the rodeo grounds as the place to look. There was no question about whether Sam would take part in the rodeo; he would be there. The only question was about the number of events he had entered. Confidently Clyde made his way to the rodeo grounds, and first to the corrals on the north side of the arena; these were the corrals behind the bucking chutes, and the fences were high. He stopped in front of the bulls: instantly there was a rush out of the herd. A black Brahman bull stood away from the others, poised like a deer on his slender legs. His head was up; his horns were the color of tarnished silver. He stood motionless while the other bulls moved in the corral, their humps tossing.

Clyde nodded with approval and walked on to the west end of the arena, where the roping chutes were; and there he met Sam, sitting quietly on a black horse Clyde did not know. Sam waved, smiled, and stepped down; he handed the reins to a boy standing beside him and came across to Clyde. His hat, shirt, levis, and boots were new; his round broken face showed a controlled excitement. "I'm up in the first flight of calf ropers," he said, "on a borrowed horse. I got to stay here, Clyde. God damn! I'm riding a bareback horse and a bull!"

He seemed calm enough. There was talk about the mustang colts: Sam was always careful to introduce topics which they could share. It appeared that the colts were well broken now; the children of John Ambrose, owner of the ranch where Sam worked, had been riding them for a month now. It was time to settle with Cathcart, and Sam would tend to that as soon as the rodeo was over.

"But you know how it is, Clyde," he said. "I couldn't do anything while the rodeo's on!"

The rodeo began with flags and a parade. After the pa-

rade came the calf roping, and Sam was the third roper out.
He broke fast on the black horse and made a perfect throw
in the middle of the arena, but he had bad luck with the
calf; it was a yellow Brahman calf that sulked against the
rope and would not jump. Sam fought hard, but needed
twenty-seven seconds to tie the calf. Stiffly he rode out of
the arena.

The action from beginning to end had the quality of ritual.
Each motion was prearranged; nothing was left to invention,
all was imitation. It was very satisfying for Clyde, who knew
what it was the cowboys imitated: it was the old functional
life of cattle herders. Thus, the cowboys played in such a
way that they seemed to be working. They were serious, intent, and even grim. The carousing that happened later was
merely carousing.

"I'll just try it for myself one of these days," Clyde said
to himself, remembering how Sam had told him one day that
he had all the strength he needed for the purpose. "Big as
you are, Clyde, you could dog a steer with the best of 'em.
You got the power. What's the fun in teaching school?"

After the calf roping came the saddle broncs. The big
horses bucked hard, but of the first six riders, only one was
set down before the whistle, so that Clyde became a little
bored with the monotony of the riders' successes. Ten years
before, Clyde had been told, the Albo rodeo had been an
amateur rodeo; riders and ropers came from nearby counties,
crowds were small, and most of the people knew one another.
Now, with fewer cowboys in the country, and more tourists, the storekeepers of the town had seen fit to import professionals. Announcers, clowns, riders, even the animals were
professionals, with the difference that the men enjoyed the
performances while the animals did not. Rodeo was like baseball now, a game for experts to make money in, and only a

few of the range cowboys, rarely gifted men like Sam, could compete with them.

"It's a good game," Clyde told himself. "But, as games go, I like the mustangs better. No profits in the mustangs." He felt quite cheerful: he could not have the old days as they had been, though he might imitate the little he knew of them, but he could still enjoy the games handed down from those times. The games, like the mustangs, were reminders of possibilities, and he could choose them or reject them as it pleased him. It was a little harder for Sam, who knew no other games, who was a little old now for choosing or rejecting.

After the bucking horses came the bulldogging, and after the bulldogging the bareback horses. Sam came out on a small bay horse who bucked well, and lasted out the ride; there was applause when the pickup man came to take him down. After that, Clyde waited only to see Sam ride a bull. This was the last event, but Sam came out first and was set down quickly. It was the black bull Clyde remembered, who had horns the color of tarnished silver. He jumped only once, and then stood with his head down, watching Sam, and a front hoof pawing the beaten earth of the arena. The crowd fell silent; Sam sat where he had fallen, gravely watching the bull, not moving until the bull moved; and the bull did not move until the clown came with a rubber balloon tied to a stick. The clown drew the bull away; Sam rose to his feet and began to look for his hat; but with the passing of tension Clyde became aware of tension.

"That was a little tight," Clyde said to a man standing beside him. "The bull might have done something." Then Clyde went home, pleased because Sam had taken a second in the day money for the bareback riding, and because he was to meet Sam that evening. It was a good enough homecoming. There would be talk that evening with a good talker.

Unfortunately, Sam was not to be found that night at the appointed time, at the appointed place. That was a bar known as the Silver Shovel, within whose darkness Clyde drank two bottles of beer before he gave up his quest. He was not angry or even surprised, because he knew that Sam was drinking, and knew that Sam was unreliable when drinking, but he was restless enough to spend a little time wandering before he went home. He entered barbershops, drugstores, and bars, and patrolled the west side of the street, where most of the bars were, and finally found, in front of Nick's Bar, Sam's wife, Bonna June, with the baby on her hip, waiting patiently.

Her name was a country name, and it suited her. Clyde could remember, from summers spent on his uncle's farm in Kansas, many such girls, many such young wives: they were quiet, pleasant, ungraceful; they felt at home only on the lonesome precincts of their farms. They did not talk much to their husbands when other people were near, and they did not know how to speak to other men, but they could enjoy other women, and Clyde had sometimes heard their talk among themselves. They talked of cake recipes; they admired the dresses in the mail-order catalogues. They were quiet, obedient women.

Bonna June greeted him with a fine smile and told him that she was to meet Sam here, but that he was a little late. She seemed happy, though a little uncomfortable, and Clyde guessed that she was a little hesitant about the propriety of speaking to a man not her husband on the main street of town. The baby was awake: it was a bald little girl with blue eyes.

"He'll be along!" Bonna June said. "He just gets a little excited at rodeo time!"

There was nothing for Clyde to say. It did not seem the

time to mention the fact that Sam had made an appointment with him also, and it was not his place to offer to escort Bonna June home. He resolved to speak just long enough to be polite and then leave; but as he was making up his mind, he heard Sam's voice raised in a shout from behind the double doors of Nick's Bar. There was no mistaking the voice; Bonna June's head jerked sharply around.

"You goddam, gut-eating, calf-butchering Indian!"

In a flash Clyde took on a new piece of information about Sam: that, like his frontier forefathers, he hated Indians; but there was no time to do anything with the information but take it. There was noise inside the bar; from the noise as from a catapult a man crashed through the double doors and tore off up the street, running in long heavy strides. Clyde barely made out a glint of black hair and dark face under a street lamp. Startled, Clyde paused a moment, looked at Bonna June, whose face had gone lumpish with fright, and then stepped past the swinging double doors into the bar.

Even in that darkness it was no trouble to find Sam. He was sitting against the end of the bar, rubbing his jaw and cursing. As Clyde came in, he began to rise.

"God damn," he said. "I'll be go to hell. Somebody hit me!"

He shook his head as he came to his feet, and began to grin; between the distended lips, the broken yellow teeth were bloody. Then he laughed aloud and turned to the bar. "Drinks on me!" he called. "Everybody got to drink on me!" Reeling a little, and sensing Clyde near him, he turned. The room was full of men in big hats, the rodeo riders, some quiet, most of them laughing to see Sam rise with such spirit. "Clyde!" Sam said. "I didn't know you was here! I just got hit a terrible wallop, Clyde, a terrible wallop! Come here, have a drink. Where's that Indian?"

"Rimmed out," a voice said from the rear of the room. "He's back on the reservation by now, I reckon!" There was laughter in the room, and Sam joined it; he bent over and slapped his thighs, and went from that into a little jig. "Rimmed out!" he snorted. "Rimmed out! I guess he didn't get a drink after all!" The bartender, a thin young man, was washing glasses behind the bar; he seemed untroubled.

Carefully Clyde explained that Bonna June was outside. After a moment Sam straightened his hat, put money on the bar, and took Clyde by the arm. They went out together, to find Bonna June still waiting, as patient as ever, her fright gone.

Sam bent down and touched the baby's bald head, laughed and made clucking sounds with his tongue. Then he said hello to Bonna June. "How was the show, honey? Come on, now, I'll put you to bed over at my sister's. I've still got some celebrating to do. Come on, Clyde. We'll take the girl home and then go somewhere and talk about the rodeo—talk about mustangs too, by God! I saw old Dick Tatum a while ago, and he's invited us over again. Come on, now, girl, we got to get you to bed!"

They set off up the street, Bonna June a little behind. Bonna June walked clumsily with the baby on her hip; she smiled forward at Sam and asked no questions. Clyde remembered some of the things he had read about American frontier wives, and shook his head; here was a frontier wife walking down a main street of the twentieth century. Apparently she had a very clear idea of what her place was, and of how her life was to be lived.

The journey went off smoothly, like something rehearsed often before. Bonna June and the baby were delivered at the door of a small frame house on a side street. Sam opened the door for them, told them to sleep well, and clapped his hands for Clyde to follow him; and then he was off again into his celebrating.

"I learned celebrating from my old daddy," he told Clyde in the first bar they reached. "There was a good cowboy! And had his own place too, back there in New Mexico. One time he had near three hundred horses. But come a Saturday night in town, or a rodeo, and he was gone. It's the cowboy style, Clyde. It's always been that way."

Sam disliked whisky, but he drank it dutifully. There was a suggestion of ritual in his celebrations as in his work: he was a man who knew what he was supposed to do because he knew what he was. He spent himself carelessly because his father had done so, and because he felt it was expected of him; and enjoyed doing it, Clyde could see.

"I tell you, Clyde, I'd just like to rodeo all the time. Back there after the war I spent near two years rodeoing, and we had high times all the time. I'll have 'em again too, you bet. When I get a little money ahead, and a good horse to work with, you'll see. I'll fix up a rig. I'll get me a good horse trailer and build me a little house on the bed of that truck of mine, and we'll be gone to the shows all the time!"

Clyde stayed with him for almost three hours, hoping to persuade him to sleep in preparation for the rodeo the next day, but he could not do it, and finally gave up and went home. Before that time, however, Sam managed to purchase drinks with his rodeo winnings for something like fifteen or twenty men in several bars. He acquired a woman, a blonde child wearing buckskin riding clothes and cowboy boots; she sat on his lap while he talked excitedly, calling out to the rodeo riders to ask about future shows and to praise great horses seen or ridden years before in Texas, in New Mexico, in Arizona. When Clyde left him, he was explaining to the

girl what his father had told him about Billy the Kid and the
Lincoln County War.

Clyde left a little bewildered by Sam's energy, but somehow pleased by him. It was no credit to Sam that he cursed
Indians, but it was comforting to see him shake off the blow
as part of the evening and go on as before; not many men
were capable of that. Sam's code was a strange code, but it
fitted him; he was at home among the cowboys. Clyde
walked home shaking his head from time to time, a little
pleased that he did not suffer from Sam's social obligations;
the unsocial night was restful. At the door to the Silver
Shovel he thought he saw Dick Tatum talking to a woman
obviously a whore, but he did not pause to make sure. He
saw a heavy body wavering near the woman's body, a big
hat, a cigar, and thought he heard Dick's voice, but he hurried on, feeling that he would have nothing to say if he
stopped.

v

The early-morning chill was gone. The sky was empty, blue,
while Clyde sat on his black horse waiting for mustangs to
come up a canyon. The plan was different this time, but
otherwise Clyde had the feeling that he had returned to something pleasant in his past. The canyon was quiet, and Clyde
remembered how he had come to it: as before. The route had
unreeled itself like a familiar movie, each scene contriving the
next scene, the Wilson Valley giving way to the Piute Mountains, and after that the wastes of Fishbone Valley, and the
road, and the empty light; nothing changed. It was a country easily returned to; the paths were simple.

The plan for the day's hunt was simple too. There would
be no attempt, as before, to corral a band of mustangs. Today

they would rope. There was a band of six mares and colts and the black stallion they had chased before. The band watered at a spring in the lower reaches of the canyon. The plan was to relay the band up the canyon, running them hard, and hope to catch a few at the head of the canyon. It was Dick's plan, and Dick would begin it by starting the mustangs on their way. After Dick came Will Scott, and after Scott came Sam, who would move the mustangs to Clyde, whose job it was to try to turn the band back, or at least to hold them long enough for the others to catch up.

"It's kind of a wild way," Dick had said. "But Sam ought to get a throw, and the perfesser too, and maybe if I can find a short cut to the head of the drive I'll get one. We want to just burn their old asses coming up the canyon. Something'll happen if we do that, I reckon. Sure. We'll see."

It was clear that Clyde had been given a privileged position; he would have the best chance. "One thing for sure," he told himself, "I won't get left behind again!" It occurred to him that Dick was testing him, but he did not mind that. The black horse was in fine condition, hardened in on grain, his wind good, his feet newly shod. "And I'm ready too," Clyde muttered. "A man doesn't get too many chances like this!"

Carefully he surveyed the lay of the land. The canyon ran roughly from north to south, falling to the south into an uninhabited desert valley which had no water. Below him the canyon walls were steep but not high, and spotted with junipers. Above him the canyon opened out onto the upland, spreading like a fan; and splitting the canyon bottom was a gully where the spring runoffs made their way. The gully was perhaps fifteen feet deep, with crumbling sides; there were boulders on both sides of it, and loose rock, but the ground was fair ground for fast travel on a horse. The trick would be to ride down the canyon at the right moment, crossing the canyon and showing himself to the running horses; then he might hold them for a few moments. After that, he guessed, he would be on his own. Neither Sam nor Dick had told him what to do then; they had left it up to him.

"I'm just supposed to do something," he told himself. "It's a game today, and they're all playing, and maybe the biggest part of the game is to see what I'll do. Well, then!" He slapped the horse's neck. "We'll by God try, won't we!"

He did not have to tell himself to stay cool; he had been a soldier, he knew the importance of control, but now, after waiting thirty minutes at least, he was beginning to feel the tension grow. He had a good position; he was a little way up on the west wall of the canyon, so that he could see for almost three quarters of a mile down the canyon, but he knew that after the mustang band came in sight he would have little time to think about what he should do. He squinted; he examined every bush, every juniper on the canyon floor, and saw nothing except bushes and trees intact in light.

He picked up his rope and shook out a loop; the loop hung flat and true. He spun the loop over his head and dropped it out to the left, and then re-coiled the rope carefully, letting the coils rest loosely in his left hand. Gingerly he hung the rope over the saddle horn again and looked down at it. The rope was in perfect condition; it would provide no excuses.

There were no more preparations to make. He had reset the blanket and the saddle and inspected the bridle. The black horse stood quietly, resting, head down.

Clyde began to be worried; it had been a long time now since the others had left him, and it was possible that the horses had abandoned this part of the country. Dick had said

there was a spring where the horses watered, but there were other springs, even in this dry country. It was no trouble to imagine what the spring down the canyon might look like now: a trickle of water, a wet place in the ground near it; deep narrow tracks of mustangs, and a scattering of sun-dried dung. Clyde had seen such springs before, and now the image in his mind almost convinced him. He became fretful and bored; he looked around him, searching ground and air for distraction.

He was surprised to notice how much there was to see. There was a gray lizard on a rock above him; he could see the pinpoint of an eye. There was movement: the lizard appeared on another rock a little closer. He had the color of the rock, but his body was defined as clearly in the perfect light as the legs of a spider on a white wall. Again there was movement, and the lizard disappeared. Curious, Clyde scanned the rocks, the sand, the decomposing lumps of granite. Nothing moved. Seen close, the hillside was a chaos, and Clyde looked up and away from it.

Above him sailed a hawk. The hawk's wings were locked, he drifted on a current of wind; his shadow changed across the floor of the canyon. A moment passed. The hawk soared out of sight behind a juniper tree at the top of the canyon wall.

Idly, and without much interest, Clyde looked down the canyon. He was a little puzzled to notice that some of the trees were hard to see; there was a haze about a clump of juniper trees far down the canyon. He could make out the twisted lines of the trunks and sense the green of the needles, but he could not see the shape of the boughs. He blinked, thinking that his eyes had momentarily clouded, but when he looked again, he could not see the trees at all.

The haze thickened; now clearly it was dust rising. Me-

chanically Clyde picked up the rope and shook out a loop, while the black horse came awake, shifting his big body and snapping his ears forward. Clyde flexed the fingers of his left hand, adjusting the grip of them on the reins, feeling the limber hard coils of rope.

There was a cloud of dust for him to look at now, but he could not see movement in the cloud; it lay in the middle of the canyon, it was coming right at him. Then it disappeared, dispersed itself.

"They're in the gully now!" Clyde said.

Time passed, but each second seemed to throb into him like something alive; he felt each second, and he found himself counting. At the number ten the dust exploded again, this time within a quarter of a mile, and he caught his breath. Under the dust, and as if he were standing near the track at the end of a race, were the breasts and heads and front legs of horses. There was a shock of sound: it was the sound of horses' hoofs, a close-coupled sound of running.

He felt himself moving; he was vaguely aware that he had come down off the slope into the canyon bottom and crossed the gully; and then he was still again. He could feel the black horse strain against the reins.

The wild horses were free of their dust now, running close together straight up the side of the gully, and there was a strange shape just behind them, a shape which showed itself suddenly as the upright torso of a man. An arm was raised, whirling; the arm came down, and the quiet canyon air was riven with the squeal of something caught. The form of a horse, black, like a silhouette, reared suddenly from the running band, twisted, fought, the front hoofs pawing; and then Clyde saw the rope drawn tight from the horse's neck to the saddle of the man behind; and saw no more, for the horses were upon him.

He was aware that he had taken the right position; he seemed to be near the center of the canyon. The horses broke suddenly to their right, away from him, and came on; and then for a moment they seemed to pause, to hesitate, even as they ran, and Clyde felt their hesitation; but they did not pause for long, and Clyde knew what he must do.

He swung the black horse to the left, dug hard with his heels, turned, and was running in the band of horses. He saw the backs and necks of horses, his eyes blurring with wind. He could feel his black horse moving powerfully, he could feel the rhythmic sway and grappling of the great muscles of the hips.

Heat rose from the backs of the horses; the air above them was alive with smells of sweat, dung, urine, sour exciting smells, as Clyde remembered vaguely that it was necessary to choose one animal for his target. To his right was a sorrel colt, his eyes popping, but he was thin in the hips and Clyde dismissed him. To his left were two bay mares, both small, and he only turned his head at them, but in front of him, running easily but breathing hard, was a black mare, the biggest animal in the band except for the stallion who ran in the lead. "That one!" Clyde thought, looking at the black mare and feeling his mind go blank. His emotion broke like a tide in the direction of the one black mare in the band of wild horses.

After that, he felt himself disappear into the wild motion of the chase, though his senses remained alive as angered snakes. He saw a cut on the left hip of the black mare. It was blood, veiled by dust; his eyes comprehended each particle of dust. Across the loins of the black mare and running backward across the hips there was a live quiver of sweat, and he felt it as if it were sweat on his own body. In the crease of the hip the sweat precipitated a vein of dust and sweat, a yellow line like an old scar. Mane and tail were shaggy, tangled, and he could see burs caught in the tail.

For a moment, while he felt his right arm somewhere above his head twirling the rope as it had been trained to do, he let himself go in admiration of the running mare, grew dizzy with love for her wildness; and then he felt his right arm come down almost of itself, as if it were someone else's arm. The rope uncoiled from his hand, the loop settled on the neck of the black mare, and his hand jerked in the slack. He had made a catch, and suddenly he felt awake, as if he had been asleep.

He began to think again. He had plenty of slack; he would not need to dally for a moment; and then he decided to apply a little pressure to slow the black mare down, remembering all that Sam had told him about ways of diminishing the shock for the caught animal. He snapped on his dallies, feeling them clash against the horn as he reined in.

There was a shock against the saddle, and the black mare's head rose. He moved along; the mare ran again; again he stopped her.

After that, aware that the other horses were gone, that he was alone, and remembering what he had been told, he managed to tie the mare. He found a big juniper and forked it with the rope; the black mare swung to it, and he had her. While she fought the rope, he slipped half-hitches over the saddle horn and stepped off. A moment later the mare fell.

Working quickly, he untied the big halter with its cotton rope from the saddle, slipped the halter on the mare's head, tied the throat latch, and removed his lariat rope. The mare was beginning to kick as he tied the cotton halter rope to the juniper tree with a careful bowline and went back to his black horse, who stood quietly, flanks sucking in and out like a bellows. And then he rode the black horse down into the gully,

out of sight of the mare, to let her recover. It was in his mind
how Sam had told him that wild animals could die easily
from being caught, from what Sam called, in his simplicity,
A Broken Heart, Captivity.

vi

The rest of the day belonged to the weeks and months that
followed. Nothing after the chase equaled the chase; it was
natural for Clyde to propose another, for later in the fall or
for the spring, and the others were willing. In the talk that
followed the chase, amiable proposals passed from one man
to another—Sam wanted to try for a buckskin band he had
heard about, Dick Tatum wanted to look at a blue stallion—
and the proposals served to remind the hunters of the hunt.

In his devious mild way, Dick Tatum made it plain that he
considered Clyde acceptable at last, for no other reason than
that Clyde had roped the black mare. He was almost fatherly
in his praise of Clyde's action. "I seen that black horse come
down into the canyon and get in amongst 'em, Sam, and that
black horse was moving. Old Clyde here let him feel the spur,
I reckon. How did it feel, Clyde? Pretty swift, looked like.
And he got a good mare out of it, too." Clyde was pleased
with the praise, and pleased suddenly with Dick, but he was
embarrassed also, remembering his queasy feelings about
Dick.

While the talk ran on, Clyde wondered where those feelings had come from, and could find no reasonable source for
them. Dick was suspicious; by his own count, he had far too
many enemies; he was not handsome or impressive; he slept
with whores. So much was known; reviewed in a new con-
text, in the warmth which came with praise, it seemed a
small sum, no more than might normally attach to the moral

history of many other men. "Nothing to be worried about, anyway!" Clyde told himself. Carefully he watched Dick, but could find in him no traces of the dim unpleasantness which had been so vividly there on other occasions. Dick was very calm. He talked about ranches. After a time Clyde surrendered himself to the talk and its pleasures, and to acceptance of Dick, which was in its way a pleasure too.

The little cabin, to which they returned for supper, was bright, warm, and like a home. The table, worn with use and years of washing, and the chairs and the old oil lamp all had the look of things set down in their proper places; the faded calendars gave no offense. In the cabin's lively warmth Clyde found it easy to think about the ranches which Dick described; for each ranch he could form a persuasive image. The image persuaded him that he would like the place the image stood for, and in his mind the house and lots he owned became causes for the beginning of a new life in a new place. On a ranch like the ranches described by Dick he would someday live a life like the best parts of the life lived by Sam. Thirstily he listened to the talk, and did not forget it after his return to Albo. Imagined ranches retained the green of summer as real autumn darkened into real winter.

School had started the week before the hunt; once again Clyde was obliged to teach children what they did not want to know. From Monday through Friday he rose early in the cool autumn days and carried his notes and books to the high school; talked, counseled, listened to clumsy answers, and went home again. Four afternoons a week he went out to a little pasture he had rented and worked with the mustang mare. He had the use of a corral, but the work went slowly, and he was uncertain what to do with the mare when the work was done. The mare was four years old approximately, as judged by her teeth, sturdy and teachable, but not so handsome now as she had been on the day when he caught her; but the mare reminded him of possibilities each time he saw her.

Sam had trained the colt he had caught, in about three weeks, to a reasonable toleration of hackamore and saddle, and sold it to a friend; but he still had the bay colts caught in the spring, and he heard nothing from the rich man Cathcart. Letters brought no answers; telephone calls found Cathcart always somewhere else, looking at his cotton near Bakersfield, inspecting asparagus fields on his island in the delta of the San Joaquin River, conferring with important people in Sacramento. Late in October Sam went to one of the Albo lawyers.

Sam was uncertain and hesitant about what he called Going to Law; he took Clyde with him to a lawyer's office. There was an awkward parley. The lawyer, a grave young man who smoked cigars, professed himself ignorant of horses and horse-trading, and advised against starting a suit; but he suggested that he would be willing to write a letter, and Sam was satisfied. There would be no charge: the lawyer was glad to be rid of them.

Surprisingly, the letter caused action. Early in November the manager of Cathcart's Fishbone Valley ranch came to Sam with the news that Cathcart would be down for a visit on the next weekend. Once again Sam called Clyde. Together they made the trip, on Sunday, in clear cold weather. The familiar route was chilled for them by the cold; it was a melancholy afternoon, and the appearance of Cathcart's ranch did not improve it.

The ranch was freshly painted, white, with green trim on gates and doors; it had the sanitary look of a model dairy farm, but there were only two milk cows in sight, three horses, none impressive, and almost no beef cattle; there were a few steers scattered in the desert alongside the road, looking lonely in the empty valley. It was a show ranch, clearly, kept for a game or for prestige. Cathcart's airplane, a Stinson commercial model, reflected the cold light from the airstrip. Cathcart's Cadillac—driven down, they discovered later, by the secretary, so that Cathcart could travel in suitable dignity after he arrived—was parked under the cottonwoods near the main house.

The ranch house was decorated in an elaborately Western style. Cattle brands were burned into all the doors; Navaho rugs hung from the walls and were scattered about the floors. Cathcart himself was wearing expensive boots, fresh-looking levis, and a red flannel shirt when he received them in the living room; but in the middle of the living room was a portable bar, made of aluminum, and the room had the smell of cities. Cathcart smelled of an expensive shaving lotion, made to shed the fragrance of pine forests in metallic apartments, and he wore a diamond ring on the third finger of his right hand.

In spite of rugs and cattle brands and the smell of pine forests, the room was a city room, transported whole from a city atmosphere, and Clyde felt uncomfortable in it; Sam was bewildered by it. Together they sat down while Cathcart greeted them; he was busy about the portable bar, touching a hidden lever so that a tray of bottles ascended from the complexities of the machine. He offered them brandy, and they took brandy; and then in an efficient, kindly manner he settled the matter of the bay colts.

"I got your letter, Leathers," he said. "And I'm sorry I put you to the trouble of arranging it, but, by God, I've been busy! It seems like every season's a busy season for me lately! Now, you say you've lost time on those colts that you could have used to break horses for other people. All right. And of course there's the original cost of the colts, and the cost of feed. You're sure they're broke well enough for my kids to ride?"

"You bet they are!" Sam said. "I guarantee 'em."

"All right, then, Leathers. How about five hundred dollars? I think that's a fair price."

Sam waited a few moments; clearly, he was a little confused. Cautiously he turned the big brandy glass in his dark rough hand. Then he accepted the price and drank some of the brandy.

Cathcart was pleased. He began to talk about the race horses he planned to send to Tanforan for the winter season, and Clyde sat back with the fine brandy to watch him and compare him with Sam.

Sam sat carefully in an easy chair done up in maroon leather; he sat erect on the front of the chair, with his hat in his hands. His raw red face seemed to stop an inch above his eyebrows, at the hat line; the rest of his forehead, protected from sun for many years now, had the look of a broad white scar under his thinning hair; and he seemed confusedly angry. The protuberant blue eyes looked sharply out into the ingenious indirect light of the room.

Cathcart moved easily from the portable bar to the fireplace to a chair, restless but unhurried, the master of the house. He was perhaps fifty years old, Clyde guessed, but he did not look it. His face had a deep tan, so that Clyde was forced to think of beach *cabañas* at Rio and sun lamps in the Fresno Athletic Club. His body was soft, even in the stiff clothes he was wearing, but not fat, and Clyde guessed that a masseur might rest somewhere among Cathcart's belongings. Cathcart spoke softly but decisively and showed at all times the preoccupation of the man of affairs, moving Clyde to decide that his manner was meant to suggest that this was a man who might have to leave the party at any moment to read his private teletype.

Clyde kept silence: what was important was that Cathcart could buy the colts, but nothing else, from Sam. It was a comforting thought. The sterile ranch, with its freshly painted fences, fine barn, alfalfa fields, and elaborately Western house, showed very clearly the limits of Cathcart's purchasing power; they showed that Cathcart could not buy a way of life. Clyde was sufficiently comforted to be amused. He felt a kind of gratitude to Cathcart for constituting, in himself and in his possessions, such a precise demonstration.

"What it takes is money and skill together," Clyde thought. He did not have to tell himself that he had money and was attaining skill, for this knowledge was cherished knowledge, always available and always pressing upon his ambitions. Clyde relaxed with the brandy and felt content. It was true that rich men like Cathcart ran up the prices of ranches with their careless spending. Ten miles north was the ranch of a tycoon who had made a fortune by selling automobiles. Five miles south was the ranch of a man who owned six hotels in five cities and a brewery in St. Louis; and Dick Tatum had remarked casually, on the night before the last hunt, that the man who owned and leased the range where they hunted mustangs owned also some twenty thousand head of cattle in the San Joaquin Valley and twice that many sheep in Arizona, New Mexico, and California. All this was unhappily true, and Clyde disliked the thought of it, but he knew that rich men did not own all the ranches and never would. He had Dick Tatum's word that many ranches lay untouched by worldly riches in remote hills and valleys.

The meeting broke up when Cathcart's secretary entered

the room to say that Cathcart was wanted on the telephone; it was a long-distance call from Los Angeles, and the secretary was grave when he announced it.

"That'll be that goddamned sugar-beet man," Cathcart said mildly. "He's been after me with his proposition for three months now. Will you boys excuse me a minute?"

While Cathcart was out, Clyde thought about the fact that he had never told Sam about the house and lots, and it occurred to him that he should tell him soon, on the chance that Sam might hear of a decent ranch or farm. By the time Cathcart returned, Clyde had decided to tell Sam at the first reasonable opportunity, but he felt no sense of urgency. Winter was coming with its long nights for discussion and hoping. There was plenty of time.

Cathcart was affable to the end. His smooth rich voice pursued them past the door and down into the yard. "Those colts ought to give my kids a lot of fun," he said. "They'll like the idea of riding colts that were caught in a real wild Western way. Here's your check, Leathers. I'll have somebody pick the colts up in the next week or so. By golly, it'll be a good Christmas for those kids of mine, won't it?"

On the ride home Sam expressed dissatisfaction with the settlement. He was much in demand as a horsebreaker; he could have taken perhaps eight horses in the last five months, at seventy-five dollars a head, if he had not been tied up with the colts, and there was the cost of feed on top of that; but after a while he took out the check, looked at it, and began to talk about the things he could do with it.

"I can settle up some debts, Clyde. You got to keep your credit clean, boy. I know all about that. And I'll buy some Christmas presents for the girl and the baby. And after all that I'll put the rest in the bank. One of these days I'll have enough to put down on a little place, Clyde. A man's got to save if he's going to do anything! You can't go on working for wages all your life if you ever want to do something! I got my eye on a few little places right now where I could keep my own chickens and raise a little hay and break my horses. You'll see, boy!"

December brought the first snows of the year; there was even snow in Albo, and in the mountains the great drifts were rising. But Sam paid no attention to snow or cold; one day he came into town for Clyde and took him out to the Ambrose ranch to see a new horse he had bought. It was a fine horse, and Sam was pleased with it: a black quarter-horse stallion, three years old, powerful, quick, and light on his feet. He had cost Sam four hundred dollars in cash, plus his big bay horse and an old saddly; but he would make a cutting horse, Sam was sure of that, and a man who had a good cutting horse could make a living at the shows any time. It was easy.

vii

The year mounted into winter. Storms rose above the Sierra; clouds bellied down over the peaks, sometimes bringing rain to Albo, sometimes bringing a skift of snow to the doors of houses and sporting-goods stores. The town grew quiet. On weekends skiers from Los Angeles passed through the town, going north on Friday night, south again on Sunday night, but they did not stop for long, and then only for meals. During the week the town's life congealed in the cold. Snowplows worked overtime on the narrow roads to the mines in the mountains, but some of the miners were laid off, and work slowed on the construction of the new reservoir and power stations to the north. In the barbershops men talked about the snow, for it was a heavy winter, and about the opening of the fishing season.

Clyde settled down in the cold season and labored away with his classes. He continued his work with the mare, but only went to her twice a week; and he did not see Sam often, for Sam was busy with his stallion in most of his off hours. He heard rumors that Sam was drinking more than usual and having trouble at home because of it, but he was not much worried. Winter for cowboys was always a slow season, Sam had said. If cowboys could sleep through the winters like bears, they would be able to stay out of trouble; that was the way Sam put it; but cowboys were not bears, they grew restless, and it was natural for them to drink and play wild games. Now and then the wild games happened in town, with Sam as the comic hero, and Clyde, having an explanation for the wildness, only laughed at the proper moments in the stories and went on about his business.

It was a little different when Sam came to him one night with a plan for buying a homestead in Fishbone Valley, for this was an eccentric wildness: the homestead was one of those they had passed on their trips to Dick Tatum's. Clyde could not forget that Sam had condemned these places, not once but several times, and laughed at the people who had been foolish enough to experiment with them. Sam's enthusiasm was the more disturbing because Clyde could recognize in it an enthusiasm similar to his own, though, unlike Sam, he had not yet focused his emotion on a particular place. Mildly Clyde tried to question the project with unanswerable questions.

"Where would you get a pump?" he asked. "What about money? You'd need money for seed, wouldn't you? And to live on until you got a crop?"

Sam answered with blithe talk about bankers: bankers had money which they loaned; he would find a banker and speak to him. Sam seemed for the moment unaware of difficulties, as if difficulties could not exist for a man who had a good project on his mind and good intentions in his heart; and Clyde sympathized with his attitude, for it was part of Sam's attractiveness that he was reckless, careless of himself, while most men were not; but Clyde had a cold feeling that Sam was bound headlong for disappointment. It occurred to him for the first time that it might not be wise, or worldly-wise, to tell Sam of the house and lots, and he felt a kind of treachery in the thought. To keep such a secret seemed unfriendly, and yet Clyde could find no opportunity to open his tale. Sam was too violently committed already to his own plans to listen to the plans of anyone else. He could hardly wait to take Clyde with him to inspect the homestead, and there was no way for Clyde to refuse.

They went on a Saturday, Clyde feeling cautious and uneasy. For a long time he had cherished the dream of the place in the country endowed with quiet and with friendly animals, and lately the dream had settled into a wistful calculation which might eventually give way to action. While he worked through the winter and waited for the spring, he had almost decided, almost made up his mind, almost written a letter to the lawyer in the Illinois city who collected rent for him. He knew Sam's plans were likely to prove foolish, but they were plans like his, and when they came to the test, his own plans came to the test also. The trip was a chilly answer to some of his longings.

There was snow in Piute Pass, and a strong wind; they needed chains well before they reached the summit and for a long way down the other side. Sam's truck had a heater, but it did not work. Currents of cold air, working through crevices in the floor, were with them all the way, and Sam's excited talk did little to warm the atmosphere.

"The girl could keep chickens and a milk cow, Clyde, and

maybe feed a pig or two. I could raise hay to sell and enough besides to feed my horses and some cattle. And, God damn, with all that time, I could make a living breaking horses and going to a few shows! That black stud is going to *make* a cutting horse, Clyde. I tell you, boy, I could do it, and I'll tell you another thing too. I just naturally want to do it. I'm godamighty tired of working for wages. A man's got to start somewhere, don't he?"

Fishbone Valley in winter seemed more empty than ever, and the homestead, when they came to it, more bleak than in summer's heat. Sam pulled the truck up in front of a bare gray unpainted cabin, and they got out of the truck to stand in front of a neat unpainted door.

"This is it," Sam said. "You see that old wire? That's the line fence. The brush ain't too thick, is it, for a place that's been let go for three years? A man could get some good out of that wire too, just by restringing it. And she's got a good soil—you could tell if the ground wasn't froze. I've asked farmers around. They all say it's a good soil in through here. All you need is the water. Anybody will tell you, Clyde."

Wind swept the empty valley. Down the road Clyde could see a gray box jutting up out of the brush, and that was the cabin on the other homestead; when he looked the other way, he could just make out the blur of bare trees at one of the valley ranches; and all the mountains were covered with snow, and even the upland country of Dick Tatum's range bore its covering of snow. Musingly Clyde remembered Sam's telling him that in winter the mustang stallions broke ice from the springs for their mares. It warmed him a little to think of mustangs in snow with their rumps to the wind, for they would stay alive somehow and be waiting when the warm spring came. He could be sure of the mustangs, he told himself. They would not disappoint him.

There was little to see of the homestead. The cabin contained an old table and one chair. Outside, there was the abandoned hay rake, with its wheels at crazy angles from the axle, and many of its tines gone; the old wire, grown rusty, sprung from the posts and coiling wildly into thickets of brush; and the privy, its door hanging open, rattling as the wind shook it. Sam inspected everything. He explained that all he needed was a pump to make the fine soil show a green. "Give me the water, and I'll make this land do something, you bet!" he said. When Clyde suggested that pumps were expensive, Sam merely shook his head and began to talk about what his grandfather had done in New Mexico seventy years before; and then, as they started back to Albo, he was off into reminiscence of his youth, and Clyde let him go. It was a familiar saga which Clyde had enjoyed before.

"My grandpa just took that range and put his horses and cows on it," Sam said, "and didn't have to go to the banker like me. He and his two brothers took their homesteads back to back, and had something. And when the brothers left, the whole thing came down to my daddy and his brother, and it would have come on down to me if I'd a stayed in that country. But I was wild. I had to go off and leave all that. I had to be a cowboy, and work on those big ranches." The stories came forth in loving detail. There was a cycle of stories about school: about the schoolmarm who kept a stick of kindling on her desk to smack the big boys with, and how she once knocked down the biggest boy—"a big rank boy, big as you, Clyde, and just full of fight"—and hauled him out into the schoolyard by the heels; about riding burros to school, and tickling them to make them buck so that the girls would be flustered. There were stories of hard times, when thieving was the chief support of most families, so that Sam's father always kept his good horses in a special corral near the house, with dogs chained to the gate; when the family lived on lean beef and flour during one hard winter.

"It's a poor country, Clyde, even when you've got some land, and I'm glad to be out of it. God damn, she was a poor country, and didn't get any better as time went on, seemed like, but it was a place where a man could feel at home, and know the people, and have something to do. I tell you, Clyde, that's what I'm thinking about in that homestead. And with a place like that, my own place, I could make a few shows now and then, and maybe earn a little money with it too. Hell, now, with the girl at home, and the baby, I can't hardly seem to go anywhere, and you know I live for horses and for working horses, Clyde. It ain't enough just to run a few mustangs every now and then, though I'll be goddamned if I don't think I'd like to make a good long trip this spring if I can get off long enough. How about that, Clyde? We could get us a pack outfit together, and we got plenty of horses. We could take a week to it and really sweep the mountain, boy!"

It was a fine suggestion, Clyde thought. Together they built it up, shoring their plans with enthusiasm and even setting a date. They agreed that sometime late in April ought to be a good time, and after this possibility had been exhausted, Sam went on with his stories even more warmly than before, while Clyde thought how pleasant it would be to spend his spring holiday in desert hills, patrolling the springs where mustangs came to water and watching them run through their freedom. With the grim homestead momentarily forgotten, the ride home was pleasant with talk, so that Clyde was able to forget Sam's extravagance about the homestead for the rest of the day and for most of the next week. But on the following Thursday, when he stopped in at the Leathers cottage to borrow a bridle from Sam, he found Bonna

June alone with the baby and Sam gone two days already.

Bonna June was firm, but clearly somewhat disturbed: Sam had been away for two nights and two days, missing his work, and worrying her a little. "It's just his winter drunk," Bonna June told him. "He did it last winter too. He'll be back. The banker wouldn't give him the money for that homestead he's so crazy about, and he went off drinking on Tuesday. Have you seen him?"

It was an uncomfortable scene for Clyde, but he waited patiently through it. Bonna June seemed not to mind his knowing that Sam had strayed, however, and gave him two cups of coffee before he left. "It's the way men are," she said, almost laughing, "specially that Sam Leathers! Which don't mean I won't say a few things when he comes back! Leaving his wife and baby like they were somebody else's. But he's wild—you know that, Clyde. I guess that's why he's a good cowboy. And he likes to go to the rodeos, and he can't do that much when he has a job like this. Oh, he'll be back pretty shortly!"

She was almost perfectly complacent, so that Clyde was able to go away feeling that she could probably take care of herself; and Sam returned the next day. Clyde found him in the barn shoeing a horse at five o'clock. There was a scab on his nose, and a welt under one eye, and he was quieter than he normally was, but otherwise not much changed. Twice he mentioned the week-long mustang hunt they had talked about on the way back from the homestead. "It's something, anyway," he said. "I could do that. I reckon I could afford it. We could have a lot of sport, couldn't we, Clyde? And right near home too, where we've both got to stay, I reckon. Well, I'm willing. There won't be nobody charge us to run mustangs, anyway! They're still free, I guess."

viii

By the middle of February it was a record winter. Three times in January, blizzards stopped trains in the railway passes in the Sierra to the north; Highway 40 stayed closed once for almost three weeks, and the mountain roads were always uncertain; once Albo had a foot of snow which lasted for three days, and this had not happened for many years. Clyde sank easily into a life of houses and buildings, watching the weather. He had come to Albo from three years in Los Angeles, and he found the snowy mountains and cold air pleasing after the rain and murk of that southern city. He remembered the winters of his boyhood in Illinois, the long gray days, and remembered also his trick of thinking ahead to spring and summer.

He thought about the mustangs wading in snow under the cedars. Their coats were shaggy now; splinters of snow were stuck in the matted hair, and their backs were cold with the cold wind. Mares staggered, colts died; in the spring he might find bones and scraps of hide left by the coyotes.

He could see the mustangs when he closed his eyes under his reading lamp. They stayed in their mountains because men held the valleys, keeping trees or hills between themselves and the wind; but in the mountains the winds were changeable, curving, erratic, and no hill could really stop them. Quietly the mustangs pawed the snow, picking at grasses and browse, chilling their lips against the cold earth and the snow. They stood with rumps to the wind, the long tails blowing past their hind legs and whipping against their bellies, while the stallions kept their watches.

It was a hard winter, but the strong ones would endure and be there for him in the spring; and he was grateful to

them, not for what they could do, or for any use they might
have, but merely for being there. He spent many nights with
Sam, talking over plans for the week-long hunt which
would be the greatest mustang hunt this country had seen
for many years. Sam's enthusiasm grew steadily. Work on
the Ambrose ranch was slow in the winter. No one hurried
to it; fences were mended, gates re-hung, and saddles patched,
but there was always plenty of time, and Sam's attention was
free to wander into the future. Now and then he spoke bitterly of bankers, often he spoke of the pleasures of traveling
the rodeo circuit, but he seemed resigned to his job. Only in
talk of the mustang hunt did his spirits rise. "It's a thing I'm
looking forward to," he said once, "because it's right out
where I can look at it. But we got to get ready for it,
Clyde!"

And the preparations did in fact begin in March as the
weather grew warmer. The barber, Jonas, and Will Scott
both agreed to go, and Sam obtained the ritual permission
from Dick Tatum. With diligence Sam collected five complete pack outfits, pack saddles, rigs, kayak boxes and bags,
and an abundance of cotton rope, and persuaded friends to
let him have the use of three horses. He would also take his
sorrel horse (the stallion being too great a problem with other
horses); the others would take their own horses and the two
mustangs caught in earlier hunts. Nine horses in all: Sam was
pleased, and said they would be ready for anything. In the
first two weeks of April Sam patched the pack outfits and
made three heavy horse halters; his energy never flagged.

But he was having his troubles at home. His black quarter-
horse stallion had come along very well as a cutting horse,
and Sam was anxious to take him to cutting contests, but
Bonna June was afraid to let him go, and resisted him. There
were muted scenes which Clyde occasionally took part in.

Once, when Clyde stopped in to talk about the mustang hunt, Sam produced a magazine which contained two pages of pictures of cutting horses, showed them to Clyde, and grew excited about what cutting horses could do for their owners.

"Look at this little mare Mexican Lady, Clyde! She was entered in her first contest last August, and she's already won three firsts and a second. Look at her watch that calf! And it says here they just started her on cutting early last year. See that, girl?" He waved the pictures at Bonna June. "It looks like I'd better be getting that black stud out to the shows pretty soon, don't it?"

"We'll see," Bonna June said. "I think he's got a lot to learn!"

A little later she walked up behind Sam and patted him on the shoulder, telling him that she had not meant it; but she did not give in, and Clyde remembered that she had always been a little reluctant to speak of the black stallion. It was no great wonder. Sam's truck needed two new tires, and the motor sounded rough, but there was no money for these things. The baby carriage was rickety; sometimes Bonna June spoke wistfully of a new washing machine.

On Saturdays, according to his custom, Sam went to Albo to drink, but occasionally he went during the week also. Once he was arrested for driving while drunk. Another time he crumpled a fender of his truck against a lamp post. Clyde, watching these things, accepted the thought of what Sam's life was, and what it might become, but made no attempt to change Sam's ways. For though Sam controlled a great variety of traditional patterns of action, or was controlled by them, he could not discuss them.

It was traditional for the wife to walk behind with a baby on her hip while the man was talking; it was no accident of varying speeds of movement, and meant no more than that the woman was obliged to show the world that she knew her place. So with Bonna June. She was happy to have Sam in sight. It was traditional for the man to drink on Saturday nights, and for the wife to wait patiently, talking with relatives or friends. It was traditional for a man to support his wife, to manage a web of habit and change just solid enough to keep a wife on the level of the wives she knew, and Sam was careful to do this; he had an eye for the clothes worn by his friends' wives, and he encouraged Bonna June to use the mail-order catalogues.

And it was traditional among Sam's people that a man sometimes wandered and was tolerated in spite of it. Clyde, thinking of the claims of the quarter-horse stallion, and of the opposite claims of Bonna June and the baby, believed that Sam might run away for a time. It was a thought easily come by.

Clyde could see it happen. Sam would range the rodeo arenas, searching for the fine moments of inspired and excellent performance which made the only parts of his life he really cared about, the successes which warmed the cowboy rituals and made it a pleasant duty for him to buy the drinks in the evening. The life would be the standard life; it would have the appropriate dust and sweat, and the appropriate smells, of leather, of dung, of split-open bales of hay, of coffee boiling over an open fire behind a grandstand. There would be women: they were scenery for the nights, occasions for laughter the next day at the corrals. There would be talk of the glories of the past, of rodeos in little Arizona towns, of fights, of famous storms, of wild cattle peeking down from mountaintops. After a time Sam would come home, unchanged, intransigent, perhaps a little hungry.

Clyde envied Sam his chance of possessing all this, for he did not doubt that such a life was exciting, but the envy was edged with irritation and unease. There was that in Sam, and in his way of life, which suggested that Sam could achieve trouble as readily as excitement. But Clyde told himself that worry was not fact, and thought of other things; kept his peace, and waited for the hunt.

Spring thrived in April as the days lengthened. There were cold days and a few days of rain in Albo which was snow in the Sierra, but such days were rare. Snow was melting in all the mountains, the creeks were big with white water; now and then a canyon passed a flood down onto the roads below. Twice there was water across the highway north of Albo. In the meadows outside of town, cattle and horses sometimes stood in water to their hocks, splashing awkwardly, while calves and colts floundered. Lawns in Albo began to be green again. Housewives appeared in their yards, carrying hoes, rakes, trowels.

In the last week of April the days were sunny and warm. In the afternoons when school was out and after supper Clyde traveled busily from place to place, making preparations for the hunt. He bought groceries and stored them in Sam's cottage, bought meats and packed them away in his own refrigerator—a side of bacon, beef, salt pork—and spent whatever time was left in working his black horse and the mustang mare, toughening them for the chase.

Everything was ready on the Saturday chosen for the departure. Sam was nervous and a little irritable, too anxious to have everything in perfect order, but no one minded. Jonas the barber was happy; he had purchased a new rope for the occasion. They rose early because they would have to make two trips with the trucks to move all the horses. By six o'clock the first caravan was on its way.

There was rain in Albo and in Fishbone Valley, but it was a light rain which no one feared. The trip moved swiftly toward the mountains at the south end of Dick's range, up a dirt road, until the road gave out at a deep rain-washed gully some five miles from the canyon they sought. There they had to stop. There was no way around the gully.

It was a disappointment, but no one complained. The skies were still clouded and the air was cold, but the men all had the feeling of holiday. There was a conference. Plans were changed. They would unload horses and gear and supplies, make the second trip, and start riding from the gully.

"It just means we got to do a little more riding than we figured," Sam said. "We can leave the trucks here just as easy as anywhere else. And, God damn, we came to do some riding, didn't we?" The difficulty seemed to please him and goad him to quicker movement. Horses and supplies were unloaded, and the horses staked out. Clyde was appointed to keep watch while the others took the trucks back to Albo for the rest of the horses and the remaining supplies. After a quick silent bustle of activity the trucks were on their way, and Clyde sat down with his back against a kayak box to wait, smoking, lazing in the cool air, spelling out for himself the elements of his anticipation.

The whole of Fishbone Valley lay before him, dark under the dark sky; he could see with some clearness for almost forty miles. The tops of the Piute Mountains were gone in cloud, and there were hazes clumped down at odd places against the lower reaches of the hills around the valley, hazes which were rain falling, but the broad middle of the valley was dry still and clear. The ranches were smudges of darkness in the brown desert, so far away and dim that he found it hard to think of them as ranches.

The country belonged to him and to the quiet horses. No one else was watching it as he was watching it. He turned his head and looked up at the mountains they would enter later in the day; they too were clouded, but he did not think of clouds. He contemplated the image of wild horses on a windy slope.

It began to rain again, softly. A cloud drifted among the joshua trees. The horses stood quietly, heads down, their backs darkening with the rain. One of the hazes he had been watching in the valley merged with other hazes. He told himself that the hazes were rain falling, and that there might be more rain still, and snow in the mountains, but these thoughts did not worry him. It was spring; there had been many sunny days, and there would be more. Tomorrow would bring sun, likely, for the winter was over.

The others returned at eleven o'clock and were still cheerful; again there was activity. By noon they were ready to go, the soft rain falling still. Sam took the lead, with three pack horses strung out behind him; Scott came next, with two pack horses, and Jonas and Clyde came on behind. There were little shouts, laughs, cries.

After two miles the rain was colder, clouds were thicker, the valley behind them lost in darkness, but jokes moved up and down the line, humorous complaints about the weather. Sam, turning in his saddle, shouted stories back to the others, about rains he had been in before, and how he had resisted them. He shouted about a river in flood which he had crossed once as a boy. In his high voice he shouted that the river had been the color of a sorrel horse, of the horse he was riding now. But gradually the talking ceased; the air was growing colder.

As they rode on, it became apparent that it was more than five miles to the entrance to the canyon. The road ran off in front of them into cloud; they could no longer see the mountains they were traveling toward. The rain sharpened, falling in heavy drops which rattled on the canvas pack covers. A wind began to blow down on them. After a time there was hail instead of rain, and the hail frightened the horses, so that they resisted the lead ropes.

"This weather's getting a little rank now!" Sam called. "By God, let's just drive these old horses!" Jauntily he stepped down and removed the lead ropes from the pack horses. "They'll go now," he shouted. "Just keep after 'em!" The pack horses, free of the lead ropes, leaned together. The canvas-covered packs bumped together. The hail turned to rain again, which came in gusts as the line of horses moved slowly up the road, into the wind.

The canyon walls appeared out of the cloud suddenly, like something made by the clouds. The road swung to the right, in under one of the walls, and the wind lessened. They were in a space of quiet, which Clyde found impressive: it echoed with the sound of the wind. He shook his head; his ears seemed to ache, as if they had grown used to the sound of the wind. Once again there was talk.

"It won't get no worse, this time of year!" Sam shouted.

Jonas said something about the weather of barbershops, and Scott spoke something not quite audible, which seemed to have the word *road* in it.

They were traveling straight up the canyon now, and the canyon walls were cliffs; turrets of red earth rose in the darkness as Clyde looked ahead. According to the maps, the road made a turn to the left, up a side canyon, and now he began to be able to see a gap in the canyon wall on his left, and he grew almost cheerful.

Feeling the absence of the sound of the wind, he could hear many other sounds. There was the sound made by the horses' hoofs, going down in mud, coming up laboriously with the mud sucking at the hoofs. There was the sound of pans rattling in one of the packs. There was still the sound of rain pelting against the canvas pack covers, and there was, from the distances ahead of him, a new sound which he could not identify.

At first it was the faintest kind of sound, and he paid it no attention; it had some of the sourceless quality of an echo, it traveled light within the earthen cliffs. But it did not disperse itself, and after a time Clyde began to listen for it, and to hear it above all the other sounds. He watched the other men to see if they were listening, but he could not make them out. Heads bent, they leaned forward in their saddles.

And then the sound grew loud, as if by some trick of the land, as if a barrier had fallen. The sound became a roar, and Clyde knew what it was. The road left the side of the canyon wall, ascended a little rise, bearing to the left, and went out of sight up the side canyon shown on the maps; and from the top of the rise Clyde and the others looked down at a river flowing through the gully at the bottom of the side canyon.

It was a yellow river, and it flowed through the road. Foam splashed against the new-made banks. Clods tumbled to the water, and sections of earth, and the gully walls. Clyde gasped a little, with surprise and with pleasure; it was a desert flood, and he knew how it had happened. Rain in the mountains had melted the snow, so that snow and rain together could pour in this flood. Clyde shivered a little. He had heard about such floods, but had never expected to see one. In the darkness, with the rain falling, he gloated on his luck; this would be something to remember!

But there was a trip to make, and after perhaps two minutes of consideration Sam took the lead in making it. He sent Clyde out to the right to keep the pack horses from going downstream, told Scott and Jonas to drive from behind, and led the band out into the yellow river. Then there were shouts, cries, gestures. Clyde got his black horse down into the water, plunged in, and slipped downstream before the

shock of the water. Waves splashed against the horse's belly.
After a moment the black horse held, and Clyde raised his
free hand as the pack horses moved to the banks. There was
confusion: the pack horses turned, milled against each other,
tried to break back, as Jonas and Scott shouted and cursed.
For a moment the horses plunged against each other, fearing
the strong water, and then suddenly began to go. Awkward
under the packs, they skidded over the bank, and quivered
with fright when the water touched them. Clyde's mustang
mare tried to come downstream, her eyes feverish above the
waves. Once she fell. A wave broke high on the pack, spilling
yellow foam across the canvas cover, as the mare struggled
to rise. Clumsily she rose, shivering, her sides dark and sleek
and dripping from the wave. Fearfully she made for the opposite bank, reached it, and trampled up through the yielding
earth, so that Clyde was able to look for the other horses and
see that they had come out already. Businesslike as ever, Sam
was moving on. The trip continued.

The yellow river was an adventure, and even in the chill
which came after it Clyde felt it so and praised his luck. Sam,
riding in the lead, had said nothing, nor had the others, but
Clyde did not mind. He was pleased with the trip's beginning.

But after the river the rest of the day was anticlimax, even
when, toward evening, several miles up the canyon, it
brought snow. The snow replaced the rain by imperceptible
degrees and finally manifested itself only by its softer falling.
It came in heavy flakes, and silently; there were almost six
inches on the ground about the cabin which was their day's
destination. The end of the day was a confusion of tasks to
be done with cold hands in an atmosphere of gloom. The
other men resented the weather, and their resentment showed
itself in sullen anger.

The next morning there were patches of blue sky to be

seen through rifts in the clouds, making everyone cheerful, and making Sam talkative again, as he had not been since the snow, but the patches of sky disappeared by eight o'clock, the day grew cold, and the snow began again. Within an hour the snow was piled up a foot deep around the cabin, around the chilled ankles of the horses, and another dark day began.

It was a time for consultation. Around the wood stove in the cabin the talk began, with Sam the leader. The men were unhappy, Clyde thought, but not without hope. Jonas, a sturdy man, though softened by the work he did, seemed a little bedraggled. His new boots were muddy and stiff. His smooth town face did not look harsher or stronger with the day's growth of beard, but merely dirty, unkempt. His way of talking was to repeat what Sam said, changing it a little and nodding his head violently. Scott, having taken a week of his vacation for the trip, seemed to be looking ahead to disasters and a week wasted.

Sam was angry; he resented the snow, and shook his head when he looked at it. "It's the worst luck ever," he said. "We can't stay here, boys, because they's no feed for the horses. They're looking poor already. And when the snow melts, the ground'll be so wet a horse can hardly move on it. And it's spring too! The worst luck ever, that's what I say!"

Sam was restless, and Clyde guessed that he wanted above all to get moving, to take something in hand, to go somewhere else where the trip might have a better chance. The talk continued for half an hour, and it was decided to move on up into the mountains; they had a tent which could keep them dry if the weather continued wet. After the decision Sam brightened a little. With work to do, he appeared to forget his troubles.

The snow continued throughout the day, falling in gusts. The junipers and cedars on the canyon slopes took on edges of white for their green boughs. Laboriously the hunters packed their horses, having trouble with the stiff ropes and pack covers; slowly moved off up the canyon. They traveled about six miles into the mountains, working their way up through the canyons, and made camp near an abandoned corral.

There was trouble about the camp site and about the proper way to put up the tent. Scott wanted to set up the tent near the spring they had reached; Sam wanted to pitch the tent against the old corral. There was a mild argument, which grew so warm on Sam's side that the others grew embarrassed, but Scott gave in before serious trouble could start. He bowed his head and almost smiled, remaining cheerful all the while, and Clyde admired him.

The tent went up clumsily. Everyone was slow, cautious, sullen, and the work which had to be done was done with little skill. One pair of hobbles was missing, and a new pair had to be improvised. Clyde's black horse tore up his feed bag. It was an unpleasant evening, cheered only the supper Sam prepared in his Dutch ovens.

After supper Sam contrived a few brief moments of anger at Jonas when Jonas spilled a pot of coffee, and allowed himself a period of angry silence afterward. He sat on a kayak box, with his hands between his knees, his broken crooked face hidden by the brim of his hat. Clyde offered him a cup of coffee when a fresh pot had been prepared; he refused. Now and then he looked up past the firelight to shake his head at the encroaching clouds.

When finally he spoke again, it was only to complain of the weather, in a bitter fashion as if against a mortal enemy, so that Clyde could not approve or even sympathize. He talked intermittently about the weather for half an hour, and then began attacking the rich man Cathcart as a swindler who could not let a poor man have a chance. Toward bedtime he switched to bankers, and cursed them. He did not talk of mustangs, and the night expired sadly, with the hunters tossing restlessly in chilly beds.

The next day, however, came sunny and warm. By one o'clock in the afternoon the snow was gone from the canyon floor, from the canyon walls, and remained only high up, on the peaks. The morning was spent in minor chores, with talk of mustangs beginning, hopefully at first, and then more confidently as the warm sun melted the snow. Sam grew almost cheerful as he replaced a front shoe on his sorrel horse. At two o'clock, with the hills brown again, trees green, it was decided that they could scout the country with some profit.

For the first time since the early hours of the first day, everyone was happy. Merry talk passed; ropes were shaken out. Surprisingly, they found the ground down canyon already dry enough to provide good footing for the horses, and this in itself was enough to make talk for an hour.

In the bright, faintly moist air they rode the country below them, canyons, canyon walls, the lower reaches of the peaks, all the while talking happily; and then, as they turned a corner, came on a little bay stallion. He was alone. From a distance of two hundred yards he watched them warily.

Quickly, in whispers, Sam gave the others a plan, and it started in silence. Clyde and Sam rode off up the wall of the side canyon and dropped down into the main canyon. Clyde went down to the junction of the two canyons to turn the little stallion back, while Sam remained above to do the roping. Jonas and Scott, waiting at least ten minutes, were to bring the stallion down the side canyon.

The plan worked well. Clyde had just found his position when he saw the stallion coming. Shouting, waving his arms, he turned the stallion up the main canyon and ran him hard until Sam, coming in fresh, was able to ride up and rope him. By the time the others arrived, the stallion was down, hitched to a tree.

The men were pleased, and talked about how the hunt had begun at last. They watched the stallion and gloated over him as a kind of guarantee of good hunting in the coming days. "It's a start, anyway," Sam said. "He's kind of a little thing, and I'll bet he's old as the hills, but, by God, he's a start!" "Our luck's turned," Jonas said. "We'll give 'em hell from now on!"

All went well until they started to move the stallion back to camp; then he fought the rope and halter. Three times he went down and got up to fight again. The fourth time he went down, he did not rise; he fell forward on crumbling front legs, his body going loose, so that his head bumped awkwardly against the ground. A great breath swelled in his chest, stayed, and then collapsed. No other took its place, and the stallion died quickly, his legs stiffening. His left eye, brown, webbed with veins, turned upward to the warm sky like a polished agate.

Quietly, reverently, Sam got off his horse to remove the halter from the stallion's head. Slowly he coiled the lead rope and tied it to his saddle. "I guess we can leave him here," he said. "The coyotes will take care of him. We shouldn't've stayed so close to him, I guess. But the wild ones will do that. A wild one will die on you."

ix

The next day there was snow again, and the trip collapsed. Out of soft voluminous clouds the snow fell in heavy flakes, to pile up against the tent and rise against the corral. By ten o'clock there was almost a foot of snow and Jonas was beginning to talk about going home. Scott, a tougher man, kept silence, but Clyde was sure that he too would go home; he was only waiting for someone else to suggest it.

Sam gave in to anger in such a way that it seemed each single snowflake hurt him. He would not listen to the others, and when he talked it was as if he were talking to himself. At noon, when the snow stopped for almost an hour, he brightened a little, but the snow came on again to make him sad, and continued through the day.

With night the sky cleared and the weather turned cold, but the change came far too late. Steadily during the two hours after supper and before they went to bed the hunters moved toward agreement that they should give up the hunt. Sam showed his consent by the way he carried himself and by his excessive worry about the horses, but he had already forgotten the trip and was thinking of other things. Blindly he talked; bad luck was his theme. He held Clyde in a corner of the tent and spoke of the troubles in his life, while Clyde had the feeling that he would have spoken in the same way to a post, or a tree, or a horse. He was patient with Clyde; he showed elaborate care in making his explanations.

"A man has just got to have it all on his side these days," he said. "It won't do to just have most of it, like horses, and feed for 'em, and a place to work 'em in, and something to chase with 'em. No, by God. A man has got to have it all. That or Irish luck."

Clyde sat quietly and listened. He could hear the wind blowing down from the mountaintops while he considered Sam and Sam's troubles. The trip was done for now, that was clear, and Sam had damaged by his anger that which he could not help; a sour melancholy held the tent. The anger had hurt the trip, and Clyde had resented it. Now, listening to Sam, he began to forget his resentment by understanding what had caused it.

"It ain't enough to have a strong back," Sam went on, "and be willing to work, and know how to do it. What's a man to do if he ain't got money and the weather on his side? I reckon he'll mostly rot, in a little town, in them little jobs, working for wages."

It was partly true, Clyde thought. Poor Sam—who could not find a place or time proper for the only work he knew, who could not live without fine moments always near.

"And a man naturally wants to be where he can have a good time doing what he's got to do, Clyde. Ain't that natural? I like to rodeo, I love to rope. It's all I live for, that and the horses I do it on. And now seems like you can't even do that any more. Catch something, and it dies on you. Catch a tough little mustang stud, and he dies on you. And there ain't much left to catch anyway."

Grimly Clyde nodded his head, though not in agreement with Sam but with what he knew of Sam, a different thing now from what it had been. "Sam can't have what he wants," Clyde thought, "a happy day every day, and thinks it's only bad luck keeps him from it. Thinks it while he drinks, thinks it while he buys the quarter horse, thinks it while he asks the banker for money. Lord!"

"And look at the country!" Sam said. "They say it can't take so many head of cows now as it used to. Well, what's the matter with the country, Clyde? You've got education. What's the matter with the country? What's happened to it? When I was a boy, there was feed everywhere down there on my daddy's place, and now they write me and say the land's running down. And look at this snow! You never get the weather when you want it!"

Clyde thought of his house and lots, and of the ranch for

which he had so many images; he thought of the blue mountain which filled a part of each image. It occurred to him that he had perhaps confused a liking for Sam with liking for the image, and forgotten all the while that an image was an image. "I could still do it, though," he told himself. "I know there's places. I may do it yet. I even want to do it. Old Sam has got his troubles, but I don't have to have them too." And yet he felt his idea of the life he desired grow dark around the edges and blurred in the middle, where Sam and his ways had once been firmly fixed. "Everybody's not like Sam!" he told himself, while he remembered that Sam was wild and that he had once admired the wildness. "And I'm not in any hurry," he told himself. "I can take plenty of time to make up my mind."

The next morning the formal decision was made. There was a brief conference, in which the talk was characterized by an imperfect cheerfulness. It was agreed that the horses would have to be taken to better feed. The horses became the excuse; there was talk about their lean flanks. Sam suggested that they go home by way of Dick Tatum's camp: he and Clyde could take the pack horses while Jonas and Scott went back for the trucks and brought them to Dick's, and that way the horses could be given a feed of hay that night.

All went quickly after the conference. Jonas and Scott rode off happily, shouting jokes back over their shoulders. Sam, not talking much, moved quickly through his work and quickly into the journey. There was a little more snow that day, and rain again as they neared Dick's, but Sam said nothing about either rain or snow, and made no complaints about bad luck.

Dick was a relief after the melancholy camp in the snowy mountains, so that Clyde was grateful to him as soon as he saw him. Dick appeared in the door of his cabin when his dogs barked the appearance of the pack train at the gate; he was putting on his hat, he was a round solid figure in the gray light. Deliberately he walked out to greet them, deliberately he helped them unload the horses and throw out a feed of hay.

"The snow's good for me," he said, "but I reckon you fellers didn't care much for it. Was it pretty wet up there? I reckon I've had a good two inches of rain here at camp."

The dry cabin was pleasant after rain and snow. Dick lounged back and forth in front of the stove while the others listened to him. He was clearly pleased to have company, pleased to have the news which company could bring him, of the weather in the mountains, of the weather in Albo, of what was happening on the ranches of Albo. He was a good host, after his fashion; he served fried beef and biscuit for supper, and talked on.

Sam was attentive and polite, but restless. While Dick talked of ranches, Sam listened, but when he spoke it was about future rodeos and about the increasing popularity of cutting contests. Clyde, sitting in a corner out of the way, watched the two others, remembering that once he had disliked and distrusted Dick and had no questions about Sam. He contemplated the change in his opinions, which was not a reversal, but which involved a sudden illumination. For Clyde's examination, Sam sat still in the light of the oil lantern: there was the broken face, its lines blurred now by beard; there the protuberant blue eyes, and the hat line like a scar. He had not changed; he was now what he had been. Only in Clyde's mind had there been a change, and now he blinked in the murky light, gauging the change. Sam was a man who could be what he was doing, who could disappear into his successes and be happy there. "He just forgets himself when he makes a good throw," Clyde thought. "You

can't talk to him, he's hardly there. And he never really re-
members himself or forgets where he can go." Clyde shook
his head, and thought: "It's nice, it must be exciting, but it
won't work all the time. Look at him. Sometimes you've got
to sit, and that's when Sam looks sad."

It was a relief merely to look at Dick, who could be comfortable in a dull time, who could abide the weary hours and
unlucky days. "Like an old rock on a mountain," Clyde
thought. "Things push him around but don't change him
much. And he wants what he has a chance to have." Dick
moved slowly within the cabin, a bald-headed grizzled man,
his tough body sagging a little toward middle age. "There
he is," Clyde thought, "and that's the way he'll be the next
time I see him. You can count on him. I wonder why I didn't
like him at first." Again Clyde shivered a little with embarrassment, wondering at his folly. It occurred to him that he
had disliked Dick because Dick was unlike Sam, as if it were
impossible to admire one without misjudging the other; but
this he could not believe. He only wanted to dislike neither.

Then it occurred to him that he had disliked Dick merely
for being what he was, and not something else, after his long
life on ranches; for having arrived at middle age merely a
sturdy, reasonably honest man equipped with certain special
skills. Dick was a man not different from many others Clyde
had known, and he had appeared at a time when Clyde had
believed that spectacularly happy men emerged from ranches
as from a nursing place for happiness. Thus disappointment
made dislike, and now Clyde squirmed a little, thinking of a
new kind of folly.

But he was glad to have Dick near. It was pleasant to listen
to his homely talk with its concentration of shrewd ambition.
He listened while Dick talked of a spring he wished to re-

open for the next summer. It was a spring high up on the
shoulder of a nameless mountain; if it were open, it could
serve the tougher cattle, the ones who traveled farthest,
while they wandered after distant grasses.

Jonas and Scott failed to come that night, and the next day
Sam was worried because he was anxious to get back to
Albo. He wanted to take a horse and go look for them, but
Dick dissuaded him with calming words. Sam stayed because
he did not wish to argue with his host, as he told Clyde, but
he could not sit still. While Dick was off repairing a door on
one of his sheds, Sam moved restlessly about inside the cabin,
playing with scraps of leather, and finally took Clyde outside
to show him a thing he had made. It was a sling. Childlike, he
dug stones from the mire beside the door and showed Clyde
how the sling worked, the stones whistling away into the
gray air. "It's what old David used on G'liath," Sam said.
"You read about that in your Bible. We made these when we
were kids, we used to herd stock with 'em when we had to
go afoot. Look here, Clyde. You got a lot of power with one
of these things. For power, a nigger-shooter just ain't in it
with a sling."

At this moment the trucks appeared on the main road and
turned in at Dick's lane; Scott waved from the lead truck.
Sam, suddenly alert, waved back and nodded his head
fiercely, but did not move. "All right, then!" he said. "Looks
like we'll get along home after all." Gravely he turned his
head down to look at the sling again. He held it stretched
out between his two big hands. "It's quite a thing," he said.
"But then there ain't any use for it any more, I guess. It's just
a powerful way of throwing a stone." Gently his fingers
rubbed the rough leather. "Pretty, though. When we were
kids we used to have a lot of fun with slings."

x

Sam ran away from home on the third day after the end of
the hunt; this was the fact. Bonna June admitted no such
thing when Clyde talked to her; she arranged a decent pre-
tense and stood firmly behind it; but she was willing to let
Clyde know what had happened because he was a friend.

Clyde, having gone out to the Ambrose ranch to talk to
Sam, to pass an empty time, found Bonna June and Sam's
sister and the sister's husband loading furniture from the cottage into a pickup truck. The blue-eyed baby was playing
with a battered magazine under the clothesline and making
no noise. Already loaded in the truck were the mattress, the
blankets, the radio, three boxes of groceries, an old trunk.
Bonna June was just coming out of the door of the cottage
with the electric clock in her hands.

The moment came instantly to life with all its embarrass-
ments and difficulties. Clyde could not leave, because he had
been seen. Bonna June could not hide. She was carrying the
clock, it was a responsibility which she felt, she had to find
a place to put it down. Sam's truck was nowhere in sight, and
the usual clutter of ropes, bridles, and pieces of leather which
was normal on the porch of the cottage was all gone.

Bonna June was calm and brave. While she told her story,
she watched Clyde fixedly, as if to show that she had nothing
to hide; and the story was a simple story. She and Sam had
decided to take a chance on their cutting horse, she said; Sam
was going to the rodeos. He had taken the truck, the stallion,
and the bay gelding; he had quit his job at the Ambrose
ranch. Now Bonna June was going into town to live with
Sam's sister until Sam returned at the end of the rodeo season. While the story went on, Sam's sister and the sister's

husband stayed in the cottage; the story was told in a portentous quiet.

"Sam's a real good cowboy!" Bonna June said. "If anybody can make money at the rodeos, he can, and if he makes some money maybe we'll be able to buy a livery stable, or maybe a little dairy where Sam could have time for his horses. There's lots of things we could do with a little money, Clyde."

The packing was almost done, but Clyde offered to help and then did what he could. He tied down a piece of canvas over the load, and waved good-by to Bonna June as the truck pulled away. It was an end of something, and Clyde felt it so, but he could not feel surprise. Such things happened. Apparently they happened with some frequency to people like Sam Leathers, and it was always possible that Sam would indeed return soon enough to pick up his family and his life where he had left them.

In the next week Clyde managed to sell his mustang mare; he got sixty dollars for her from one of the druggists in Albo, who wanted her for his fourteen-year-old son. The mare was gentle and fairly well trained; Clyde was happy to be able to find a home for her. School took up again; the boys and girls came chattering and laughing to the classes and sometimes listened to what he said. One of the girls sent him an announcement of her engagement to one of the boys. An Indian boy in his American-history class was suspended from school for coming to his classes drunk, and Clyde attended to the matter of getting an apology from the boy so that he could be reinstated. When the term ended, in the first week of June, Clyde was left to himself.

He was left to himself with a decision which had formed itself quietly since the last days of the great hunt. He had decided to leave Albo to return to his old job in Los Angeles,

where he could have better students and higher pay. He had
not settled the matter of the ranch or farm, and did not want
to; he merely told himself that it was time to move along.
Because of the house and lots in the Illinois city, he had
money enough to carry him through the summer without
working, and because he felt no need to hurry, he stayed on
in Albo. Missing Sam, he spent most of his days reading; now
and then he exercised his black horse. On weekends he filled
a pack and took his fishing rod into the Sierra. One Sunday
he drove to Cedar Grove, another town in the Wilson Valley, to watch a rodeo.

In July he admitted to himself that he was waiting to see if
Sam would come back. Early in August he began to have
doubts. Dick Tatum came to see him one hot night, and they
spent a pleasant time drinking beer in Clyde's apartment; and
Dick only shrugged his shoulders when he heard about Sam's
departure. "It's the cowboy blood in him," Dick said, "that
and being young enough. I reckon Sam's not more'n thirty-
five, is he? That's young enough. But he'll get over it. I did.
Sure, I used to be a pretty good bronc rider myself, Clyde. I
took a second once at Phoenix. Why, Sam might even come
back to this woman here in Albo—you can't tell. I even did
that once myself. He's a good hand, that Sam, a real good
boy. He won't lack for jobs when he decides to settle down."
Dick stayed the night, and left the next morning on his way
to Bakersfield for a conference with his owner. Cheerful,
sweating a little in the morning sun, he talked until the moment of his departure.

In September, with the days still hot, the nights getting
cooler, Clyde left Albo for Los Angeles. He left the address
of his new high school with Bonna June; he sold his black
horse to the druggist who had taken the mustang mare. He
worked hard through the fall, enjoying the pleasures of the

city when he could, and was reasonably content. In December there was a letter from Sam, postmarked from Albo, written in a tall ungainly hand, with many spelling errors. Sam had fared well enough at the rodeos during the summer; he had sent money home, and returned with almost three hundred dollars. The stallion was making a fine cutting horse; another year and he might be a steady winner. Sam had got his old job back at the Ambrose ranch; Bonna June was expecting another baby. It was a cheerful letter which Clyde was glad to have, because it recalled for him the fine day of the second hunt, and the broad open country where the mustangs wandered, and the yellow river running through the road in the dark canyon, but it was news from another world and Clyde did not quite know how to answer it. He was busy with his work; he was thinking of taking up skiing during the Christmas holiday.

He answered the letter by saying that he hoped to make a visit to Albo at the end of the school year, in June, when the weather was hot, when with luck he might have time to travel. He could think of nothing else to say. At about the time he was sealing the letter, he had a momentary vision of the high Nevada desert, empty in its perfect light. It was a familiar vision, and it made him sad, but after a time it passed.

PART 2 🖝 *The War*

WOUNDS

A RIFLE BULLET striking bone hits with a fine hardness, followed instantly by a numbing shock; and then down you go.

When it happened to me, I felt my left leg for blood, thinking to gauge the wound, but could not do it, for the blood was running imperceptibly in my heavy trousers already soaked with the rain. I moved the knee, where the bullet had hit, and said to the man ahead of me: "I think maybe I'm hit, by God! Now what do you think of that?"

It was a November night in the south of Holland, with low gray clouds billowing voluminously close to earth. In the flash of a shell bursting you could see the pale misty bottoms of the clouds, and the rains came stirring out of them against your face with a feeling of impalpable moist depths. Up ahead of me were woods, from which the rifle shot had come; behind me a ditch, its waters flowing black like sooty Acheron itself; and all around me was the war—my war, one of the old ones now—littering the earth, making an ominous dark.

I lay with my face to the ground, padded where my cheek

touched it by leaf mold and withered grasses; we were in a pasture, surely, and there was a soft wind. In a little while it was time to go on, and so I rose, finding that I was not badly hurt, and continued marching through the night. Now and then I wondered that a bullet could knock me down and still bounce away, but I was growing used to perplexity and did not mind it. I had no thought of taking my sulfa tablets, for I wanted to save them for a major wound.

Toward morning we dug holes that started water seeping from the earth like wells, and when the dawn came we discovered ourselves in a cultivated field, plowed now and harrowed down, that was bordered on two sides by a dike lined with poplars, and on the third by a clump of houses. These were gray houses, blurred by a faintly falling rain; there were narrow windows and doors, and tile roofs the color of dirty copper. Each house had its trees, black and unidentifiable, glistening with the perpetual damp. The people were gone, I was sure, from those houses five hundred yards away, who have now long since returned to make the fields ripen again in heavy crops of sugar beets and grain.

There was no sign of life, though we had been told that Germans held the houses, and so that morning I thought about the farmers, hiding with their families. It was possible they hid in haystacks, or in the little pine forests of that country, and I could guess how it might be for them, for each chilly family huddled beneath a dripping tree. But of course they were far away; they did not exist, and at nine o'clock that morning came something which did, a British plane, strafing the houses for us. In an instant I had eyes for nothing else.

The plane was a Spitfire, of slim body and wide wings curved at the tips, and its course was to swoop low, fire the machine guns, and rise again. I crouched in my hole, legs folded into the water at the hole's bottom, and stared upward with joy. On the plane's second pass there was an answer from behind the houses, the steady, jarring hammer of 20-millimeter anti-aircraft guns firing synchronously; there would be a flak wagon behind the houses, that was it, a tracked vehicle with four guns in a turret, and so I grew frightened for the plane and its pilot.

But for two more passes the plane came low and then roared away in safety. I rejoiced, and forgot the icy chill gripping my feet and lower legs. The sound of the motor was loud and sweet on the downswing, and I could almost feel the delicate sheen of oil masking each working part in that slick harmony; I could sense the pistons firing in a row, and the electric messages of control vibrating along the wires. And of course I had a notion of the pilot, who would be a thin-faced Englishman like some of the British infantry officers I had seen; he would have a soft voice, and a depre-cating way of moving his hands, and be from Kent perhaps, or Lancashire, places I knew from training days.

And then the plane was hit, on the fourth pass, as it was pulling out: one moment there was the screaming sound from the motor as the pilot started his climb, and then there was a silence, hoarse with meaning. The plane climbed ever more steeply, until it became apparent that the arc of its climb would fall back into a circle leading to a crash. Quite distinctly I made out the markings on the upper surfaces of the wings: there were the emblematic rings of white and royal blue and red, and numbers in heavy block forms. For an instant there was a soft glitter on the hood over the cock-pit, an aerial shadow of death.

Who was that pilot? I could never know. At the beauty of his fall I sighed. Down he came, and there was a crash at which any man might blink.

Deeply I flung myself into my hole, bringing my forehead close to the earthy smell of water. After the crash there was an explosion, and then the familiar sound of splintered metal going by, a rough *whirroo* that leaves a hard quiet in the wake of its passing. Cautiously I looked out of my hole and saw, not a hundred yards away, the wreckage with smoke clumped upon it and slowly rising. There was nothing to do or say; the man was dead. In the shallow pool of water nearest my hole I observed a few patches of oil film, spattered there by the explosion. They widened; they grew floating there, unchanged by damp, in subtle colors I could not really see. There was a smoky blue perhaps, and a touch of orange or red; the colors had a perfect polish and no reflection in the gray morning.

Later that day another company attacked the houses, and we moved on to the dike with the poplars, where we stayed for a time in shallow holes. Toward nightfall a barrage of 120-millimeter mortars fell on the dike, killing the two men in the hole next to me, and thus stirring the officers to move again. We climbed out of our holes, and I looked at the bodies laid out under somebody's shelter-half; the feet projected from under the canvas, toes up, and the feet looked alive; one left foot was naked and bloody, the shoe blown clean off, exposing the horny toenails of the infantryman. We marched a long time that night, and finally arrived at the still-burning ruins of a barn, near which we dug holes again, for the third time that day.

There was an orchard all around the barn; little trees with sleek black trunks stood there in crooked rows, and our holes went down into a heavy earth that had a pleasant fragrance of rotted apples. The resiny smell of burning timbers carried to me a memory of campfires, and so it was not long before I had the feeling of holiday. My knee was stiffening, and I was wet and cold, but I became cheerful, and with a friend named Curry I decided to go closer to the tumbled fires of the barn. Our idea was to warm ourselves, and we were happy with that idea.

"If there's any shelling, we can duck back to our holes," Curry said. "But I'll bet the Germans are just as tired as we are."

"It's a fool thing to do," I said. "But let's do it. Damn it, I want to do it!"

Cautiously we made our way, staying clear of the German side of the fire so that we would not make silhouettes; and we were stopped only once in our progress, when a horse came charging through the position. There was a commotion behind us; the horse came looming into the light of the fire, clumsily galloping, swaying from side to side. He was high and dark, and somehow marred, moving like a creature stiff-jointed and old, and he stumbled against one of the little trees; then he screamed in terror, and we could see that he was badly burned. He had no mane or tail, and carried a sweet smell of burnt flesh into our holiday air. Again he crashed into a tree, and screamed, and then we knew he was blind. His eyes were singed wounds in his bony head, and he tossed his head as he galloped, as if to shake away the terrible darkness.

He galloped through the position from one end to the other, and disappeared into the night. I was a little shaken, but Curry restored my confidence. "Somebody'll shoot the old thing before morning," he said, "and put him out of his misery. Sure they will."

In a few moments we were back on our quest, and very quickly found what we wanted, an orderly fire, burning in a little stack of the poles used in that country to prop hayricks. It was warm there, and you could stand close without discomfort; and there was shelter from German eyes in a still-untumbled corner of the old barn itself.

"This is the place," Curry said. "By God, I'm going to take off my shoes and pants and get 'em dry."

We set about it, and in fact we stripped off all our clothes, in a gesture of high spirits, and set them out to dry. We drove stakes and placed our shoes and socks on them; I improvised a coat-rack for the shirts and jackets, and Curry arranged a way of stretching trousers between pairs of stakes. We had a game of co-operation, and so in a little while it was possible to enjoy feelings of harmony and peace.

Curry was not my best friend in the squad, but he was a good friend, and we had an understanding. He came from the same sort of family I had come from, and from the same sort of town. He had two brothers and a sister; his father was a purchasing agent, his mother had been to a small college in Michigan; and he lived in a suburb of Detroit. He had been drafted from the University of Michigan three months before his nineteenth birthday, and now he was awaiting his twentieth birthday. We were two of a kind; we understood that we were fortunate in everything except being in the war, and we were getting used to that; and of course we were pleased to be together, to be able to exchange identical sentiments about the unhappy incidents of our life.

Soon we had canned rations bubbling on the embers at the edge of the fire, and all about us were clouds of steam rising from our clothes. Naked we could stand the cold air of night, and even enjoy it; the wind raised gooseflesh on skin grown oily and bitterly resistant. We sparred a little, and in doing this I got several twinges in the knee that only made me happier. I looked at my wound, which was too small holes, each well covered by a crisp black scab, and a moderate swelling to the left of the kneecap. The wound was gen-

uine, clearly, and yet no hindrance to lightheartedness and
running.

Ah, that was a time! We leaped in and out of the firelight
in that cold soft Holland air, and ate our rations as children
eat at picnics, voraciously, so as to gain a quick release to the
games of the woods. We were fierce, like children, and felt
scorn for our friends crouching in holes, their bodies clotted
in damp cloth. Indeed, we were happy, and I will never forget the feeling.

An end came, as it had to, but at first it seemed not serious.
A light shelling of 120-millimeter mortars began to fall on
the edges of the orchard, and as we headed for the holes we
had dug, it was plain that the pattern was moving toward the
fire. We left our clothes, naturally, and ran naked, crouching
close to earth, and there was no danger, for we had time.
The holes were close to us, not twenty yards away, and we
were all but safe until Curry fell. Perhaps his bare foot
caught on something a heavy shoe would have brushed aside;
perhaps he stepped on a hot ember and by flinching from it
lost his balance; but he fell, and the pattern of the barrage
abruptly included him.

It was a light barrage. Moments after I reached my hole,
where one of my other friends was waiting for me with arms
braced to catch some of the shock of my diving fall, the barrage was over, and I rose quickly to see what had happened
behind me. I was breathing sharply, feeling excited and
happy, and so I needed a few moments before I could see
clearly. Meanwhile I heard Curry's voice speaking rapidly in
a normal tone, though I could not distinguish words. I was
perplexed; I looked around, and called the word "Curry"
several times into the hush which follows a barrage.

Then I saw him. Like a white flower in the night was the
whiteness of his body, and very clearly I saw a spout of

blood rising from the base of his throat. And heard him: "Lordy, Lordy," he said, "somebody, the blood's going out of me like water out of a hose. For God's sake, somebody, come help me. Do you want me to die here like a stuck pig?" The tone was almost humorous, and showed the control of the considerate patient who wants not to be a bother.

"I'm coming!" I shouted. "Curry, Curry, I'm coming, hold on!"

I scrambled out of the hole and started for him, charging low as if to knock something down with my shoulders; and I had made perhaps eight or nine yards of the distance when I heard the whispering fall of a mortar shell as the barrage began again. Down I went, as I had been taught, to hide myself against the stained old earth; flat on my belly, hands over my head, and listening to the explosions and whistling flights of shrapnel. The barrage was a little heavier this time, but shorter, and I scarcely had time to think about it before it was over.

I got to my feet a little slowly, with belly and chest darkly washed by a fine, silt-like mud, and began to trot toward Curry, but even before I reached him I saw that there would be no reason for haste. He had been hit again, and was dead now. He lay on his back, arms outspread against the rainy Holland earth. His hands and face were dark, with the weathering that comes to the devoted infantryman.

I could not see the wound that had first caught him; there was no spout of blood to define it now, and a wrinkled sheet of blood was settling all along his throat and collarbone and down his right shoulder. The wounds of the second barrage I could scarcely miss, for they were a great slash across his right thigh and a rip all across his belly, out of which now tumbled bowels and intestines.

Quickly I saw it all, and will not forget it, the death, the great wounds, the white body and scarcely used sex of this boy who had so great a part of his life ahead of him when he died.

In a little while other soldiers came, and a blanket was stretched over the body. I went back to the fire in the hay-rick poles and slowly dressed myself, not brushing away the mud from my chest and belly. I was feeling sad, and empty, as I have since felt a few times after rising from women.

Before I went to my hole for sleep, I dressed the body of my friend in the clothes which had dried while he was dying. I wanted whatever was left of him not to be cold, and so I did what had to be done with his spilled guts, and bundled the slippery coils back into the still-warm cage of muscle and tough hide. I got him together, and got him dressed, and thus had what I wanted, the feeling that I had done the few things left me to do.

And then I went back to my hole and started to be cold in a way I had not known before. That night I shivered with cold for the first time in my life, and it seemed to me that I could feel the moist night air seeping into my bones, corrupting the sweet, secret marrow. It was a fancy, but the next morning I was stiff and ailing, and had trouble making the day's march.

I had a recovery to make from Curry's death, however, and so I worked away at it, and was beginning to succeed by four o'clock, when my knee started an action very like the throbbing of blood, except that it was pain moving there. I was glad to have the pain, for it seemed a way of getting along with Curry's death, a way of settling accounts with whatever powers might be.

Also it was true that the pain persuaded me that my wound might soon be serious enough to take me out of the war for a while, and that was a thought which must cheer any soldier of the infantry. Toward dark we stopped near a big farm and were told that we might expect the company cooks that night with hot food and newspapers, and so we knew that our war was about to cease for a little while. We had seen no firing all that day; we were growing cheerful; we dug great holes, and found pleasure in the labor.

I dug with my friend Olney Arnett, a Tennessean, and we constructed a masterpiece of comfort in the field. We were on a little hill, and so we could go deep without getting water; we went down four and a half feet, in a hole seven feet long and almost five feet wide. We thatched the bottom to a depth of a foot and a half with fragrant hay taken from the barn at the top of the hill, and covered everything against the rain with our two shelter-halves draped across a pole stolen from the same barn.

We had a rough equivalent of a cabin with roof and ridgepole; we fastened the sides of the shelter-halves with well-packed heaps of dirt, and were ready to weather out a gale. "It's the best hole we've had for a week or more," Arnett said. "Just think how it's going to be to sleep in it tonight!"

A furry little mist was in the air, to moisten the face and the backs of hands, but we were sure there would be heavy rain that night, for there was always heavy rain in those nights. We would need our cave. In constructing it, we had achieved something good, and so we could have the pleasure of shared accomplishment. Arnett had for some time been my best friend in the squad, and therefore in the world, though we were not at all like each other; and so my pleasure in the task was augmented by the pleasure of having Arnett take part in it. He was a farm boy who had subtle arts of whittling with a pocket knife sharp as a razor; he knew bird cries, and the Tennessee names for all the trees and grasses of ancient Europe; he came from an old people long rooted in a single county, and he knew strange songs that puzzled me. He was a sturdy boy, not the kind to give in to his circumstances; braver than I, and more calm, so that he could regard the details of our life in the war with a reluctant good humor, where I was given to furious rages.

We were at odds in everything except the necessary arts of living together, but in these we could be at peace. Having finished our hole, we walked like loving brothers to the farmhouse where I had been told to come for treatment of my knee. There we found an agreeable officer who made arrangements for hot water and cloths; he was the platoon leader of the second rifle platoon of our company, and thus it was an act of special condescension for him to forsake his responsibilities to think about easing my pain.

It was a trick to get my trousers down past the huge swelling that had come into my knee, but we managed it, and then Arnett moistened pads of clean white cloth into compresses, which he laid delicately over the sore places. I sat in a chair, with my left leg propped on another, and might have been a little king of that high, narrow room.

Close to my hand was a fire burning in a little porcelain stove. On top of the stove was a canteen cup of coffee, prepared especially for me, with a little of the lieutenant's whisky in it for flavor and comfort, and a big pot of water for the compresses. There had been no destruction in the room; the woodwork in windows and wall moldings was highly polished and dark; the chairs which ringed the old table were plain and hard, but not uncomfortable, and there were two steel engravings on the walls, each showing a skater dashing brilliantly down the winter ice of a canal. It was a Dutch interior, immaculately polished and rich, and not much altered by the litter of soldiers. Rifles leaning against the walls did not really change the look of it, but they were sufficiently present so that I could have a momentary sense of belonging to the room. I was at ease, and could have been happy greeting guests.

When the cooks arrived outside in their two-and-a-half-ton truck, Arnett went to them and got a noble supper for me. I had tomatoes, bread, and two kinds of meat, with a sweet stimulant composed of one part canned milk and sugar, and one part black coffee. The tears almost came to my eyes as I sat in the hot room holding the heavy cup. My skin was alive with the pleasure of warmth; my whole system was growing soft and joyous in the pleasure of being tended to. Two hours I spent in this way before I had to go outside again, and when I left I felt fortified and strong. The cold air, blown against my face by the night wind in such a way as to suggest the rain which was coming, only served to remind me that I had a fine shelter to take myself to, and so I joked with Arnett and even made fun of his country ways as we walked slowly along. When we got to the hole, Arnett offered to take part of my guard that night, and I accepted; I would keep watch for the first three hours, until midnight, and then he would be responsible for the rest of the night. I was grateful, and thanked him.

At the open end of the hole I propped myself up and set my rifle on its sling, sights up, the barrel pointing north. Beside it I placed my three grenades and Arnett's two. For a while I listened to Arnett burrowing in the hay on his side of the hole, and then, when there were no more noises from him, I occupied myself in watching the sky. At ten thirty I was dismayed to see the sky grow clear, exposing a crystalline darkness and a few stars. I was angry, thinking there might be no rain to test the cave and give me the sounds of rain addressing a roof above my weary head. For half an hour I had this distress, and suffered bitterly, until the sky closed again and I could prepare myself for enjoyment.

At midnight I woke Arnett, and he rose cheerfully. He arranged his hay so that he could sit wrapped in it to the waist while he was keeping guard, and then said good night to me and began softly to hum an old tune.

I was ready for sleep as I crawled slowly into my hay. Deep in it was the musty fragrance of summer; I distinguished three kinds of flower smells, and even found, with darkened fingers, a dry little bur soft to the touch that might have been a clover blossom. As I settled myself, I could feel a pollenous dust crossing the skin of my face and tickling the back of my neck under the shirt collar. I became dry in feeling, as if I too had lain curing through the wet autumn, in the high old barn on the hill.

In a little while I became warm also, and therefore ready for bliss, but for a while no bliss came. My left leg was stiff and sore from the ankle far up into the thigh, and there was an untouchable coldness in the toes of my left foot. There was a steady pain. I could not sleep, and in my wakefulness I remembered the tragic stories of my soldier's life.

I grew angry; there was no rain, and so I softly cursed the weather, for a long time, until at last the rain began. It came hard and beating, just what I wanted, and yet it did not bring me sleep. I heard the drumming on the canvas, and in the not-quite-thorough darkness of a night in the midst of war I could just make out the canvas sagging with the accruing weight of water. I had what I wanted, and yet it did not suffice, and so my spirit for a while approached despair.

Disappointments were severe in those troubled days. I was having an unpleasant time in that sweet hay, and then a thing happened that changed everything in an instant. The heavy rain at last grew too much for the moorings of the shelter-half on Arnett's side of the hole; he had stretched the canvas too near the horizontal, and left no way for the water to run off, and so there were surely ten gallons of water gathered above his head. I did not see what happened, of course, for my eyes were closed, but I knew what it was. Arnett, sitting motionless, his face composed under his helmet, eyes watching out into the night, was allowing himself to remember his mother's face, perhaps, or the look of her kitchen; and then the shelter-half pulled free and loosed those gallons of Holland rain on his head like a flood sent from on high.

"Gre't God A-mighty!" Arnett said, spluttering like one drowning. I opened my eyes and saw instantly what had happened: Arnett was floundering, shaking his dripping head and shoulders like old Neptune himself rising out of troubled waters. He tried standing up, and said: "My God, I'm drownded, the goddamned roof . . ." And then he sat down again, his haunches splashing. "Oh, no," he groaned. "Oh, goddamned no!" Weakly he raised his right arm and then let it fall. "I'm all wet," he said. "And on a night like this I'll never get dry!"

I half sat up, but then my leg hurt sharply, making me fall back. I shivered, and raised my shoulders, awaiting the shock of icy waters from Arnett's disaster, and for a moment I felt a savage fury that he had been so clumsy in building his side of the roof. "God damn it, Arnett," I called, and then stopped out of regard for our friendship. "Arnett?" I said again. It came to me that I was not yet dampened, and this was an enormous surprise. Cautiously I felt around in my hay, looking for signs of water; but there were none.

"Arnett," I said. "My God, I'm dry! It all fell on you, you poor bastard!"

"Son of a bitch!" Arnett shouted. He was standing now,

thrashing his arms about wildly. "Son of a bitch! Son of a bitch! You goddamned water, you rain, may you fairly die, you goddamn, cold, mis'able water!"

His hands fell to his sides, and he shook his head. "Oh, no," he said. "And I done so many *good* deeds today." Slumped over, he stood without moving, and suddenly I began to laugh.

He had helped me, he was the best friend I had in all the world, but I laughed at his misfortune as I have rarely laughed in my life. Tired and dejected, he stood without answering while I laughed with fury. After a long time he threw his wet hay out of the hole and sat down again, on the bare ground, to resume his guard, and I laughed even then. His silence was nothing to me; I could not care; and long after the night had grown quiet again I was still chuckling, deep in my warm hay smelling dryly of wild flowers and clover.

I went to sleep without our speaking to each other again, and I slept a flowing, tide-like sleep that carried me with perfect ease into the wakening chill of the next morning. It was joyous sleep, and I was presiding over it as it happened, with some part of me that will be forever wakeful. I had enjoyment, and knew I was having it, and knew further that no man could ask for more from the earth and the curious things which grow upon it.

I woke in the morning cheerful, with the full expectation that my life would soon improve in all its conditions. I was certain that good luck was coming; and so it did. Arnett had got over his disaster, and held nothing against me, so that we were friends as before. He helped me out of the hole, and caught me when I fell; he was sympathetic when it became apparent that I would not be able to walk all the way to breakfast at the cooks' truck.

I was a cripple now; there was nothing left me but to say good-by to my friends and go to the hospitals. I went with the cooks, sitting in the cab of the truck with the driver and the mess sergeant. I was sorrowful at leaving all my old friends, but anxious to see what the hospitals had to offer, and so I traveled in great serenity of spirit; and of course it happened that the hospitals offered a great deal, enough to please any rational man, any soldier of the infantry.

At the first hospital there was a warm room filled with long narrow tables, at which doctors were working over other wounded men. On one of these tables I had my knee opened and dressed. I was warm once more, looking upward into bright unfocused light, and, being really not badly hurt, I could enjoy the sharpness of the doctor's scalpel. I could feel the edge with a shock of pleasure, knowing that the edge was exposing corruption and cutting it out. Without looking, I could feel the small flow of blood which followed the course of the knife, and enjoy that too, for I was only losing a tainted blood that any man would be happy to have out of him.

Then there was a ride in an ambulance to yet another hospital, where I stayed for a few hours in the late afternoon while a train was making up to carry a load of wounded to Paris. I was in Belgium now, far from the fighting. Over my supper I began to dream about the great luminous city to the south, and I could not quite believe in my good fortune when I was taken to the train at eight o'clock that night.

Events were passing me by, they happened so swiftly. I was borne from one fine place to another like a little boy on a roller-coaster, wild with joy, unable either to get off the car or make it stop. All the faces were friendly, all the machines aided my comfort. I was technically a walking wounded, and so I traveled in one of the standard carriages, and there the seats were fine, for the carriage was of the first class.

Suddenly from walls broken and crumbling I was transported to walls beautifully finished in polished wood. With two other wounded men I established myself in luxury, with my left leg propped up on a little bench the nurse had brought in for me. I was astonished by the dark and glossy walls, and charmed by the patterns of flowers and trees inlaid under the final shellac; the images might have been reflected there, such was the effect, as if the walls had been the shut windows of an old house that mirror the rich, decaying gardens outside. The benches we sat on were covered with a heavy tapestry, on which were a parade of silver bushes and marble fountains, with little golden deer delicately walking by.

I was dazzled, and then, of course, sleepy, but sleepy in a pleasant way; I only wanted to be fresh for the wonderful things the next day might bring. The train rolled southward, whistle screaming as in a dream of fast night trains, and we reached Paris before dawn. Then there was a ride in an ambulance, and disappointment that I would not see Paris that day, but the disappointment did not last.

There was a faint daylight at the hospital doors, and I knew I was entering a fine old building redolent with peace and charity. Above the doors, in a frieze, were sculptured naked angels and cherubic infants; they were gray figures almost lifelike in the hesitant light. Pigeons fluttered near, and as I entered the building I understood that the pigeons had the right to enjoy the mottled purity of the carved stone. Who would worry? The stone would last.

Inside, there was a rhythm of care to draw me in, and I knew I had reached an end. Here I could rest, and be comforted. I was put to bed between sheets of English linen, under blankets of English wool, and the skin of a noble woman could not be finer to my touch than those humble fabrics were. I was fed on a pink ham, surely from the best of Virginia smokehouses, on yams, and asparagus smelling astonishingly of spring; and I was given fine coffee, in a white crockery cup. I talked to a nurse, who smiled at me; she was busy, and she was plainly a dutiful type, but I was her duty, and so in a way she belonged to me.

There was so much to be grateful for that I began to feel guilty, as if no single man could merit such care. Men were dying within those walls, I knew, for I had seen rooms closed behind placards which said that no visitors were allowed, and I had sensed, on my passage upstairs to my ward, several ominous movements of nurses and doctors; they would be walking softly, as if on tiptoe, and solemnly like priests, and they could not fool me. Death was all about me, and might even have left its stench in some of the darker corridors and more distant rooms. And of course I was curious, remembering stories I had heard of other military hospitals; I wondered whether I would have duties in this strange, delightful place, and so I asked the doctor who came to see me, as soon as he had finished his examination.

"Will I have duties here, sir? Like making the bed and scrubbing the floor, say?"

"Of course not," he answered. "Don't even think about it." He was a short, dark man wearing gold-rimmed spectacles; a major, a middle-aged man. He looked shrewd and good-humored, and it came to me, as a summation of all my pieces of wonderful luck, that he was a man I could trust; and so I spoke quite frankly.

"What will I have to do here, then?" I asked. "What *should* I do?"

"Why, just get well, son," he said. "That's all. And enjoy yourself. Don't you like it here? Well, then, enjoy it, there's your duty. Maybe later on you'll be able to go out and see if Paris suits you. It's easy. You'll see. Don't you know how to be happy any more?"

"Happy?" I said, and took thought. "My God, in all my life I've never been so happy!"

Indeed, will I ever be so happy again?

FRIENDSHIP

WHEN I FIRST knew him, Lev was first sergeant, hated by everybody except the sergeants who played cards with him. He was a faraway deity in his orderly room, and at company formations. He was a Jew, and looked like one, with a hooked nose that seemed all hard bone down to its very tip, but only once did I know anyone to call him Jew in anger, and that time was a victory for Lev, as things turned out.

It happened at Camp Kilmer when we were on our way overseas. A quarrelsome Southerner in my platoon, a private first class named Duval, returning late one evening from a pass to New York City, came across Lev and his cronies at a game of Hearts in the day room. Duval was drunk, and so he dared to ask for a place in the game, which was going along comfortably with four players. There was a silence. I looked up from my letter, and half a dozen others grew quite still over magazines.

"We're playing partners," Lev said after a moment, raising his large, unblinking eyes from his hand. He was quite firm; it was known that he and his friends never played any game with partners.

"Come on, Sarge, le'me sit in," Duval said. "I know that game. I'm a good Hearts player." He was leaning forward a little, a light-heavyweight approximately, known to have sought fights in bars, and respected for his strength and recklessness. "Don't hard-ass me, Sarge," he added. "Ain't we goin' overseas to fight the war together?"

Gravely Lev looked at the members of the game, each in turn shaking his head in response. Then Lev looked up again and said: "We don't want you in the game, Duval. We only play with the first three grades here—staff sergeants and up, that is."

Again there was a silence, and after a moment, as it became apparent that Duval would not leave, I saw that something more was coming. Lev began dealing the cards; his lips were drawn back a little from his teeth, and for an instant his tongue appeared, licking his lower lip in a gesture which reminded me of a cat just come in from the out-of-doors.

The edge was all to Lev, for he was at home amid the trappings of his power. In the next room his clerk was laboring over the company papers. In the barracks most of his company was asleep within reach of his care, and at each side of the table were his friends expecting him to defend the privileges of the noncommissioned officer. The man at Lev's left said something about the Queen of Spades, and Lev responded with a little chuckle, saying: "He wants to know where the Bitch is, and nobody'll tell him." There was a laugh, and its effect was to seal the game into its ritual.

Duval's face grew red. He lifted his right hand and looked at it intently, and then said quickly: "That ain't no way to treat a man." He was stubborn; now he proved it. "You didn't have to say it that way, Sarge."

"I'll say it again if I want to!" Lev said sharply, not even looking up this time. "And don't point your finger at me."

By this time there was a look of helpless rage in Duval's face. "I ain't leaving," he said. "I'll be damned if I will. You don't give a man hardly a chance, Sarge!"

"If you don't lay off, I'll give you something, though!" Lev said, and laughed boisterously. "Oh, I'll give it to you!" He raised his head and stared insolently at Duval, secure in his high place: who could be more at home than a first sergeant in his own company day room?

"The hell with you, then," Duval said. He paused, and took courage from the thing already said. "God damn it, Sarge!"

"All right," Lev said. "All right—all right!"

"With you, Sergeant Lev. *First* Sergeant Lev, by God." Growing bolder, Duval looked around the room, smiling at the men he knew in order to claim their support. "Lev?" he said. "What kind of a name is that, anyway? God damn it, I know what kind of name it is. It's a Yid name, ain't it? Sure it is." Again he looked at the others in the room, to rally their approval to his cause. "Come to think of it, there ain't no reason why a white man would want into a Yid card game anyway."

Lev, without scraping his chair against the floor, and without making any kind of stir with his feet, had risen; and there he was. He moved out away from the table, walking straight up, with his hands at his sides, the fingers closed enough to be hook-like and alert for seizing. "Okay, Duval," he said. "It's a Yid name, all right. Watch yourself. I'm coming at you." A little skip appeared in his gait, and suddenly he was no longer quite walking. His right hand, still open, came up to his right cheek, where it hovered, and his left arm, weaving a little, like the head of an angry snake, extended itself in front of him.

Square and solid, Duval awaited him, scowling, and so for

perhaps three seconds there was the prospect of a fight in the company day room; but there really was no fight. Lev had the movements of a fighter, the strength, and the willingness to commit himself, and he had these qualities with such intensity that as they happened they quite extinguished our sense of a combat.

Duval did not strike a blow, and was himself hit perhaps two dozen times in the space of twenty seconds. He was hit first in the nose by a swinging hook, and there was the sound of the nose breaking like a cracked board; then he was hit in the belly and over the heart, in a flurry of punches, so that he was doubled over on himself, like a man bending down to tie a shoelace; and then he was hit twice on the jaw, once on the left, once on the right, and from these blows he began to fall; but since he was a tough, strong man he straightened up first, so that he toppled slowly, and then he was hit once more, by a sliding, dropping right-hand punch that sliced open his left eyebrow as a razor might slice open a ripe tomato.

At the end he was sitting dumped awkwardly on his hams, with his legs sprawled out crookedly, as if they did not quite belong to him. He was conscious; his right eye stared waveringly up and down at nothing, while blood streamed down the sightless pit of his left eye and spread out across his cheek and into the corner of his mouth, that now was opening and closing rhythmically, like the mouth of a hurt fish.

"All right," Lev said. "All right, then, all right." He stood scowling down for a moment, his lips drawn back from his glittering teeth, his tongue working busily across his upper lip, as if he might be thinking about tasting the blood of his fallen enemy. For perhaps a minute he stood so, looking as I might imagine a veteran gladiator to look after surrounding the armored man with his net and finding his life with the barbed trident, while the crowd roars, and the Emperor, pleased a little, reaches out to touch the pearly thigh of a favorite boy.

Then Lev nodded once, approving, and turned to me his large bold eyes. "Go up to my room and get the little leather bag—it's like a suitcase—out of my green barracks bag. And hurry, God damn it, before this kid bleeds to death on our goddamned floor."

I hurried, and returned quickly, having experienced a curious sensation of guilt on rummaging through the belongings of such an exalted personage. The bag was like the cases that doctors used to carry on calls, and in it, so we all discovered when Lev opened it on the day-room floor, were several kinds of hospital equipment, including a little steel case of scalpels. One of these Lev used to touch up the cut over Duval's eye, and then, with a large needle and something which looked like a coarse thread, he sewed up the cut, using a complicated sewing stroke that I could hardly follow. After that, he cleaned out the left eye with a glass eye-cup and delicate touches with a little cylinder of rolled-up gauze, and washed Duval's face, with an economical tenderness of movement startling in that atmosphere of ancient hate.

When he was done, he had two of the watchers take Duval up to the barracks, leading him like a blind cripple, and then, clearly pleased with himself, and feeling rich, as any man might after such a scene, he returned to the game. For a moment he stood above his chair, appreciating it, and, I think, appreciating the opportunity for pleasure which would soon be laid out before him once again. "Good enough," he said, and sat down.

He composed himself, arched his back, and slowly rotated his head, eyes hooded but glittering above his hawk's nose; and then he spoke once quite clearly to the whole room. "I'm a Yid, all right," he said. "But I'm the kind that always runs to a fight, and that's the worst kind, men. Whose deal is it?"

Then he bent to the game; and that was the man he was in those days.

How much more he might have been I could not know for certain, but nowadays, thinking back, I have the feeling that there was a great deal to know. Certainly he was an imposing first sergeant—and we were proud of him, in spite of our hating him as all first sergeants must be hated. He was a possession we could mention knowingly to men of other companies in the battalion, and they had heard of him, usually, or at least heard rumors about him. He was an elegant marcher and a master of the manual at arms; when he gave the drill, he caused a precision in the movements of men who under other voices tended to slackness; and of course he was proud of what he could make us do. He liked his job, and clearly liked his company, though he was never heard to say so. According to our rosters, his full name was Murray B. Lev, though there was a rumor that his best friends were allowed to call him Moe, on occasion. He was one of those powerful, middle-sized men who seem to summarize the physical intensities of the male principle; he was hairy, with dense black curls matted over his chest and back, and fine silky hairs lying flat on the backs of his hands; his cheeks had a bluish tinge, and he shaved regularly twice a day, even after we entered the combat zone. He had a solid body neatly rigged, and could hardly move without suggesting grace and competence. He carried himself alertly, and his cold brown eyes took note of everything that happened in his little world. He seemed always ready to take advantage of an opportunity, and ready also to design an opportunity if that ever became necessary.

There were women to please him everywhere he went, it

was said, but he was close-mouthed in such matters, and not even his best friends among the sergeants were allowed to follow him when he left camp on his Class A Pass, to be gone until reveille the next morning. Twice at our camp in Colorado he brought a pretty blonde girl to watch a parade, but I never saw him with a woman at any other time. He was a skillful lover, surely, but, like most men of that breed, he traveled by darkness, covering his tracks, and never took the same route twice in succession.

His past was not quite a mystery. He was from Chicago, and since he was in his early thirties when he was first sergeant, it was certain that he had lived variously in that dark city before he entered the army. He admitted owning what he called "an interest" in a bar on East 63rd Street, so I was told, and said he had "an income" from a hand laundry on 53rd Street. He did not talk about his civilian jobs, but he would admit earning money with golf at Jackson Park, and that seemed reasonable. He was a fine athlete; he was the shortstop on the regimental baseball team that won the division championship, and in our last season before we went to Europe he batted .419 in twenty-seven games.

He could play golf, I'll venture. Had he lived through the war, he might even now be standing in the shade of a palm tree on the practice green of a resort course in Florida. He would be amiable in the bright, watery light reflected off the Gulf; he would be available for a game, certainly, and he would bet if challenged, and win by a stroke on the last hole, to take all the money. After that, he might buy the drinks and listen modestly to the conversation about the major-league baseball team training at a nearby town.

He was a natural citizen of twilight worlds; it was inevitable that someone should suggest, after seeing his doctor's case at Camp Kilmer, that he had probably been an abortionist in Chicago. He talked sometimes about Barney Ross, the Jewish welterweight champion from Chicago, and once, so it was said, refused to deny that he had worked as a corner-man for some of Ross's opponents. There was a tradition among those of us who cared about sports that Lev's father had been a friend to Abe Attell, the marvelous old-time bantamweight champion from San Francisco, who, growing soft, and aging, had represented the gamblers to the Black Sox of 1919.

Nowadays, as I think back, it seems entirely possible that Lev might have gone the way of Attell if he had lived long enough: Attell, who carried himself unmarked and un-beaten through hundreds of fights, and finally came around to secret meetings with Gandil and Jackson and Cicotte in a Chicago hotel room. We must guess that Attell was a friend to the gambler Arnold Rothstein, who was soft and fat and clever, and so might Lev have become a friend to a fat and clever man.

I think it could not have been otherwise, had there been no war. Lev had talents, and so he was bound to use them. But the war came to provide a new ground for those talents, and so he became a wonderful soldier, famed for bravery and ferocity, and known for his extreme devotion to his com-pany.

In fact, he was happy as a soldier, there can be no doubt of it. He was proud of his uniform, and had many, so that he was able to change twice and sometimes even three times a day. He was proud of his soldier's skills, and it was nothing to him that he was hated, for that was part of the job.

The chief symptom of his happy life in the war came in the curious nature of some of the friendships he made; and particularly in his friendship with a nineteen-year-old Okla-homa boy named Jim Bob Allison. This was a slender, sturdy

boy who had lived most of his life in a town called Cedar
Springs. He was innocent, goodhearted, and intelligent, just
what a boy from a country town is supposed to be in America. His face might not have looked out of place under a
Boy Scout hat, and he had the appearance of one who could
make fire with a wooden disk, a stick, and a bow.

He was no athlete, being a little awkward and too long in
the leg, but he had a face which was just about right for the
skinny end on the high-school football team. His face was
squarish, with a narrow bony jaw that might in time take on
a formidable curve; his mouth was full but firm, the lips always lying close together, with a faint suggestion of coming
maturity, and he had a straight nose which, with his clear
blue eyes, gave him an attractive look as of a boy whom any
girl's mother would be willing to trust on sight.

He often talked humorously about women, wanting them,
but he was bashful and unasking. In Cedar Springs he had
sometimes been in the vicinity of girls at ice-cream socials
and picnics given by the Kiwanis Club, but he admitted
freely that he had been one of those boys who make an uneasy group on the outskirts, hooting the well-combed boys
who dare to approach the girls. He was a boy for the out-of-
doors, and it was true that he had fished for catfish in the
Canadian River where it passes through Hardin County, and
had killed his first deer at the age of sixteen, in one of the
southern counties of the state, on a trip with his father and
two uncles from Ponca City. He was a boy for the straw
hat and bib overalls, and he had worn these, and gone bare-
foot too, of course, moving through his boy's life like some
wise man's memory of Huckleberry Finn.

And this boy became a close friend to Moe Lev in the het-
erogeneous complexity of the American army, where seeing
them together became a normal sight, touching somehow,

and faintly alarming, for each had much to learn from the
other. They were thrown together initially by the fact that
Jim Bob was for a while the company commander's runner
and so spent most of his time near company headquarters,
where Lev ruled. Jim Bob was noticed, but of course he was
not close to Lev so long as we were in training, for Lev
would not befriend a mere private first class at a time when
he was teaching discipline. Jim Bob was willing to learn,
however, and, like many boys of that army, he became star-
tlingly professional in the way he regarded the army and his
duties in it, largely because he had never known another job;
it was the only life he had ever had away from home, and so
he felt for it the respect and admiration which boys properly
reserve for their first major commitment. He read the manu-
als, he drilled carefully, and he was a good marksman; thus
he was available for Lev's regard when the time came.

That time came gradually, after we reached France. It was
not long before Lev ceased to be hated in the company, this
being a normal phenomenon in most armies, I suspect. Once
the shooting started, his harshness during training could be
seen to have its uses, and his toughness was clearly valuable
when there was a town to be attacked or a river to be crossed.
He risked dangers he did not have to risk, and so in time,
after we had moved up out of northern France and Belgium
to the border of Holland, we came to have a strong feeling
of respect for him.

Jim Bob became one of his most outspoken admirers, and
learned to say judiciously: "Sure I like him. You goddamn
right I like him. Ain't he the bravest man in the battalion?
Everybody knows that." He would speak of Lev's exploits
as if he were speaking of an honored brother or a hardy, loving father. "Do you remember when he set off the TNT
against the wall of that stone barn on the Belgian border?"

he would say, and wait for his audience to recall whatever images they might have of that time, when Lev, under fire from a nearby house and from two snipers in an adjoining wood, had blown an enormous hole in the wall of a stone barn, so that one of the rifle platoons could attack the Germans hidden in the barn. "Yes, indeedy," Jim Bob would continue. "We *all* remember that time, I *guess*. And how about when he led the charge against that Panther tank in the woods last week? 'A course there was some others went with him then, but most of them went because old Lev was there to say 'Come on, let's go get that son-of-a-bitch!' " It had been a notable triumph: Lev had taken a group of eight men and destroyed a Panther tank and five German infantrymen who had been accompanying it, with no losses to his group.

There were other exploits, and Jim Bob made the most of them, and made no secret of his admiration, so that Lev came to be in a position where it was difficult for him not to like Jim Bob. Lev became a famous soldier in the regiment, and in due course was awarded both the Bronze Star and the Silver Star. Furthermore, he was a stable and consistent man, a soldier to be admired by his fellow soldiers. We had our share of heroes, there in our north European war, but only a few, like Lev, were truly sound. The others tended to be brave with a certain desperation for a few weeks or a few months, goaded into risk by some eccentricity in their motivations. Such men could be violent and effective, but they often wore themselves out with their violence, growing tired and fretful and even fearful sometimes.

When that happened, the hero became a normal soldier or a psychological casualty, while Lev continued as he had been, expressing the deepest and truest bent of his life; and, naturally enough, affecting those around him, altering them sometimes in a quite startling fashion. Jim Bob, for example, being a hero-worshipper, taught himself war rather quickly, and then, more slowly, emulating Lev, taught himself a fine hardness of intention. Lev did not believe that a proper soldier should surrender unless he was wounded in such a way that he could no longer fight; and so Jim Bob accepted this belief, and one night proved his acceptance in action.

We had reached Germany in late November, and were engaged east of Aachen in the heaviest fighting we had yet seen. Jim Bob was sent with a message to a rifle platoon besieged in a factory, and was present during the German attack which broke the platoon's resistance. There was a Tiger tank to push the door in, and there was a large force of SS infantry. Our platoon leader and platoon sergeant were killed, along with half a dozen others, and of the remainder some ran away and some allowed themselves to be captured; but Jim Bob hid himself under a heap of waste rags, keeping his rifle ready, and stayed there for almost twelve hours, until the factory was retaken by another of our platoons. He stood up then, dusty and begrimed, and I remember how he looked. He was tired, his eyelids were heavy, but his eyes were bright; he was leaning on his rifle, and with his free hand, the left, he was making brushing movements at his jacket and pants. He looked a boy, but a boy precocious in a hard world, and he was not at all dismayed.

Naturally, Lev was pleased. It became known that he had a special regard for Jim Bob, and the two of them began to be seen together rather frequently. They shared rations out of boxes and cans; they sat together when we had a meal from our own kitchen; and many times they dug holes together, sharing the narrow earthen walls. They talked, of course, with Lev telling stories of big-city adventure, and Jim Bob explaining country ways of fishing and hunting; and these conversations came to be a part of the company's legend about itself.

And through all this Lev's instruction continued. Jim Bob acquired a willingness never to stop fighting, and the knowledge that there always came a time when decisive action was necessary. "Somewhere in a fight there's a time when a man has got to do something, and then he'd better do it," so Lev said, and demonstrated in his actions. Thus, when Jim Bob happened to be surprised on a message-carrying mission by a stray German rifleman somehow left behind in the general retreat to the Rhine River, he took care of himself very nicely. He had been caught in the open, with no cover; the German was hidden behind a tree, lying down with almost the whole of his body protected; but Jim Bob moved rapidly to his right on the open ground, rising, running, and falling to fire a shot, and then doing it again, until finally he had got far enough to the German's flank to have a clear shot at him; and then he killed with a bullet through the neck, afterwards like a hunter dipping his fingers in the blood from the wound, for it was first blood.

It was a rare thing, that individual combat, in a war of running and hiding and big guns fired from far away, and the news of it spread rapidly. Again Lev was pleased, and for several days he spoke admiringly of Jim Bob's exploit, returning Jim Bob's compliments. His favorite remark was, simply: "The kid's got that old ticker, men. If he had the built, he'd of made a hell of a fighter, that kid would."

High praise; and of course it came back to Jim Bob multiplied and rhetorically enforced. He became, over a period of time, what Lev wanted all of us to be, a soldier who would not run, and who was capable of fierceness, and he had his reward one day in the outskirts of Cologne, when Lev took the trouble to save his life. Jim Bob, returning from one of the platoon leaders, whom he had visited with a message, was knocked down and stunned by a mortar shell exploding close to him. It was an accidental barrage, a piece of guess-work by German gunners trying to do their best with an impossible situation; and none of us knew how long the barrage might last.

Lev, in the first let-up, ran out to Jim Bob and picked him up, put the limp body on his shoulder, and trotted to the safety of the house where the company command post was hidden in a cellar. There Jim Bob revived; he opened his clear blue eyes like one born again, while outside the barrage resumed with greater intensity than before.

"Look at the kid," Lev said. "The kid's all right. He don't look it with that baby face, but he can't fool the old man. I knew plenty of tough fighters that had a baby face—sure, they were even the kind that liked to see blood!"

Jim Bob sat up, greatly moved, and, after a few moments of getting up his determination, said: "Then you must have brought me in. I don't remember what happened after . . ."

"Sure I brought you in," Lev said.

"Then you're a brave, good man, Sergeant Lev! I want to say—" But he did not really know what he wanted to say, and so he paused, resting in what he had already said.

And that was the way things were when we reached the Rhine, where the character of the war began to change. We had a few days of rest in Cologne, during which Lev was awarded a commission as second lieutenant and given my platoon, which had lost its platoon leader just west of the city in the last of our attacks there. It had been apparent for a long time that Lev would have to accept this honor, though he had been heard to protest against the possibility. I was by then a squad leader, having moved up through the ranks as one squad leader after another had fallen or died, and of course I was glad to have Lev control my future, for he was known to be careful with his men. I was further pleased that Lev brought with him, to take over another of the platoon's squads, Jim Bob, newly promoted to staff sergeant for the occasion. By this time they were close friends of the war-time sort, having shared enough intense experience in a few months so that they would never run out of matter for talk so long as the war lasted.

There was a chance of awkwardness in the fact that Duval, once Lev's victim in the famous fight, had become the pla-toon sergeant, and in fact there were a few difficult moments in Cologne, before we returned to the fighting. We were quartered in two big houses whose owners had stripped them to the walls, and we were not comfortable there; our footsteps had a flat, vicious sound on the polished floors. We were caged by the barren walls, and thus it was impossible for Lev not to make his presence heavily felt when he arrived with his bright new insignia of rank. He spoke his requests in the normal style of the combat zone, of course, which was a friendly sound, but it was difficult for him to use a friendly sound on Duval without seeming apologetic. "We'll have to find a time to talk to those two new men," he would say, and look perplexed, while Duval guardedly watched him. Or: "I'll have to go up to the Company CP for a briefing, Duval. I ought to be back soon."

The whole platoon was close at hand; there was no chance of privacy in which the two might parse their differences. During the first day Lev turned rather frequently to me, as to a neutral observer; we had been coming closer together during the months just past, and he had several times allowed himself to talk to me at some length, but now he let me feel that he was somehow dependent on me. That I liked, for it was an achievement to be of use to such a man. I understood that I was expected to serve as a mediator, and so I tried to make up conversations to include both lieutenant and sergeant.

There was not much I could do, though I intimated to each man in turn that the other was willing to forget the bitter quarrel in their past; and this may have helped. Duval, who had lived in both Alabama and Georgia, was a proud Southerner, a farmer, a man who had kept coon dogs; he would never understand Lev, and certainly he would never be able to ask for a reconciliation. But he was a good soldier and an honest man; he could hold a grudge, but by that time I am sure he recognized something wrong in his speech to Lev before their fight; he had been driven to words he might not have found in other circumstances. He was not inflexible; he may even have admired Lev's skill with his hard brown fists. Toward the end of Lev's second day with us we were all happy to notice an easing of tension, a softening of official courtesy.

After three days of fighting in the Remagen bridgehead to the south, all old differences had been forgotten, and Lev and Duval were close and friendly as if the past had never been. Certainly there had existed a great violence to hold them apart in other days, in that other world where there was no war, but a greater violence bound them together in a time of combat.

In fact, there were only a few of us who could know that old time on the American shore, for of the twenty-five men in the platoon at the time Lev took it over, only seven had been in the company when we left Camp Kilmer to come to Europe: Lev, Jim Bob, Duval, and myself, with three others. We were the old-timers, and that fact was a bond.

Within ten days of Lev's arrival in the platoon we even had a game of Hearts, the four of us, Lev, Duval, Jim Bob, and I, lions and lambs all squatting together in a hole in the ground. It was daytime, of course, the front having moved out ahead of us for several miles, under the attacks of our armor; over us, a blue sky, and all around the smell of sap running in the trees, and the sound of wind in the first leaves. We played for perhaps two hours in the middle of the afternoon, with Lev a little more quiet than he normally was, and Duval carrying himself quite delicately, like a young man on probation in the family of a new girl friend. Jim Bob and I, being spectators at the formal making of a peace, were able to be a little more loud than the principals, and a little more obviously joyous.

The newly cut earthen walls smelled damply of spring, and a little later of cigar smoke, when Lev distributed the last of his little stock. At the end of the game we all sat back comfortably smoking.

"This is nice," Lev said. "This is all right," nodding his head emphatically, his guard down, his face gently smiling like that of a father at the head of his family table.

"Why, it is," Jim Bob said. "I never smoked a cigar before."

"It's a damn good cigar," Duval said. "A good, free-drawing cigar, by God."

Things began to go very well in our platoon after that, with our organization firm and the men well hardened; but of course it was not long before the character of the war changed most dramatically. Within a week of the breakthrough from the Remagen bridgehead it was apparent to all of us that the war was coming to an end. We had very few fights, though some of them were bitter; for the most part, we traveled to the east like explorers, riding on trucks or tanks sometimes, but mostly marching. We were in a green and pleasant land, and we lived on the fat of it. In little villages of the Rhineland we found eggs, and hams, and fragrant country breads, which we enjoyed on the spot where we found them. We stole fat chickens, after the immemorial style of soldiers, and carried them to our night resting places, where a way could always be found to roast or broil them. There began to be women available to the more resourceful men among us, and surely we must have left some swelling bellies in the wake of our advance.

The war eased off on us, and then, quite naturally, it happened that our own army began to oppress us once again. There came an order from regimental headquarters that all men were to shave at least once a day, and that irregularities of uniform were not to be tolerated; there was an order, very fiercely phrased, which forbade any soldier or officer to fraternize with any German civilian. To these exactions Lev surprisingly paid no attention. "That stuff was all right before. We don't need it now," he said, and we remained comfortable.

And once when a young officer from battalion headquarters attempted to reassert the old power system by driving my squad from an attractive house in a Thuringian village, Lev appeared to stop him. It was a fine evening in late March; above us was a pale sky, all that was left of a great arching day; in the air was a little smell of cooking, and the cheerful voices of men settling down for a night of rest. I was busy with my squad in the front room when the neatly uniformed first lieutenant arrived. We had a goose cooking in the kitchen, and a case of Rhine wine open on the floor of the front room, and we were as cheerful as infantry soldiers can ever be.

"Who's in charge here?" the lieutenant said from the door. He was young; he was wearing a little mustache, and he carried his automatic pistol in a flamboyant shoulder holster.

"You men!" he said. "I'm afraid I'll have to commandeer this house for Battalion S-2! You hear? I'm sorry—"

He moved a little to the side as Lev came in from outside; and then Lev, seeming almost clumsy in his movements, as if he did not intend them, eased the young officer out the door, not touching him, but rather suggesting direction and force.

"Ah, Lieutenant Lev," the officer said gratefully. "You see, I've got orders from the boss—" and he waved his right arm gaily. "You know how it is!"

"Of course," Lev said. "You want the house for yourself."

"Well, yes," the officer said, in a tone which suggested that gentlemen could agree without worrying themselves over what the men might think.

"It's a nice house," Lev said mildly.

"Why, yes, it's all right," the officer agreed, not quite so comfortable.

"But you can't have it," Lev said. "These men got here first. Their company captured the goddamned town! And we lost a man here too. So you think of something."

Lev sounded quite cheerful, but not very reasonable, not quite open to argument.

"I don't see, Lieutenant . . ." the other began. "After all, Lieutenant, I outrank you. . . ."

"You do, at that. I can see it."

"And so by regulations . . ."

"Regulations?" Lev said. "Regulations?" He laughed harshly, stepped back, and seized his crotch, in an old city gesture of derision. "Here's your goddamn regulations, you son-of-a-bitch!" Lev was an officer, all right, but no gentleman, and so there was no way for the young battalion officer to reach him; but he tried.

"I want the house," he said, keeping his voice steady.

"Sure you do!"

"I mean it, Lieutenant. I want the house!"

"Then take it, kid. But let me tell you I'll fight you for it, and not with my hands either. So go ahead—so think of something!"

It was a challenge to a duel, though I have no idea whether Lev would have fought it. But he did not have to fight, for it was not long before the young officer backed off, growling fitfully, and even swearing.

It was a clear victory for us over all others, for Lev over battalion headquarters, and so we celebrated it that night by getting drunk down to the last man.

The incident became an emblem for us of the coming end of the war. There were not many Germans left to fight, and so Lev fought the tyranny which came from above us in our own army. He arranged a magnificent theft of liquor from a stock which was being reserved for officers of the regimental headquarters, and he himself led the raid. He stole rations and bargained for them with the bright intensity he had formerly shown in battle. Day after day he committed exploits of loving care.

He was fully committed to us, that was the fact, and acknowledged no other duties. He might have been a father passionately raising children, and certainly he needed us as much as we needed him. Toward the end, in fact, it seemed that he could not do without us. Once a German tank hit a house he was in with an 88-millimeter shell and knocked a wall over on him, but when he rose from the rubble, dizzy and sick, he refused the offer of hospitalization which was made to him by the company commander.

He came up smelling of the damp interior of that ancient wall; he was whitened with a light dust of plaster, and his nose was stopped up, so that he had to breathe hoarsely and with effort, like an asthmatic when the fit is on. He was dizzy from near-suffocation, and he was sick several times, crawling about in this misery like an old dog with infirm bowels, but even at this time, before he had fully come to his senses, he shouted: "I'm all right! Leave me alone! I'm going to stay right where I am! I got to stay!"

He had not been too badly hurt, in fact, though he had a cough from that moment which he was never to lose; a memory his body preserved, I think, of the cold, pulverous silence under the wall, like the silence of earth in a grave. He was shaken, but when I asked him later why he had been so anxious not to be evacuated to the comforts of hospitals, he had little to say. He seemed perplexed, faintly ill at ease, even a little unhappy. We were standing on the bank of a small river, near the ruins of a bridge the Germans had blown up in their retreat; a short way behind us was the house where the wall had fallen. Lev was leaning against an elm tree, his strong body at ease but not sagging against the finely combed black bark. Delicate prongs of pale green were showing in the branches above his head, and there was a smell of greenery, of cut hay, of flowers in the soft air. The Germans had already left that valley, with the tank which had given us trouble, and so we had the brilliant peace of a battle's end. The day was clear, and the sun so bright and mild that I could almost smell the warmth of it.

"Ah, well, comes the summer and the war'll be over," Lev said. "Back in Chicago, the White Sox will be playing at Comiskey Park, even!"

His face was cold and resolved beneath his steel helmet, and there was something statue-like in his expression, as if he were remembering an ancient tribal image of King David —the old King, the warrior remembering battles and feats of love.

"I'm sad to see the war ending, kid," Lev said. "You know? Why couldn't the war go on forever? I wish the war would go on and never stop!"

And then we moved on, as we had to, until toward the middle of April we reached the Harz Mountains, where for a little while we had again the sharp battles of the old lively war. In those small green mountains a considerable force of miscellaneous German troops had gathered, and they were ready to fight. How did they feel about things, I wonder, as they waited in the hills, in the greening forest? Below them on the plain was a vast army of enemies; behind them only the hills, and, for some of them perhaps, an ancient German memory of Druid priests at work in a leafy darkness, of warriors wearing helmets armed with the horns of bulls.

They were desperate, certainly, and they fought hard. In our first battle with them, which happened at the very edge of the hills, we lost five riflemen and an officer. The next day, in a town which lay enclosed in a canyon, we had even greater losses, and in fact had the last serious losses of the war: there we lost the last remnants of our innocence.

It was a pretty town, and might have been a resort, I think. There were several big inns; there was a hospital with a solarium on the south wing; perhaps that was a town famous for healing waters. On the square there were fine old chestnut trees in stately rows, each tree established in a masonwork pit filled with black earth. There were iron benches, and there was a bandstand, with rosebushes dependent from its latticed sides.

Spring was blooming in the square, and we would have been happy to stay there; but we—Lev's platoon and a machine-gun squad—were obliged to leave the town and ascend the canyon toward a force of German infantry supposed to be waiting there. There was a zone of gardens on the edge of town; each garden had its board fence. Then there was a little meadow, with a brook running through it. The grass was stiff and high, a purplish green. A milk cow—a bright pastel tan—stood heavily in the grass, her teats brushing against the grass tops. It happened that I passed close to her, and got a smell of the warm, rank odor of her, and of her breath, invisibly staining the heavy spring air.

Then we were in a forest of black fir, a darkness with ferns swaying in it, that sunlight riddled. Suddenly the air was cool; icy currents billowed down from the heights, which in those small mountains could not have been very far away, and certainly from the bluish plateaus we had dimly seen from the valley—lifted horizons of wavy line and watery surface. Slowly, almost gently, we made our way, in open order. Jim Bob was to my left with his squad; Lev and Duval were to the right with the third squad; I was in the middle with the six men remaining to me. We were scattered out, fearing snipers, but we were ready for almost anything.

The first problem was to find the enemy, and we were lucky in that. As we began climbing out of the canyon, we came across signs of German troops: a helmet, shiny, black, brand new; two grenades stuck in the crotch of a fir tree. There was a smell of people about, interrupting the dense eddies of forest smells. In a little while the climb began to seem ominous, and we found the enemy at about the time I began to sweat with the effort of climbing.

A burst from a German machine gun ripped its way down through the shady silence of the hillside. The fight was on; there was a sound of rifle fire as we answered the challenge that came down upon us. I was in cover behind the trunk of a tree—what kind of tree I will never know, for I was only concerned that it be thick—and I was trying to make out the contours of the little battle. That was difficult; near me were

two men of my squad, but I could see no one else. I had a
sense of heavy fire from the invisible Germans; it sounded serious this time, seeming to swarm and rise through the thickets. Now and then a bullet clipped a bough from a fir tree,
and then that bough would settle to the ground with a faint,
sighing flutter, gentle as falling snow.

Then from my right, where Lev was at work, someone
called quite clearly: "Go on up the hill. Lev says everybody
go on up the hill."

That was reassuring word, suggesting that we had nothing unusual ahead of us. I called my squad to move up, and
began making my way; that meant running and falling. I
caught sight of Jim Bob, not far to my left, and perceived
that he had already got the message; he was on his way.
And so we proceeded, and for a while I had the feeling that
we would simply ascend the hill and there kill or capture the
people who had offered us battle thus late in the war. I was
not hoping trustfully; I was only expecting what I had a right
to expect. The war was coming to an end, and everybody
knew it—even the Germans knew it, who had been coming
sadly into our lines for a long time, tired, reluctant, bemused.

Then, as I was moving from one tree to another, a bullet
shattered the stock of my rifle. The shock did not quite twist
the rifle from my hand, but it brought me up, and made me
angry and resentful. I paused, hiding behind the tree trunk,
and inspected the damage. The stock was gone, from about
two inches behind the trigger guard; there was only a jagged
stump, still quivering. "Son of a bitch!" I said. I hefted the
rifle, and it felt crazily new and strange; it did not feel like
a rifle at all, and suddenly I felt defenseless, there in that
handsome forest.

I became reluctant to move on, and so I took time to look
about me and listen; and then I heard, from the left, where

Jim Bob had his squad, a dim cry of "Medic, Medic!" and from the right, where Lev and Duval were, a cry, a mere susurrus that proposed: "I'm hurt, I'm hurt, I'm really hurt."

"Hold up, second squad," I called, feeling guilty, and began searching carefully through the area to my right, trying to find a sign from the source of authority; and so I saw a man down, not far from me. He was lying on his back, and appeared to be trying to turn over; his body made spasmodic flopping movements, like a beached fish. I looked a little closer and saw that he was covering his face with his hands. In fact, he was clutching his face, as if to hold it against slipping. His hands were claw-like, grasping, and suddenly one of the hands went red with blood.

"I got to go there," I said, and began crawling; but that was slow, and so I got up and raced for him, so that I brought up on the ground at his side. I was winded, and scared, now. I looked down fearfully and saw that the hurt creature under the hands was Platoon Sergeant Duval, struck down in what would surely be the last month of the war. For a moment I paused, thinking what to do. Then, as I was resolving to look at the wound, I heard Lev's voice calling my name. The voice was whispering fiercely, and it said: "Who is it? Who is it? Is it Duval? He was over there."

I nodded, and whispered: "Yes, Duval. He's hit, bad."

I looked again to my right and saw Lev rise up, square and firm and very soldierly, and start running toward me; he was beautifully balanced on the steep slope, and he carried his carbine as an ancient savage might carry his spear. He came fast, and dropped lightly to the ground on the other side of Duval. He had his carbine up in firing position; he took aim carefully and then fired twice. I looked to see what he was shooting at, but could see no target; you understand, I did not expect to. As I looked up the steep hill, I saw the light-

spotted shade of the forest; I had a sense of trees, bushes, gar-
lands of fern, but I could see no enemy. It was rare in that
war to see a live enemy during a battle, for the great infantry tactic of both sides was to stay hidden, to keep close to
the dark.

"There," Lev said. "This isn't going right. It's like the old
war. It's a battle. Hey, you got your rifle busted! Well, take
Duval's—he won't be needing it for a while."

Lev was looking at me over Duval's slowly writhing body,
and Lev's face was intent, concentrated, as if he were aiming
a gun. The lines of the face were clearly drawn: the big nose,
the harsh jaw, the powerfully controlled stare of the eyes,
unblinking and bright as a snake's. The mouth was cruel; the
face was calm, and Lev was no more disturbed or upset than
he might have been during a training maneuver. So it seemed
at that moment; and so it was, I believe, though change was
imminent, already setting in like a sunset against bright day.

"You're okay, kid," Lev said to me. "Now, how's old Duval?" He looked down, and instantly there was a change in
his expression. He was startled; his lips came apart slowly,
and then his tongue appeared, uncertainly touching his upper
lip. "Uh-oh," he said. "Hey, Duval, how you makin' it, kid?
It's Lev. It's your corner."

Duval's right hand was oily with blood. I touched it, hoping he might lift his hand so that I could see the wound. His
body jerked; his hips lifted convulsively, like a hooked fish
splashing at the surface just out of reach of the boat. There
was a great pool of blood under his head, and its margin,
smoothly spreading, had begun to reach my left elbow.
"Well, it's no joke, then," Lev said. "Let's get the bandage
out. Duval—old buddy?—I'm going to bandage you up, and
run a tourniquet if I have to. Hey, it's Lev, it's the old cut
man. I fixed you up before, I can do it again. Sure I can!"

His fingers went to work—they were spindly and lean, with tufts of black hair between the knuckles; and the fingers were crooked—oddly bent, and that must have been a result of the prize ring, in old Chicago times. Lev was crouching now, exposing the arch of his body to the enemy fire, if it should happen to come that way. His body seemed merely to preside over his nimble hands; his body was something for the arms and hands to hang from.

Then Duval spoke, in a voice absolutely unchanged from his normal voice. "That you, Sarge?" he said. "Lieutenant, I mean. Shoot, ah've had it." The voice stopped eccentrically; there seemed no principle for either stopping or continuing.

"Just take it easy," Lev said. "I'm with you, kid."

"Ah've had it, Sarge," Duval said, and now both his hands were bloody. "In the face. In the neck too. You can't see it. It's awright, Sarge. Ah done my best, comin' up here. You send my stuff to my wife, will you, now? And write her? Hush! Ah can't see! It must of been in the eyes too." He moaned, and viciously his body bucked; this time he turned himself onto his right side, facing me with his mask of red hands, and spilling blood—pouring it, as from a basin—onto my sleeve. Lev moved over, continuing his work, and now had the bandage out; it was the packaged dressing we used to wear at our belts. He held it poised. "Here it is," he said quickly. "I got it right here, kid. I'm right with you—"

Then there was a change in Duval; what was that change? I could not mark its happening, though I noticed a momentary tremor in leg and arm. His blood still warm upon me, he died, and his hands stayed at his face. "Hold on, kid!" Lev shouted. "Don't think about that blood. I'm a cut man, I'll fix it!" Then Lev took Duval's left hand, moved it away from the face, and slipped his fingers over the wrist; and that was to take the pulse, surely, though at that moment, being con-

fused, I could not understand what he intended. Then he
dropped the wrist, and there was a look of dismay on his
face. "No!" he said. "Why, hell, the war's ending—" Then
he bent suddenly over the body and put his helmeted head
to the still chest; his face, turned sidewise, looked up at me,
the eyes dazed and staring. Then a grimace of disgust came
over the face, followed instantly by a look of wrenching sorrow. That strong face came away from all its conventions
to look so. "Oh, no!" he said, and raised himself so that he
could look down at the body.

"Come on back," he said. "You don't have to die. Don't
die! You got the stuff, kid—come on through! Hey, this is
Lev! We had a fight, remember! You showed how you could
take it! No," he concluded aimlessly.

He raised his face to me, now purged of its old fierceness.
He held out his hands, palms up, the white bandage in his
right hand like some mysterious piece of clothing, swaddling
for a creature no longer available. "He was my friend," he
said. "I didn't have so many. You, hey. You listen to his heart
and tell me— No! No good in that." He bent his head and
lowered his hands, though the hand holding the bandage continued to rise and fall; and that was a futile gesture, the
skilled hand reaching out toward something that skill could
never reach. Lev began to cry; and so he was a strong man
abandoning the conventions of his strength. His powerful
body was kneeling now; a devotional posture had erected itself within that massive back and delicately curved those
heavy arms. "Come back," he said, "come back. I want you
to come back. See if you can't make it. Go ahead, try."

I looked away, rolled over and looked back toward my
squad, and saw, not ten feet away, the face of Jim Bob Allison intently watching. He was crouching behind a tree; his
face was white, horror-stricken. I turned over once again so

that I could look at the ground, and for some time I stared, atomizing the rich black dirt and stones and leaves. I watched the vein of a leaf. I watched a spider—the long-legged breed —ascend with stately elegance a little stack of leaves, and there pause. Lev was crying; I could hear him, and I continued hearing him for a long time after he stopped.

The battle had grown quieter, lacking Lev's purpose to make it happen; and suddenly the forest grew still, as if no battle had been there. I raised my head and looked at Lev, who now was squatting beside Duval, but facing the slope. He was looking up the hill, and his face was once again the familiar face of the warrior, the leader in battle. A speculative look was in his eyes as he turned to me, and he looked gentle. "Well," he said, "what we gonna do? I know."

He picked up his carbine and cleared the bolt; he looked down and inspected the chamber, casually running his little finger along the face of the bolt. "Look to your piece," he said. "I mean Duval's—there." He waited while I took up the rifle. "Well, check it," he said. "It's had a fall, it may have gotten dirty." He watched while I inspected the rifle, and then he said: "Good work, kid. Now we've got to get at it again. Stay here a minute. I'm going to start this battle again." He rose; he paused for a moment, standing at the side of his fallen comrade, and then slowly walked to a nearby tree; he stood behind it, not behind the trunk but only behind the green skirt of spreading boughs. He stood for a moment carelessly, and then, like a bugler preparing to sound a call, he drew his body up and straightened himself. He took the position of the soldier at attention.

"Well," he muttered, and then, in his old parade-ground voice that I had not heard for many months, he called: "Third p'toon, tench-hut! Hear me, third p'atoon! Come alive! This is Lev! You know me! Get ready now, and I'll

give the word!" Then, casually, he relaxed and looked down
at me. "Just like an old first sergeant, eh, kid? Well, that's
about all there is to it. You ready to go? I want to give the
boys a chance to get ready, 'cause we're going up this hill.
Huh! The fact is, I can't stand the war to end. You know,
that Barney Ross, that fighter—champion he was!—he used
to say that a body feint was a good thing, but sometimes
you just had to take a shot to give one, and go on in. Well,
that's what I'm going to do. I've got to do something." He
turned away, almost indifferently, and again set himself in his
position of command; and again his electrifying cry rang out
along the hillside: "Third p'atoon, tench-hut! Ready, now!
come out shooting! Now's the time. *Ee-yahh!*" That was a
battle shout, and the real David might have roared something like it as he lightly stepped into the deep shadow of
Goliath.

Lev moved out from behind the tree, his carbine at his hip;
he fired twice up the hill and began running. "Charge, third
platoon," he shouted. "Charge, God damn it! Let's git those
sons-of-bitches!"

There was firing all along our line; we were moving; the
surge was rising! And in a little while there came an answering fire, sweeping down the hill; the battle was alive! We
charged, and charged successfully. Up we went, and even
now I can remember something of the ardor that thickened
in my legs and back as I pounded up that hill. It is the joy
of life that respires in a tired body at such times, when death
is near; and sweat is a sign of noble striving. Lovers ascending
a peak of feeling are not more passionate than men when the
spirit finds a precise expression in brute movement; complex
motives running into a simple result—making a fury, melting
the bonds of normal possibility.

We assaulted the hill, and there are good American army

precedents for that. Some years after the war I read about Sheridan's gesture at the foot of Missionary Ridge in the Tennessee mountains; and perhaps Lev was not so vastly different from that illustrious soldier, who had a fierce mustache and a dark face, and said "Here's how!" drained his half-pint flask of whisky, and started up through the rocks toward the Confederate rifle pits.

For myself, I forgot my surroundings and went shouting up the hill. I fell once, but otherwise did not stop, for I felt that others were with me; I hoped that Lev was not too far ahead, and I expected that Jim Bob, somewhere to my left, was already beyond me. I fired my rifle now and then, but only in a formal military fashion; there was a battle, and firearms were being carried; it was only right that they should be discharged now and then. For some time the charge was an exhilaration of movement, a very pure joy, and then, as it reached the German positions, there began to be fighting, though I saw only a little of it.

Just to my left I saw two German soldiers suddenly rise up out of their holes with their arms held high in the gesture of surrender. They were quite close to me; their faces were blurred, mask-like, childish somehow in their anticipation; they were white, scared faces of boys, wanting to surrender; but the moment of surrender is a delicate moment which fate governs, and their fate was to die that day, and so they went down as if swept by wind—shot from somewhere to the left of me. I myself stepped on a wounded German as I crashed over his hole; and he only bent down closer to earth, crouching, covering his helmeted head with crossed hands—and his smell of an earth-bound animal, rank and fetid, came up to me. Later I saw him marching in the little column of prisoners we took down the mountain.

The charge ended for me in a gradual slowing-down as I

beat my way through a thicket. I became aware of a cobweb; I felt it distinctly, and that was how I knew the charge was over. It came to me that there was no more German small-arms fire; and, a little later, no more fire of any sort, as the after-battle stillness began reaching out from its sources, from the dead, and the hurt, and the suddenly exhausted survivors. I stopped. Bemused, I looked about me, and noticed the details of the forest with a new precision. I even bent down to look at a fern, for I was feeling quiet and content, ready to consider a new thing. I touched it; the underside was waxy, and the upper surfaces had a kindling green feel that was like some essence of life, guessed at but never before touched. I turned around and wandered back toward the German line; I walked cautiously, for in those days I never walked any other way; thus I came upon the battle's end with a certain measure of mental coolness returned. I was already having reservations about the battle, like a newly successful lover considering the obligations his victory has fastened to him. There is an aftertaste of pleasure to such moments, which yields readily to darker feelings, by a process of conversion in the normal irony of change. I was ready to be sad; I felt pale and wan, in a preliminary way, for I was beginning to be afraid about the battle's cost.

Thus I was almost able to accept the news I had from my comrades that the battle had been costly indeed; that seemed right. Seven men had been killed outright, including Lev, who had not gone thirty feet before he took a bullet dead center in the heart; and there were many wounded, so that our platoon—the third platoon—had almost destroyed itself on that little hill. But that was the way the charge happened, and I can remember imagining how, as Lev began his charge, some still-unfrightened German rifleman had carefully taken aim, waiting for his chance as the leader of the enemy came up the slope. I considered how it must have been, the German concentrating, his eye squinting, trying to stay calm so that he could squeeze off his shot. For Lev there must have been a numbing shock and, perhaps, a dim sensation of falling; and then he was down for good, who had once walked boldly on the bleak sidewalks of Chicago.

There were some little matters to tend to then. Prisoners had to be guarded, and there were six of these. The wounded had to be looked to, and this was done by calling in another platoon for assistance; and the dead had to be taken down the hill to the town, and this we did ourselves. Jim Bob it was who carried Lev, and I carried Duval, and the burden was heavy. Duval was a big man, and his body seemed to drive itself into my shoulder, as if it were really seeking the earth. I have never carried a heavier burden, but I was not unhappy, for I wanted something to do, and wanted to do the right thing. It happened that we met stretcher-bearers at the foot of the hill, and then we were able to turn over our burdens to them.

Jim Bob and I, with what was left of the platoon, some eleven men, counting ourselves, went on back into the town, seeking the square. We were tired; that was sure. We were looking for liquor, and looking for a place to sleep; and when we reached the square we found that the company commander had arranged to give us a little rest. We were set free and told to find quarters and something to eat, but we were not quite ready for such things. We got liquor and wine, and I began to drink wine, standing with Jim Bob in the shadow of the bandstand in the little square. After a time he wandered off, carrying a bottle of wine, and I settled down to the business of conceiving a drunkenness; I managed a thin, clear intoxication that worked only in my head and left my legs firm. I walked about in the square; I approached the budding roses, and smelled the grainy roughness of the bark of chestnut trees. What else could I do? I wondered about Jim Bob, and grew angry at the sun, glowing across every surface of the pretty little square.

Toward five thirty I saw Jim Bob, walking meditatively on his high, skinny legs; he was across the square, and he was looking down at a body—Lev's body, so I guessed—that had been laid out on a stretcher under somebody's blanket. Lev was gone, assuredly; he had been approaching this end for a long time, and come away from the nearness of it so often that there was a kind of justice in his being touched by it at last. I did not look at the body—that little hooded and narrow thing; I watched Jim Bob, who was having his struggles. After a while two men from another platoon marched a group of eight prisoners into the square, stopped them, and then stood leaning on their rifles, awaiting orders. In the group of prisoners I thought I recognized some of those who had surrendered after killing my friends; and I began to feel resentment and even hate.

The town was quiet. A pale bluish light was dying above the canyon, and the hills were irregularly tipped with fir trees growing thickly; it was a time when there was nothing to say. I sat on one of the iron benches, with liquor in my head, heavy and stupid, unable to move. Such quiet is not far from death, I think, with the mind intact but ineffective. I got up once and found a little branch from a rosebush on the bandstand; I took it to the bench, and there played with it, as if there might be contained in it some principle of dignified regret for the death of old friends. The leaves had not yet come, but the thorns were left from other seasons, and I let them catch at the skin of my hands.

I was all alone, surely, just as Jim Bob was all alone, but he was at least capable of action; and perhaps that defines him. In that dim evening light he looked a boy, but he could move and change of his own power; he could accept his fate as if he were choosing it, and that is a rare gift. He got up. I could see him quite clearly. He went to the two riflemen guarding the prisoners, and talked with them. Their heads inclined to him, and they nodded. They stood patiently, servants to a just intention grown corrupt in its happening; they were careless and blind, and now, if they are still alive, perhaps they have quite forgotten that day.

A faint sibilance in the air was all I could hear of that talk, but of course I knew what was being said. How could I not? I understood that Jim Bob was selecting the prisoner he thought had killed his friend Lev; and Jim Bob was preparing a revenge.

Then it was decided. Jim Bob unsheathed his bayonet and fixed it to his rifle. With the bayonet point he picked out one of the prisoners and began marching him out of the square. Slowly the figures of the two men merged in the distance. As the day weakened, they went out of sight, into an alley perhaps, where there would be the dung of dogs, and scraps of paper blowing on the wind.

Then there came a shot, bursting into the heavy silence. At the shock of it, I drove one of the rose thorns deep into the palm of my right hand, and it seemed a proper thing to do. There was another crash, incredibly loud, and I held the thorn in place, waiting for the little flow of blood which ought to come. There were eight shots in all, but it was almost fifteen minutes between the first and the last. Truly, Jim Bob was in no hurry. He was not submitting to an accident; he intended every blow of the little copper-jacketed bullets. Thin and harsh, he must have stood with the rifle held firmly, counting the rounds, and watching the effect of them.

When it was over, I sat sweating and exhausted on my bench. I threw away my sprig of rose; death had been done, and long before Jim Bob returned, I had begun the process of recovery. I was an expert on recoveries, and still am. When Jim Bob stood before me, his rifle slung over his right shoulder, I was ready for him.

"You know where I've been," he said. "I saw you watching me. The truth is—damn it, it's so!—I loved that man, and now he's dead. Dead, I wouldn't have believed it." His boy's face was shadowy under his helmet; only his outline was clear, drawn against the last light of day, and it was a dense, formal darkness in the shape of an armed man. "Well, I got even," he said. "You know."

I nodded, and he leaned forward a little before continuing; he was still on the attack. "But it was funny what happened," he said. "Up there on the hill, I mean. Who'd ever think he'd feel that bad about Duval? And that's what made him charge like that, I guess."

I shook my head, keeping silence, for I thought I understood why Lev had felt that bad about Duval. Once again I could not help thinking that war is not all bad; and to that thought I cling now, though it is a belief hard to cherish and impossible to defend in a peaceful society.

And then Jim Bob changed the subject, saying: "But I got even with the bastard that killed him—or with some one of the bastards. Yes I did!" Tears of rage appeared in his eyes and ran untended down his cheeks. "Bastard, coming in to surrender after shooting us up! Don't you ever think I didn't get something back, though, up there in the alley with that German son-of-a-bitch! It was close range—" And here Jim Bob raised his free hand and clenched it into a fist. "Close range. I could see the bullets hit him—I never saw that before. A bullet punches a man, and you miss that when you pot him at long range. By God, a bullet fairly knocks the life out of a man—it's like stomping him to death! And I took my time about it, you know that. And learned something about life, I reckon. You bet I did! And old Lev was the man who taught me how to be that way!" Then he went away victorious, a fierce boy who had done what he wanted to do, and he will have that as long as he lives.

But the next day it was plain that his hair had begun to turn gray during the night, and three weeks later, with the war all but over, his hair was streaked with broad silvery bands. His face had not changed much; it was still a boy's face, but for the white hair, which darkened the features into something resembling an image of fallen man; a handsome face, and hard-eyed, that had been quite undistinguished in other days.

For a long time I ignored this oddity, out of politeness and respect, but of course in the end we had to talk about it, if only to arrange mutually friendly attitudes toward it. I mentioned the white hair, and Jim Bob said: "It scares me. I don't know what to think about it. But maybe it'll be all right. Maybe it'll help me look older, so I can get a woman back in the States. And then it reminds me of old Lev, and how we used to play Hearts together, and I like that. Though, God damn it, he was a bad influence on me, making me mean like I am. Wasn't he? Why, he may have made a killer out of me!

"But I like to remember him. I want to remember him. He was a good man, wasn't he? The best I ever knew in all my life. Wasn't he?"

"He was a good man," I said. "Sure he was."

A MARRIAGE

❧

❧ ❧ ❧ ❧ ❧ ❧
❧ ❧ ❧ ❧ ❧

I'LL TAKE YOU and your family across the river, ma'am," Willy said, "but it'll cost you."

At evening a crowd of women and children rallied uncertainly at the east bank of the little river, the Mulde, because it was an international boundary. A mournful whispering moved in the crowd; they were watching the sentry march his post on the pontoon bridge.

"I'll be glad to help, ma'am," Willy said. Heavy and powerful, he was leaning forward, talking to a German girl who was carrying a baby on her hip. "When we're on the other side, then you come with me," Willy went on. "*Mit mir, verstehen?* That's the way we'll work it."

The girl shook her head; I saw that she was pretty. Behind her was the family that depended on her, two older women and two small girls, watching timidly.

"No," she said, quite distinctly. "That would be infamous." Then she turned her head and looked back to the east. Her throat was exposed in a supple line, and the effort of holding the baby caused her breasts to rise buoyantly; her expression was hard. To the east, in the fading light, was the high smoke of advancing war. It smudged the eastern heaven above the Russian soldiery as, in other centuries, above the wild horsemen of the steppes in their leather jackets. The girl looked at that ominous haze, and then pointed with her free hand at the two little girls. "And Inge?" she said. "And Johanna? My two little girls? Would you leave them here for the Russians to eat?"

"I'll be glad to help," Willy said. "But the order says no Germans can cross this bridge here, and so I'd be breaking the law if I let you across. Ma'am, I'll break that law for you, but I won't break it for nothing. Listen, all I want is a little loving. What's that to a pretty girl like you?"

"It is wartime," the German girl said coldly, "but I owe something to the memory of my dear husband. I cannot listen to you. What you say is—terrible!" She turned back to her family, and the two little girls hugged her legs.

"Don't go away mad," Willy said mildly. "You just think it over awhile, now."

The girl was saying something to the two women, who looked as if they might be a mother and a grandmother; then, briefly, she stared over her shoulder at Willy. Something bitter and cold flickered out at Willy then, and I fancied I saw the girl's nostrils widen.

Willy smiled, and then came over to me and got out a cigar. "She'll come around," he said. "She's got to. There ain't no way to swim those old ladies and kids over this river. She'd swim it, though, you bet." He clipped the end of the cigar with his pocket knife, and then lit the cigar with one of the three lighters he always carried. "There, now," he said. "I want to let my evening meal set a little."

Willy was our Texan, twenty-two years old at that time. He was well made and strong, and if he had gone to college he would very likely have played football—at Baylor, say, or Texas A. and M. He had a blunt-featured, Western sort of face, with ruddy cheekbones, and pale blue eyes looking mildly out at the world he meant to plunder. He came from Dallas, but he was a country boy in his origins; he had followed a plow, he had picked cotton, he had gone out on many a cold morning to fetch the cows for milking.

He was married; he had taken a wife when he was seventeen, and got two sons and a daughter on her; and, so he told us, got caught cheating just after the birth of the daughter. He came to be, as he put it, "unhappily married"; no doubt he had seen the phrase in a newspaper. "I love my wife," he used to say, "but I'm unhappily married. She is *such* a goddamned bitch." She had even dared, after his departure for the army, to take up with other men, and then written Willy about her exploits. He sometimes read her letters to me. Willy, naturally enough, occupied himself in that last spring of the war with revenge on his wife. Any woman would do for that, and so he had known all kinds, young and old. He came to be an expert on the German women.

"That one belongs to the quality," he said now. "I can tell it. She's got some breeding to her, got some hot blood. But she'll come round—she's a widow, you heard that."

I did not go to the bridge the next night, for I was reluctant to see the girl's surrender, which did indeed seem inevitable. As Willy said, "It's not as if she was alone. She's a Christian. She's got to think of others!" She did not appear at the bridge, however, and the following morning Willy became a little uneasy.

He talked to me; that was his way. When he was in action he kept silence, but when he could not act he became gloomy, and often he came to me, for he respected my education— my three semesters at a small Ohio college. I had words, and

Willy found them soothing; and of course we had some things to remember between us. During the fighting we had been good comrades; Willy had been a fine soldier, and had even saved my life on one occasion, as, perhaps, I had saved his on another. So we believed, anyhow, and respected each other.

Willy talked anxiously about the German girl, whose name was Elfrida, he had learned. He thought he understood her, but she was not answering to his expectations; he had missed her for a day, and a day is a long time. He claimed that she did not really dislike him. "In fact, she likes me pretty well. I can tell. A woman likes you or she doesn't, and this one likes me. She hates being in a corner, though. She can't stand that. God damn her, she could have found a boat, or a raft."

It seemed possible that the girl might have managed something, and so I went down to the bridge that evening, hoping not to see her; but she was there, carrying her baby, dressed in the normal fashion of refugee women, in a heavy knee-length coat, with a dark brown skirt showing beneath it. She came to meet us with a smile on her face, and clearly she had a policy. She was ready for us; and Willy began smiling kindly, so that he should appear to triumph gracefully. I stepped aside, and she smiled at me—a minute, independent smile, as if it did not really count. Then she composed herself before Willy, and said: "I am ready to bargain with you, but not for myself. Do you understand? I have money. We have decided to sacrifice it. My mother and grandmother agree that it is better we should be poor than that I should yield to you . . . to your . . . advances!"

I marveled at her, for she spoke with only a slight accent, and that not German. She sounded English, in fact, and so she intimidated me a little. Willy, too, was somewhat startled. "Money?" he said. "Where would you get money?"

"We are not a poor family," the girl answered firmly. "Ah, so, but where would I have learned to speak English in a family of bankrupts? You must not be naïve!"

"Well, your money's no good anyway," Willy answered sullenly. "Your marks are *kaput*."

"Excuse me. I am not offering marks. I am offering American dollars—here, you may see them." And she held out a leather wallet thickly engraved, which Willy took because, clearly, it was the only thing to do. For a moment his big fingers moved awkwardly on the wallet, and then they came to themselves and bent the wallet in such a way as to open the folding. For a moment Willy stared. "It looks all right," he said. "How much is there?"

"Two hundred and fifty dollars, and quite genuine. Feel free to inspect it, if you wish."

"I don't have to inspect it," Willy said.

"Insist upon your rights! I am not a cheat. I do not wish to be thought such a one."

"It's not that," Willy said, and his voice was aggrieved. "Here, take your purse—your wallet." He pushed it toward her, and she quite coolly accepted it. "Put your money away," Willy said roughly. "Put it away! What's money alongside of love? And love is what I'm after."

"Don't be a fool," the girl said.

"And don't get the wrong idea about me," Willy said. "You think I'd take money from a woman? Listen. I made my offer, and you can take it or leave it."

"It's outrageous," the girl said. "You're not an officer—how dare you refuse my good American money!" For the first time since I had known her, the girl sounded as if tears might be possible for her. "Oh," she said. "You're not—*unmöglich*. . . ." She turned, and ran toward her family. When she reached them, she seemed to gather them up and draw them along with her, and in a moment she had moved them out of sight in the crowd of pilgrims at the riverbank.

After that, we did not see her for two days; and then she turned up on our side of the bridge, in the custody of two MP's from regimental headquarters. The MP's, looking unhappy, delivered Elfrida and her family to the east side of the river, where Elfrida promptly led the way into the willows; and then the MP's came back to our side, where we got the story from the older one, a staff sergeant. "Oh, you know her—that girl with the baby? Listen, take some advice, and don't get to know her too well. I'll tell you—"

"But what did she do?" Willy asked.

"Well, not much," the sergeant said. He paused; he was a man in his thirties, with a mustache, and must have seen something of life. "She just happened to be crossing the river with her family in one of our engineers' boats when the colonel was out for his constitutional. You know how he is—he goes for a walk every morning at five o'clock. Well, he asked her where she got that boat—it's painted O.D. and has all sorts of serial numbers on it. She said it was an estate boat—belonged to a friend. Well, what about that?

"So the colonel took it up with her, of course, figuring she's bribed somebody. When she began to get a little uncomfortable, she tried to bribe him. She had American money, two hundred and fifty dollars of it—confiscated now, naturally. What could he do? Now, if she'd offered that nice body, the colonel might have . . .

"But let that go. The fact is, as we were coming out here, I offered to see what I could do, just in a personal sort of way. I may have put my arm on her shoulder, in fact, and she damn near cut my throat with her fingernails. . . ."

Willy and I were left with a sense of having been involved in something larger than we had expected, and even Willy began to be a little impressed. "She's lost her money, anyway," he said. "That'll make her come around . . . a little sooner. . . ." But he did not sound convinced, and I began to feel sure that the girl would in fact never come around. I respected her, and was already half in love with her; and naturally I wanted to believe well of a woman I loved. The thought came to me that perhaps I might do a favor for such a woman and her family. I had only to speak to the sentry. Later I might have to fight Willy, for he had made the first claim on the property which Elfrida was, but I was willing to do that. I might even, so I imagined, enjoy doing that.

I had an intention, but unfortunately I did not execute it in time. Elfrida, grown desperate, came down to the bridge that very night and accepted Willy's offer, to be accomplished on the next night. I was there on the next night; I had come to a decision, and was ready to enter the lists, but I was just in time to see Willy have his triumph.

As you know, a pontoon bridge floats on the water; it is low there, and buoyant; in the gathering dark our bridge looked like a boat closely moored. Coruscations of current rippled downstream from it; breezes moved in the willows along the bank, and occasionally there was a harsh stirring in the high old elms that grew along the east bank. I sat down with my back to the trunk of one of those elms, and wondered how it would feel to make a generous offer to a beautiful girl like Elfrida. I thought it would feel fine. Elfrida, pleased, might then reward me with love, and that would be right: virtue deserved such an answer.

Before me were the pilgrims, restless. Russian patrols were on our side of the Elbe; some had been sighted not five miles from this spot; and the main body would close to the Mulde in two days, so it was rumored. A desperate time for the German women! The crowd of them looked like a Doré illustration of a scene from the *Purgatorio*. They wore long coats that looked like sculptured robes in the evening light; they seemed to be leaning to the west, while on the bridge the sentry, a boy in a helmet, quietly marched his post, step-stop, the restless feet! To be sure, I was a little sad; and then Willy and Elfrida appeared out of the crowd.

Elfrida was carrying her baby, and my only thought was that I did not yet know whether the baby was a boy or girl. Behind Elfrida came the mother and the grandmoter, and each of these carried a suitcase and led along a little girl. The crowd fell away, and the family moved alone with its bene-factor.

It was clear that Willy knew what he was about. His uni-form was clean, he was wearing a necktie, and he had bor-rowed somebody's pistol and belt for the occasion, so that he could have both hands free, no doubt. He was wearing his combat infantryman's badge; his helmet was tipped back jauntily.

He paused at the bridge, but only to wave the family on ahead of him. He patted the little girls on the head, and they ducked away, skittishly, in normal child's fashion. Willy came on, forcing the family ahead of him. The sentry, who was a good friend of ours from the third platoon, marched his post on the other track and did not even look at what was hap-pening.

By this time I had gotten to my feet and made my way to the middle of the bridge, and there I stayed for the re-mainder of the scene. I was feeling sad, hopeless, a little de-ranged, but I was alert, you may be sure.

Elfrida held the baby in the crook of her right arm, much as the pioneer Kentuckian held his Pennsylvania rifle. She had her weight on both feet—her feet were apart, like a boxer's. Willy spoke to her, and paused; Elfrida did not move; and then Willy gently put his hands on the baby and took the baby from her arms. Those arms for a moment followed the baby, the fingers opening and closing. Willy whispered something to the invisible face of the baby, of which a faint crooning was audible to me, and then gave the baby to the grandmother. "Thank you, ma'am," he said. "You're real obliging."

Then briskly he took Elfrida's arm and started walking her toward the deep grass that grew along the riverbank to the south of town.

He was moving successfully; and then Elfrida pulled away and said sharply: "No! I won't go!"

She stood apart from him, angry, ready to fight. Her head was swaying, and her arms moved cat-like; her right hand formed a claw, suddenly, and with it she reached out, hooking. Willy did not move, and Elfrida's nails raked his face. She screamed, lightly. Still he did not move.

"All right," he said. "That's in the bargain too, just this once. What do you think it got you?"

She stood quite close to him, with her hands on her hips. Her head was back; her chin out; her bosom was heaving —ah, she composed! She knew she was creating an effect!

"You are a beast, to hold a lady to such a bargain," she said.

"No, I *ain't*," Willy said. "But a bargain's a bargain."

"A beast. A wicked, sinful— Illiterate, too!"

"Say what you like. You can't hurt me. Honey, can't you see I'm just full of love for you?"

"Oh!" She shuddered, and stepped away.

Willy shook his head, his cheek showing marks now, curving lines; and then looked down; but his big body was poised, I noticed, ready to go. "Well, I love you, honey. Don't make a fuss, now."

"It's impossible," she said. "You are too crude. Now, please, if you will excuse me—"

Then Willy caught her left arm; he seemed to reach across an enormous space; her upper body moved jerkily, like a puppet's staggering walk. "Come on," he said, and started off down the riverbank, where were willows, high grass, the dark that would make them sweat. She was with him, all her protests vain; her head went down, but I noticed that she managed once, quickly, to look at Willy, look him up and down, as not every girl would be able to do in a situation like that. She appraised him, I think, and even nodded, as their figures grew dim and became one large figure instead of two small ones—a giant huddle, merging with the night.

I remembered the bottle of brandy I was carrying—I had thought to comfort Elfrida with it. Now I got it out and drank. I was feeling like a rejected lover; I was astonished at Willy's brilliant action, and the brandy did not make me brave. I sank into myself, wanting time to pass, but time would scarcely move. I felt abandoned, like something dropped by a careless proprietor—a feeling of youth, surely —but of course in a little while I got used to it and began to look around me.

In the foreground was Elfrida's family. I watched them for a while, that little cluster of souls, and then went over to them. The grandmother seemed almost asleep; her eyes were closed; she held the baby, and with it was quiet as statuary in a garden. One of the little girls leaned against her; this child was perhaps five years old, plump and dark, with brown eyes that looked vaguely toward me and then quickly away. The mother stared brightly at me through spectacles and fluttered her eyelids. Clearly, she was frightened, but she was trying not to look so, for fright might seem an insult to the American, who was a lord of life and death there at the bank of the international river. The mother's face was blurred—she looked like anyone's mother. Her hand rhythmically gripped and relaxed on the hand of the smaller girl, and this child was drunk with sleepiness. In a little while she would have to be put down to rest on the damp ground, among the cold grasses and flowers.

The women had no significant expression to use on this occasion of their family's dishonor. Weary and bored, they were waiting for the next thing to happen. Indeed, the older women of any nation are likely to know what it is to wait outside the bedchambers of the young. It was nothing to these women that their daughter's bedchamber would be a hollow space under a willow tree.

Soon these veteran ladies would be able to resume their journey, and if dishonor went with them, they would surely not die of it. Very likely dishonor would prove merely excess baggage on such a journey. At that very moment they might be thinking how fortunate they were to have a handsome daughter who could please the fierce young men at the bridge. The Russians—ah, the Russians were very close, the drunken peasants bent on rape and plunder. . . .

I wandered off, thinking not to return until everything was over, and I got drunk, but when I came back much later, I discovered Elfrida's family in the place where I had left them. A blanket had been produced from somewhere, and the two little girls were asleep on it, under a tree. They lay on their backs, and the toes of their shoes protruded upward.

The sentry was quietly marching his post, and on the other side of the river the pilgrims were settling down for the night. A murmur of voices crossed the river from their rude beds, but there was no activity; even their fear had grown inert. Looming over them was a sourceless glow in the east-

ern sky—a pale red that would not have been out of place in
a sunrise. I looked at my watch, a large Swiss pocket watch,
loot from a prisoner. It was twelve thirty. The Russians were
burning villages and haystacks, probably on our side of the
Elbe; the peasant boys were capering jubilantly in the firelight, just as I would caper there if I belonged to that army.

I sat down in shadows by the bridge abutment, where I
could be dark. I had a drink—it tasted strong, like the air, on
that night of the blossoming Saxon plain. I thought it odd
that the brandy should taste good to me after so much of
it, but that was the way of things in that season. I was at
that stage of drunkenness where vision is penetrating—the
eye can burn its way in. Or so I felt. I was ready to watch
Willy and Elfrida, and quite naturally I was hoping for discord. I was angry at myself, and discord could be my medi-
cine; and discord there was.

They came back suddenly, the lovers. They appeared on
the road from town, and I surmised that Willy had taken
Elfrida to a house there. He could have ordered the Germans
out; that was a thing we did not mind doing. I grimaced;
Willy could enjoy her more immoderately in a house, in a
bed. . . . They were not together any more, however, that
was plain. Elfrida manifested a distance between them; she
was haughty, in the starlight. With great dignity she walked
toward her family, while Willy, tired perhaps, came slouching along behind her in his country way.

When she was beside her mother and grandmother, who
were clumsily getting to their feet, she turned to face Willy,
and said: "Have the decency to keep your distance from my
mother."

Willy stopped obediently. "Whatever you say, honey," he
answered.

Elfrida spoke furiously to her family; she took up the baby

and restored it to the crook of her arm. The mother and grandmother bent to the children and started waking them. Restlessly the children held to sleep, burying their faces against the summons.

"Peasant!" Elfrida said then, with her head down. "What do you know about love?" She took a menacing step toward Willy, as if she might again scratch him, and said: "Love is —beyond your comprehension!"

"Yes'm," Willy said. "But I'll show you yet."

"Ah! But I hate you! And I will make you pay! Your filthy bargain . . . I'll make you pay!" she screamed, and then bent down to one of the children, speaking rapid German, torrents of command, exhortation, rage. The family rose around her and suddenly took her in; and, as they began moving, it seemed clear that she was safely away from Willy, who was still standing at rest, slouching. He had a cigar going, and its glow faintly lighted up his blunt features, returning them to my comprehension. He was just Willy, after all, my old friend, an honest soldier. I concluded that I ought to rise and go to him, and so I did, and offered him a drink from my bottle, which he was willing to take.

He was glad to see me, but of course his thoughts were with Elfrida. "I found 'em a place for the night," he said. "I showed her where it is, and I reckon they'll go there. It's right nice."

"After all that?" I said. "After what she said? She's on her way to Cologne right now!"

"That talk?" he said mildly. "That don't matter much— that's just something women do. That's the way they *are*."

"But she hates you, Willy!"

"She don't hate me. Listen, she's a passionate woman. I didn't rape her. Old Willy Fletcher ain't never raped a woman yet." He looked at her, dimly, through the reddish

light of the cigar, and said: "Come to think of it, she loves
me. She scratched me again, but she scratched my back, and
you know what that means."

There was nothing for me to say. In a moment Willy
turned away from the river, and said: "I'm tired. Let's go
home." And then we went away. I finished my bottle while
I lay on my back in bed, in the big country house where
our company was quartered, and the next morning I woke
with a headache which I was able to welcome.

I felt I had it coming; I desired punishment, and in due
course it came. After breakfast Willy went off to Elfrida,
"to see about my woman," as he put it. We had scarcely any
duties, and we were free to go where we liked during the
day, so long as we did not run away. I chose to stay in the
big house, gloomily hoping that Willy would have a disaster; but when he did not return by noon, I went into the
town looking for him.

The town was very small, and it had not been fought over;
it was intact, and full of people hiding. The doors of the
houses were always kept shut against wandering soldiers,
even during the day, and the only signs of life were the children who occasionally got outside of the houses to make a
racket in the street. I feared I had an impossible task, for if
the family was holding itself within doors, I could never find
it. I felt defeated, in a preliminary way, and so I was striding
along rather angrily; and then I came across Elfrida's two
daughters, in a minute front yard, playing in a sandbox.
They looked up at me, expectantly and fearfully, like puppies.
I slowed my walk. Their eyes followed me, the heads perplexedly turning. The girls had brown eyes perfectly dispas-
sionate; their expressions were such that I knew they had
stopped having a good time because I had come near them.

I was uncomfortable, and then it occurred to me that I

had never before seen a sandbox in Europe—I was looking at an oddity. The sand was damp; the box was a simple affair, nailed together, and had a familiar, American look to it.

"*Wo ist dein Mut—*" I began a question, and then paused. From somewhere behind the house came a sound of hammering, rhythmical and slow.

It was not a sound I was used to hearing in Europe. I was vaguely alarmed. The children were watching me, their mouths open—not afraid, but ready for something unpleasant. I hurried away, along the side of the house, and heard their whispering behind me. I reached the corner of the house and turned it, and there was Willy, on a ladder, hammering at a plank which he was holding across a window. He looked down: he had nails between his teeth. He bobbed his head in greeting, and then took the nails out of his mouth.

"I'm patching up this old window," he said.

"I see you are," I answered.

"The glass is busted out, and I couldn't find any shutters to fit—" He nodded, and said: "Just a minute now." He drove two more nails, and stepped down. The window had a look I was familiar with—the look of abandoned houses whose windows have been boarded up against tramps and wandering boys. Houses on the outskirts of town, they have shade from rich antique trees.

"I'll bet you made the sandbox too," I said, and Willy began to look uncomfortable.

"Oh, that," he said, shrugging. "That wasn't nothing. The supply sergeant loaned me the tools and nails." He lifted his hammer: it looked new.

Then the back door opened, and Elfrida came out, looking as women do who have just washed their hair. Her face was tanned—golden in the faintly dusty sunshine—and as I saw her clearly for the first time, I perceived that she had a fine, high-bred look, as, let us say, we would like Austrian countesses to look. She was wearing a cotton dress, light gray.

"Beautiful," I murmured.

Willy, at my side, was restless, uneasy, and may have been wondering if he had gone too far in giving comfort to the enemy. Elfrida paused on the steps, frowning, and seemed to nod at me. Then she swept past Willy and went up to the window. She spread her legs a little and stamped her feet into the dust. With hands on hips, she inclined her head back and stared at the blank place where the window had been.

For perhaps twenty seconds she stood so, and then she stepped rather delicately, fastidiously, past us, back to the door and through it, closing the door quite softly. The baby was asleep, very likely; a household had begun to function.

Willy was looking sheepish, not at all the conqueror now. He hefted the hammer, and I noticed that he had a good way with it. "A feller wants to make himself handy if he can," he said.

Silently I nodded.

"She needs me," he went on. "A woman needs a man. Well, damn it, I told you she didn't hate me!"

For quite a while we stood there, Willy reluctant and ashamed, and I trying to get a sense of things. I was once again astonished; I could not keep up with developments, and so I decided to go back to my bottle. I got drunk that afternoon, and stayed moderately drunk for several days. I wanted away from Willy, and I managed it. I did not even see him for three days. When I came to myself again, I was shaky, and startled by things. The Russians had arrived at the river, a whole regiment, so the rumor went, and their presence manifested itself as minor changes in our view. Across the river there was a trench, perhaps a hundred yards back from the bank; I could see the parapet, a light tan slashing the green of the fields. There were anti-tank guns with black slender barrels trained on us, one every two or three hundred yards. Now and then a soldier appeared momentarily on the parapet—a clumsy figure, lifting a pick or shovel. Sometimes a head appeared in silhouette over the parapet, and several times I saw horsemen cantering along behind the trench; and perhaps these were Cossack scouts.

The Russians kept out of sight most of the time, and maintained two sentries at the bridge. These were always friendly boys carrying submachine guns; it was impossible to talk to them. They smiled, they made extravagant gestures, their pidgin German was not like ours.

The pilgrims had vanished, like small animals gone to ground. On our side of the river there were family caravans constantly setting off for the west, and we had a rumor that the international boundary would soon be moving westward also. Our life had changed during my drunkenness; we had new oddities, and Willy and Elfrida composed a remarkable one, for they had become fond lovers. I first saw that fondness one night when Willy enlisted my help to move some U.S. Army canned goods to the lady's house; which is to say, I helped him steal these things from our company kitchen. We waited until the cooks had gone to bed, and then invaded the kitchen of the big house. We hauled our plunder to Elfrida in a wheelbarrow which Willy had borrowed somewhere, and all this was a lark, naturally.

We had to become quite solemn, however, when we entered the room where Elfrida was waiting. There were two oil lamps on a table, and Elfrida was standing in their light. On the table was the baby, naked, like a Cupid in oils of the cinquecento. He lay on a white cloth, and beside him was a basin with water in it, from which a light mist was ascending.

Elfrida looked at us, observed the nature of our burdens, and said: "I am about to give the baby a bath. His name is Heinrich, and he likes his bath very much." She smiled shyly, and touched the tiny boy. She was sweating, her temples glistened.

The bath was a ceremony, auspiciously begun and managed. Elfrida gently lifted the little body and immersed it in the water; she held the head above the surface with her left hand, while with her right she accomplished the ritual ablutions. The boy's body had a golden sheen after the water touched it; the arms had currents of white down, and the face held an expression of bliss. The lips were slightly parted —they were not smiling. The eyes were open, but were not seeing; the baby's world was, as it were, printed upon them, and was no more than the touch of warm water, of the mother's cautious hands, of the gentle air.

"He has good color," Elfrida said. "I have always given him baths in the sun—how do you say, sunbaths?"

"That's a fine-looking boy," Willy said. His face was calm, discreet, and it came to me that he could well judge of baby boys. He was a man; he had fathered sons in faraway Texas.

Elfrida raised her head and smiled at Willy. "It's nice that you should like him," she said. "*Schöner Heinrich!*" She bent quickly and touched the baby's forehead with her lips; and then, straightening up, she took the boy from the water, and set about drying him and diapering him for bed. Her hands moved comfortably with such work, and Willy and I stood about helplessly. We made a joke about our theft. We laughed; and we understood that for a time we did not greatly matter to the scene we found ourselves in.

When the baby was put away in the next room, Elfrida turned her attention to us, and it was something heavy, something resolute that came to us. First she went up to Willy and said: "Thank you very much for bringing us food." Her voice caressed the sentiment, making an endearment. Willy blushed. "You're nice," she said, *"sehr nett,"* and reached up to touch him lightly with her fingertips where not so long ago she had clawed viciously.

She then turned to me and said: "Thank you for helping us, dear friend. We will not forget you!"

It was up to me then to depart, and I did this, but I felt foolish to leave such a woman, though she belonged to another.

Willy had her to himself, but it was not apparent that his enjoyments were unclouded. He had taken on responsibilities which required energetic tending. It was no small matter to feed such a family, and he had to look forward to the problem of moving the family to the west, for by this time we had heard that our division was to be moved away from the international boundary. And Elfrida herself was difficult. She was capable of scratching seriously in her passion—"She *hurts,*" Willy said. "My back is raw from her fingernails!" —and she did not always keep her appointments. She was elusive; Willy found her mysterious. Still, they did well together. Willy was strong with youth, and Elfrida bloomed, as brides are supposed to do. She developed a marvelous color, a brilliant self-confidence. Willy improved her wardrobe, by judicious trading in the village; some of the refugees had brought pretty things with them. Willy offered coffee, cigarettes, and canned goods, which he stole as he needed them. He found Elfrida several dresses, two pairs of silk stockings, and a pair of shoes, and he ordered other things from the States.

Such attentions had their effect. Elfrida ceased to look like a refugee. She began to look like a well-maintained wife, and she began to assert a kind of wifely authority with Willy.

There came a time when she was able to request him to take her and her family to Halle. We had a rumor that the division was going there, and she expressed a desire to anticipate such a transfer. Willy of course wanted her to go, and so he came to me with his plan for borrowing one of the company's trucks.

"I really like that woman pretty well," he said, "and I want to take care of her. But I need some help. How about it? Would you go along?" I could scarcely refuse, for to do so would be to deny the old friendship of the war; and, besides, I wanted to help Elfrida.

Again we had a lark. The first thing was to plan a route to Halle that would avoid battalion and regimental head-quarters areas, where traffic checks might be expected. This we did by scouting the country, in a jeep temporarily stolen from our own battalion headquarters company. We found a route, and marked it on our maps; then we returned home feeling excited and cheerful. The next thing was to find a place for Elfrida's family in Halle, and this proved more difficult. Willy took over this task, and needed two days for it. He wandered heroically; he came back each day dusty and tired. One day he traveled by jeep, borrowed this time from regimental headquarters, and the next day by motorcycle; he had found a German army motorcycle cached in a shed, and, so he claimed it, it ran perfectly. He made an interesting figure as he departed: the big man lightly crouching, absolutely bent on traveling fierce and fast, the machine's rear wheel sending up spurts of dust behind him. When he came back, he had a bump on his head and some bruises, one great violet affair on his left arm; he had fallen off the machine in a corner; but he was happy, for he had found a house in Halle for Elfrida and her family.

He was full of enthusiasm, as if he were considering the

problems of his own true family. He spoke of the house as if
he had just conversed with an enthusiastic broker. "There
ain't a window lacks glass, there's furniture, and there's even
carpets. By God, there's a garden out back that has roses!"
He let me doctor his wounds, which were several large
scuffed areas on his back, where the hide had been polished
raw by gravel in the roadway, but he would not stop talking
about his house, and about the joy which he expected Elfrida
to take in it. "By God, it's even a pretty big house, and in a
nice neighborhood," he said. "You'll see when we get there.
It's a place for the quality—I had hell running that other
family out!"

Then he asked me if Elfrida would be pleased by such a
house, and I said she would be pleased. I was daubing at his
back with tincture of merthiolate, and he was touchy about
it. I had a good view of him. He was hurting, his bruises were
dark, and he would admit to a headache, no doubt the result
of a minor concussion, but he would not consider these matters seriously. Beside his great concern, they did not seem
real.

"Willy," I said, and touched him with my pink daub of
cotton, "everything happens to you!"

When he left me to go to Elfrida, he had a dim and hopeful
smile on his face, for he wanted his news to give pleasure.

The next night was chosen for the family's migration.
Willy and I made an arrangement with one of the company
truck drivers, an old friend of combat days, and that night at
ten o'clock I drove our truck to the rendezvous agreed upon;
this was a road junction perhaps half a mile from town. At
ten thirty Willy arrived with the family, trooping in out of
the dark, the family cautious and scared. We helped them up
into the truck and hurried away. While I drove, Willy kept
an anxious eye out. We expected difficulties, for we were not

used to having our own way, but nothing happened. Our route unreeled itself, coming up out of the dark—road signs briefly black and white under Willy's flashlight, crossroads pale and still. We made the trip without headlights in a little more than three hours, and found a garden smelling of roses at the end of it, and a high, narrow brick house. Inside, behind blackout screens, Willy lighted oil lamps and shyly gave over the house to Elfrida.

"Here it is, honey," he said. "It's yours."

The family were astonished. We were in a room that could only be a parlor: the furniture was heavy, there was an Oriental rug, there were framed photographs on the walls, gentlemen and ladies in black. The little girls did not move at all, and the older women inspected the room in fierce, darting stares, blinking their eyelids. Elfrida nodded her head just once, and said: "Splendid!"

Then she came to me and took my right hand in hers. "Thank you again, dear friend," she said, looking me in the eye. "You have done a wonderful thing for us."

"You're—welcome," I stammered. I had not expected thanks, since the trip had been uneventful. I had hoped for a difficulty, so that I could do something bold or gallant while Elfrida looked on, but now I perceived that I would not have had greater thanks from Elfrida for driving our truck through a road block.

She kissed my hand. I blushed, and could not speak. She turned to Willy, slowly walked to him, and embraced him. Lightly she kissed him on both cheeks; she tilted her head back and said: "You are so good to me . . . sweetheart."

Willy mumbled, and she stepped back. "A husband could not treat me more nicely," she said, and Willy hung his head. On the way back to our village Willy kept saying: "I can't

get over it. I expected her to be glad . . . but she called me
sweetheart! What do you think of that, now!"

He was impressed, and clearly he was thinking of Elfrida in
a new way; but he could not do anything for a few days because we were occupied with moving away from the international river. The whole army was moving back to allow
the Russians into the part of central Germany allotted them
in the grand settlement. Throughout that time Willy was
very anxious, much more distinctly exercised than I had ever
expected him to be. He seemed uncommonly meditative. For
several miles during our ride in trucks to Halle he even carried his chin on his hand. He kept his brows knitted, and the
smooth, hard lines of his face looked contorted with the lines
raying up between his eyebrows. His face was not meant to
look so; he appeared to be in pain, but at the same time he
seemed joyful. I concluded that he was in love, and did not
worry about him.

Our company was set down in a block of houses in a work-
ing-class quarter of the city, and very quickly we arranged
our comforts. The regimental commander took over a local
brewery and arranged to distribute its product. Each of our
houses had a keg of beer in the back yard, and a soldier whose
duty was to sprinkle the keg with a garden hose. Volleyball
nets were strung up in a nearby field, and softball teams
were organized. Willy quickly found his way to Elfrida, and
I did not see much of him for almost a week; and then one
evening, just before he was due to set out on his nightly journey, he told me that he was going to get married.

"But you are married," I said. "In Dallas. You've got
kids!"

"I know. I'm just getting married in church, here. Elfrida—"

"In church?"

"In a Catholic church, the kind the Mexicans have down home. Elfrida's Catholic. There won't be any papers at a courthouse, or anything like that."

"But you're not Catholic! What makes you think you can—"

"I'll just fake it, that's all. Elfrida's already taught me how to cross myself. And I'll have something for the priest— that'll help."

"Elfrida's already found a priest, then."

"You bet. The whole thing is her idea, but I don't mind. She figures I'll take better care of her if I'm married to her— that's what she says, anyhow."

I thought of bigamy, and wanted to mention it, but could not find the words I needed; and Willy anticipated me.

"I know what you're thinking," he said, "but it ain't so. I'll go back to my family in Dallas, even to that bitch—I'll straighten her out when I get home. But I'm going to be married here, in Germany, at least for a while. Elfrida wants me to, and that's enough for me."

"You'll have to have a secret wedding," I said.

"Secret, you bet! I don't want nobody to hear of it. And I want you to be my best man. Listen, Elfrida wants flowers, so you and I are going to have to promote some for her. Now, I figured . . ." His plans were comprehensive; he attacked the problem of getting married with characteristic energy. He arranged for a wedding feast; that meant a compact with the mess sergeant. He introduced the mess sergeant to a pretty girl. He contracted for the church; it was a humble church in a nondescript edge-of-town parish. He organized the conspiracy—to have an illegal wedding in broad daylight, under the eyes of the army. The stern army order against fraternization had to be got around. He talked to the priest, several times. He obtained corsages, cut flowers, and bouquets. He got champagne. He stole it from the stocks of confiscated German stores which were kept for our officers in the company orderly room.

He had activity like a disease, and sported in it; and he accomplished everything he set out to do. He got himself married to Elfrida, in a Catholic church, in great privacy. The family was present, looking scared and dressed-up; the little girls were carrying bouquets of roses, and that was Willy's idea. Elfrida was very solemn in a blue dress, and did not look her best. Only Willy was splendid, in uniform and ribbons. He had shined his combat infantryman's badge with silver polish, and wangled some paratrooper boots.

I was there, unhappy, thinking that Elfrida was now absolutely cut off from me. I felt myself held in by the atmosphere of the church. Above my head I sensed a high religious dimness, coercing me. The priest's Latin was very suave, muttered like a dangerous secret; the priest himself seemed not quite to belong to what he was doing, for he had a questioning, faintly bitter face with sharp features. He had large brown eyes which now and then peeped boldly out of the ritual. Several times he glanced at Willy, and it was plain that he did not make very much of Willy.

At the end of the ceremony Willy kissed Elfrida very chastely. He touched her shoulders lightly, bent toward her, and just brushed her lips with his. I was offended, for Willy seemed to be giving in to his surroundings. Elfrida, as she turned away from the altar, had a look of radiant triumph, which for a moment she bent on me. She seemed to say: "Observe, I have done something with this clay." She made me look down, for I had no expression that would answer her. As they were leaving the church, Willy made the sign of the cross, and Elfrida nodded approvingly.

I had reason to be vexed, and so I stung them with a handful of rice. They were surprised, and Elfrida for a moment looked shrewdly at me. Willy said: "Heah, heah!" and grinned.

Then we made separate journeys to Elfrida's house for the wedding feast, and I got drunk on Willy's champagne. I wandered off while Willy was proposing toasts to his new family —the grandmother was already tipsy—and resolved to pay no further attention to Willy and Elfrida. I wanted to look the other way, and for perhaps a week I did that. I was captain of the company volleyball team, and that week we won the regimental championship. A new rumor grew strong, and I paid attention to it: we were to go to Japan, in the second assault wave, after a furlough in the States, and that furlough was a pleasant thing to think about. We heard that we would leave Germany in June, in July, in August.

I kept my attention away from Willy, but not my thoughts, and so I was ready for him when I once again looked his way. I found him happy. He had become a husband, our only one. He had become domestic. I went one evening to his house, and he met me at the door, carrying the baby. He called me in and had me sit down; he got me a cigar and a glass of brandy. Then he took a chair, and perched the baby on his knee. The baby was facing him, and together they composed an image of the familial relation. Willy clucked at the baby while the baby rolled his head.

"Ain't he a fine boy?" Willy said. "Elfrida lets me take care of him now and then."

We talked for perhaps half an hour. Willy changed the baby's diapers, and soothed him once when he cried. Elfrida did not appear, and since there was curfew for Germans at seven o'clock, I assumed she was in the house; but I did not ask. Willy was happy. There were voices from other rooms and upstairs; the household was moving around its center, and he was content.

Through June and July Willy came to have a reputation in the company for domesticity, and this was a reputation more difficult for him to sustain than his old one. He was a provider, and wanted to be a good one, but there was no legitimate work for him to do. He had to steal or promote what his family needed, and so he intrigued with certain mess sergeants and supply sergeants in the regiment. Willy could sometimes arrange a German girl for a sergeant; and sometimes, through Elfrida, he came across goods which he could barter. At one time, for example, he had French perfume, left over from the days of German conquest, with which he traded quite successfully.

He had to keep moving; he had people to see; and, increasingly as the summer wore on, he had military duties to put up with. The army was returning to normal after the confusions of victory. Training schedules appeared; formations were enforced; the officers began to withdraw into their privileges. Willy had to conduct his illegal business in the early-morning hours and after retreat; he took to rising at four thirty, and he was often out until midnight.

He found time to enjoy his family, however. He took supper with them, and this was a great pleasure to him. He sported with the baby; his custom was to take the baby as soon as he arrived, so that, where once the baby had seemed an extension of Elfrida, he now seemed an extension of Willy. I had the habit of going with Willy two or three times a week for supper, and I was impressed with the joy he could take in family life.

He had a talent for it. He accepted his family, and they accepted him, so that, on the whole, his marriage was a stable and quiet affair. The mother and grandmother respected him. He was a figure of authority to them, and he was imposing enough, certainly, as he took his ease—his big body relaxed in a heavy chair, a cigar going, his feet propped on a stool. The little girls liked to climb on him, and their mother watched approvingly.

Elfrida took great pains with Willy. She looked to his comforts. Twice a week she did his laundry and ironing; every night she cooked for him and served him, and would not sit down until he was drinking his coffee. Her devotion was almost Oriental, and she delighted in it. Together in that parlor they made a very touching composition—wedded bliss perpetually rising to its best opportunities. Willy had the baby, and Elfrida to put on his slippers for him. She had bought them herself—leather ones—and her way was to kneel before him. She kept her face attentive, and sometimes when she rose she kissed him lightly on the forehead.

So the marriage held as the summer wore on. Willy was happy—he used to tell me so, several times a day—and Elfrida was always smiling; but late in July there happened an event which made a change. In fact, Elfrida seduced me, as it were, and I had to conceive a whole new set of attitudes toward her. I was surprised—astonished. Suddenly I was given just that which I had been wanting, and my feelings on receiving the gift taught me how strong the wanting had been. I had plainly grown weak with desire; I was vulnerable and available. I accepted my good fortune as a matter of course. Not for a moment did I think of resisting it, for I had been trained as a soldier to seek out good fortune, on the theory that only good fortune could save me. I was an opportunist, and had an animal keenness for sensing a chance, a way out or a way to a satisfaction.

I hung on a hair trigger constantly; but I was not alone in

that. My delicacy was universal. All of us were like that, and so my society included and confirmed my personal style. I accepted Elfrida, and thought, instantly, that anyone else would do the same. Light does not move more resolutely through dark than my motives toward accomplishment. I thought vaguely about the war, and told myself that in wartime many things were possible that could never be so in a peace; and a murderer could not be more bitter than I was in seeking love.

With an afternoon free because of a volleyball practice that was set for four o'clock, I went to Elfrida's house, and found her restless and bored. Willy was having to be a soldier that afternoon. When Elfrida asked if I would take her for a walk, I was immediately ready to try my luck with her. We did not go far, though we talked very rapidly, and we kept to the alleys. We came to a shed that had hay in it, and Elfrida suggested that we tarry. "I would like to rest," she said. She set my heart to pounding: she was tall and fragrant; I could smell her hair, with the sun on it.

I had no care for my friend. I was aware of him; he was this lady's proprietor, but he seemed unreal. Elfrida was new to me, her normal ties undone. The curve of her hip was present to me, and her smooth round arms. She was a lady whom fortune had abused, and so she deserved sympathy; and I was full of sympathy! I longed to tell her so. I was prepared to rehearse her misfortunes at the bridge, and warmly press her hand in restitution. I was ready to talk, to make a plea, but there was no need.

A dumb resolution took me near to her, so that I could touch her shoulder. Sick with apprehension, I looked at her face. She was in a dusty light from the open door. I thought: "She has blue eyes," and then I saw that she had great violet eyes, enlarging themselves to accommodate a new feeling. She kept silence, and there was a sweetness in her pose, as of some ideal image. Her expression was meditative and remote; a little smile appeared on her lips, and I caught her.

An old story. I was clumsy, she was graceful. I frowned with concentration, and she smiled, and we made love. Her will was to have love that afternoon, and so it happened, a clarity.

When it was over, and I was dusting off her golden shoulders where were clover blossoms and dry little leaves from the hay, I asked her to love me, "Because I love you, because I've loved you for a long time."

She said: "Of course I love you. I have proved it." She turned, she put her warm arm on my neck, and kissed me. "You are a nice boy," she said. "Now I think we should go back to my house before Willy comes."

She dressed slowly and gracefully. She balanced sinuously on one foot while she pulled a silk stocking onto the other leg; her bent knee was like a jewel. She balanced again to put on a shoe, and then flexed her thigh for me, and grinned. At each stage of the dressing she looked as if she were posing for a painter—intending to look her finest. When we left the shed, she looked back at it and nodded; and then she walked at my side quite mildly. We arrived at her house a few minutes before Willy, whom she received in her customary fashion; she kissed him, she got his slippers, she brought out the baby from his nap. Then she stepped away from him, perfectly calm, and there was only a small flaring of her nostrils to indicate that she had a secret from her trusting husband.

I of course from that moment began to suffer desire in its aspect of blank pain. I wanted Elfrida to myself, that instant, but I observed that she was indefinitely far away from me.

I looked stealthily at the line of her buttocks, that not half an hour before had been under my touch, and they were as if in a painting, high up on a wall of a museum. I began calculating when my next chance might arrive, and then, of course, I feared that it might never arrive. I tried to remember everything Elfrida had said to me, for a sign that she had committed herself to me, but I could recall only terms of endearment and minute animal sounds, and these could scarcely represent a commitment.

I fiercely considered her motives, wanting to humble them to my self-interest. Toward that end, I told myself that Elfrida was a careless girl, easily deflected, but I could not accept that. I then told myself that she might love me for my good qualities, but I could not recall that I possessed good qualities. I did not make her out; her conduct was opaque to my desire. I wanted not to leave the house, and of course Willy pressed me to stay—for dinner, for brandy, for conversation. I looked to Elfrida, naturally, for a sign, and when there seemed not to be one, I felt a duty to depart. In a few minutes I left, thinking of no other thing than a way to return when Willy would not be there to interrupt me.

I discovered then that it was not difficult to find Willy away. His business enterprises kept him away from home, like the traveling salesman of American tradition who must wander farther than a knight of the grail. The very next day, at the same hour in the afternoon, I found Elfrida alone, and I asked her to go walking. She refused, but she did not kill my hopes. On the way back to the company I discovered a new ferocity of desire and began to understand how Willy had been brought under control. I felt the influence of an art which I could not understand. I grew angry at Elfrida, and I decided that anger could understand her; she had embraced me only to coax out gifts, and this was a bitter thought; but I sought gifts that night among the men of the company. Many had loot, and some of it applied to my difficulty. I bought a ring and a bracelet, and two days later made Elfrida a gift of them, which she accepted gracefully.

For these things she kissed me, and said: "You understand that I will not be able to wear them—certainly not when Willy is home. But I will get them out sometimes and admire them."

The next day we went during the afternoon to the shed with the hay, and again the following day, and my pleasures became astonishing to me. I felt suddenly healed of obscure wounds left by the war. I walked about with confidence, thrusting my head upward, and I understood that I was happy. I began to wonder if I might not somehow ease Willy out. The thought came to me that I might have Willy's bigamous marriage annulled by some German authority and then marry Elfrida myself, quite legally.

I was ready to announce myself superior to the world, until, two days later, Elfrida told me that we would have to end our little affair, though it had become pleasing to her. I became angry—like Willy, I was ready to do violence—and I questioned her hotly. We were at her house, in the parlor, sitting in the huge chairs; she was wearing her gray dress, and she looked very competent, like the old Elfrida of the bridge, leading her little family through the wilderness.

"I must think of my family," she said, very moderately.

"Then why did you start an affair with me? All of a sudden —out of the blue! Now you've got a responsibility to me!"

She smiled, and forced me to smile with her. "You are quite nice," she said. "I did not know that Americans could be so . . . pleasant. And you have done great services for us. Why should I not love you?" She was very much in command of herself, and looked somehow pleased; and of course I taxed her with that.

"You look . . . happy!" I said. "Does it make you happy to see me sad?"

"No, not that," she answered quickly. "But can't you see? I am a little happy. I am happy that we had an affair. It pleases me to have an affair just now!"

She got up and struck an attitude: one hand on a hip, the other pointing at me. She was a figure of defiance. Indeed, her bosom was heaving; she was in the grip of an emotion.

"Can't you see?" she said again. "Of course I am happy. I made him marry me, that violent man, and now I have done it—done what I wanted to do!"

She laughed suddenly, and it was a shocking sound in that stodgy, decorous room. "Of course!" she said again, smiling ferociously and displaying two rows of small white teeth, glittering. "Am I such a woman—to be trampled? Not yet! I will not forget who I am."

Then she shuddered, and her arms fell to her sides. "I am sorry," she said. "But surely you can see . . ."

I could see. She had taken her revenge on Willy, as she had promised to do; marriage her means, and I the final instrument. I thought of the sharp-featured priest; he would be sad if he knew Elfrida's accomplishment, which was surely a sin. I looked at Elfrida, fierce in wrath, and I felt cheated, as if something had been withdrawn from my experience of her— some largeness of motive that I could admire. And then, her mood changing, she came to me and took my hands and said: "But I do love you, *Liebchen*. It was not only that I . . ." She paused, and then went back to her chair; she sat down and composed herself.

"You understand, I love Willy too," she said. "After such a beginning . . . Perhaps you cannot believe me."

"Willy?" I said. "But he—"

"Took me like a robber. Yes. Like one of the bad old German barons."

"You shouldn't love him, then," I said. "It's not right!"

"Perhaps not. I have thought that. But I do."

I was perplexed, but I believed her; she looked beautiful and honest. My trouble was that I did not want to go away. "Then you're better than I thought," I said. "More generous, more fair—now I really can't leave you!"

"Ah, so," she said, and made a deprecating gesture. "It is difficult for me that I . . . It is ridiculous after everything that I should love Willy. I have come to know him; so, I can love him. He is a good man, of course. He has been quite good to me." She sighed, and shrugged her shoulders. "It is fortunate that we are all young," she said, "with so much before us."

I then returned to my pleas, which she considered and finally smiled over. She made me a gift of that smile, and when I left her I could believe that her resolution was not final. I felt illuminated; but, naturally, I took away with me some of her concern about Willy. She feared his perception, and so I feared it too. I wanted Willy to persist in ignorance so that he would continue inviting me to his house, where I might have the good fortune to win his wife again. I began to see that Willy could have perception; he was no fool, and his mild blue eyes could get through to a fact if they once became alert.

But for a time the summer continued its even way for us, a mild and healing round in a gentle weather. There came the news of the Japanese surrender, and we celebrated that; and it was apparent that soon the division would be sent home, as the vast army began to break up. Every day we had new rumors, but there were no decisions, and we stayed on; and the curious situation I had got into with Elfrida and Willy took on a peculiar appearance; it began to look formal. The occasions we shared—the dinners we took together, the drinking bouts, the storytelling—had an unstable gravity, as if we were anticipating change.

I often meditated our doings. Willy had commenced the comedy with violent love enforcing itself by violence; he had been passionate and efficient simultaneously, and that was a rarity. Perhaps Willy had a gift for this; I could believe it. He came from a people who had possessed such a gift; with it they had appropriated the indefinite horizon. Something was asleep in him to set him thus free after plunder, but he was not evil; he did not even intend any harm.

And surely Elfrida was not evil, who had only found a woman's way of dealing with her world. Perhaps her trouble was that her world came up to her touch, and could be dealt with only by some contortion of the flesh. She had known the shudder in the loins—ah, she could do something about that! She had not been afraid, and so she had managed a revenge. She had made a cuckold of Willy; perhaps she had felt a moral duty to do that, and certainly she had made herself the heroine of an adventure.

Unfortunately, she had also worked her way through to love of Willy, and so she was in a delicate position. She was compromised, and perhaps unhappy. No longer a victim, she was vulnerable in her triumph: what might happen now? Soon we would leave Europe, we Americans who had conquered it, and there would be an end; but we would not be leaving for a while, and there was time for something to happen. We had an opportunity to follow out the scheme our acts predicted, and of course we used that opportunity. In fact, Willy, following the golden baby, Heinrich, one Sunday morning came across the bracelet and ring which I had given Elfrida.

He presented his evidence that evening, just before dinner, while the three of us were sitting in the parlor. He leaned out unobtrusively from his chair and dropped the ring and bracelet on the carpet. There was a crystalline sound as their metals touched, platinum and gold, and then the jewels refracted light as the pieces settled into the nap of the carpet. "I reckon you know what those are," he said. "That boy in the third platoon had that bracelet just two or three weeks ago and he sold it to you. I asked him." He leaned back, his face quite mild. His eyes were directed out into the center of the room.

"Those are mine," Elfrida said then. "Where did you get them?"

"The baby found 'em," Willy said softly. "He was playing in your bag, and he turned the bag upside down. And I was taking care of the baby . . . at that time."

"They were my aunt's," Elfrida said. "Her husband sent them from Paris in 1940—after the conquest. Do you suggest—"

"I say. I ain't going to suggest. Honey, you're fresh out of a husband. I ain't going to argue with you. As for you, old buddy—" and here he looked at me, detachedly—"in a minute I'm going to take you outside and whup you until you can't stand."

Silence all around. I tensed myself against an attack, for Willy was clearly ready to fight, and I tried to think of something to say. I tried a denial. "Willy," I said, "it isn't so! It just isn't so!" He did not bother to look at me; he was staring hard at Elfrida, and his expression now was guarded, masklike.

"Honey, you going to deny it too?" he said.

"Of course, Willy," she said, "if you wish me to. Perhaps you should explain what I have done, however. I have done nothing . . . against you."

"Deny laying up with that son-of-a-bitch over there!" Willy roared, and got to his feet. "Deny that, you slut!" I got to my feet, thinking of self-defense.

Elfrida turned her head upward, and agony for a moment took her features; and when she looked down again, her expression was hard—I had not seen it like that since the night at the bridge. "Ah," she said. "Slut, is it? Still, I deny everything. That is my policy!"

"Come to think of it, you aren't out a husband," Willy said then, and he was grinning now. "Listen, I was already married back in Texas when I went to the church with you. I couldn't really marry you. My other wife is in the records at the county courthouse in Jim Clark County. . . ."

"Yes, I know," Elfrida said. "As if that were a thing you needed to tell me. Please, you must understand that I have eyes. I saw your way with a diaper; I knew you were a husband when you came to me—an American husband! Skillful with a diaper! Willy, don't be this way. Why must you treat me so?" Her expression pleaded with him to be decent, to be quiet, if necessary to forgive her. Willy had his back to us, and now he muttered: "Don't try to sweet-talk me out of it."

"I will say what I want to say!" Elfrida answered. "If I have lost a husband, you have lost a son or a daughter. Yours. Your own, like those of Texas. Willy, I am carrying your child. That is true." Her voice was calm, she was not trying to make a persuasion. She announced the fact, and kept her poise.

"My child," Willy said, still with his back to us, and then whirled to face us. "Mine? Or his? Or anybody's? How would *you* know, that will sleep with anybody that comes along? My child. Why, you slut, you slut . . ."

"Oh, then!" Elfrida said. "Then! Listen, peasant as you have always been! Understand that you wear the horns, please, if I may use our vulgar European expression. I, I set them there for you, in return for your favors to me at the bridge, you . . . And I have loved you, in spite of all your vileness. . . ." Her face was the cold, furious face she had put on at the bridge after Willy had taken his fee. She looked strange to me, oddly European, as if the scene had returned her to a familiar role; and then Willy, with his head down, said: "And I loved you. Can't you see? Why did you have to spoil it? You didn't have to! What did I do that was so bad? But I'm damned if I'll apologize to a woman. Women—what have I ever got from women but a crooked deal? Or the clap? Women—sluts. Be damned if I'll talk any more. You—" and he pointed an accusing finger at me— "get your ass outside so we can have it out, you son-of-a-bitch. Come on—or are you afraid to get out from behind your woman's skirts?"

He turned and went out the door, and I was following him close, for I had a rage that matched his own. I did not have time to speak to Elfrida, but I had a sense of her, upright, fierce, but somehow sad, and very weary. . . . Then I was outside, in the late afternoon light, and Willy was waiting for me. We were in the garden; there were walls about us, yielding a thick shade streaked here and there with greenness. I was ready to start fighting, but Willy had yet a few things to say. "Old buddy," he began. "Ain't you a dandy! Did you think about a friend? I guess. You thought how you could steal his woman. Didn't it count for nothing, all that we done during the war? Old buddy!"

"Don't talk to me like that," I answered, feeling my rage grow. "Don't you . . . reproach me! You businessman!

You thought you could bargain for love—for her love. What do they teach you down there in Texas? That everything has a price? . . . You businessman!"

"I saved your life," Willy said, "and I sure wish I hadn't. If you ain't the most miserable excuse for a friend . . ."

"And I saved yours, and, by God, I never would have done it if I'd known what it was. Listen, you loan shark, I don't regret anything—"

And that was all the signal needed. The fight was on. Willy charged me, head down, and clearly had it in mind to butt me, but I timed an uppercut and caught him perfectly just as he reached me, and felt something go, under my knuckles. It felt like a thin board cracking. I stopped him in his tracks. He stood up; blood was gushing from his nose, flooding his lower face; and I had the sense then to go for the body while he was forgetting it. I put four or five good punches in to the belly, one of them just under the high arch of the ribs, and I made him gasp. I hurt him with those punches and, I think, saved myself from destruction, for I slowed him, and limited him. He came on, and he had a terrible strength; I could not keep him off. He could hit and he could wrestle. One of his right-hand punches very nearly severed my left ear from my head, and later, while we were on the ground, I think he must have taken the torn ear in his teeth, for the whole lower half of it was hanging by a shred when the fight was over.

I just managed to hang on, to stay with him until he was exhausted, and that was a long time after the fight started. We fell apart, finally, like spent fighting chickens, and sat sprawling on the ground, staring at each other. Elfrida came out, bearing a bowl of water, with white cloths tucked under her arms, and her face was white. She looked deafened, as if she did not quite believe the story her ears had brought her. Distaste, horror showed in the line of her mouth; she was biting her lip, in that ancient gesture of dismay. Willy looked up, and then shook his head and drove her away.

"I won't let you touch me," he said, "and I'll kill you if you touch him."

"I'll be all right," I said, for I was not more badly hurt than he was. Elfrida went back to the house, and I stared at Willy. His face looked as if it had slipped on his bones—the whole central part of it has slewed around to the right. "And I'll be watching you," I went on. "If you lay a hand on her, I'll take it out of you."

"And I'll do the same for you!" he shouted, and winced with the movement of his jaw. Awkwardly he pawed at his lower face. Hurt, exhausted, he did not look at all dismayed; he seemed almost satisfied, having done what his code required him to do.

I touched my ear very lightly, for I could feel how perilously it was related to me now. It began to hurt, and it was as if a chord of nerves had been exposed to the fiery touch of the air. I was dizzy and sick, but I too felt a vague satisfaction. In Willy's look as he held himself against the ground, I saw something of a virtuous rage now satisfied, and it was true that he had been enlisted in the cause of family and home; he was feeling justified, that was clear, and I too felt justified, though for other reasons. I also felt ashamed—soiled, as if I had fallen into a pit. I now sat at the bottom of an unlucky event, staring up and wondering at the bad thing that had happened to a good friendship.

"Willy, I don't like . . . all this," I said.

Vaguely he looked at me. "Nah," he said.

We were quiet for a time, and then I said: "We'd better get back to the company. It's going to take a doctor to put your nose back on its root."

"And you'd better see somebody with a sewing kit," Willy

said. "That ear's hanging like a tail, there. I reckon it hurts, don't it?"

"It hurts," I answered. "I guess your nose doesn't feel too good, either."

"It feels like I got a hole in my face. That hurts." Slowly he turned his head, as if testing it to see whether it would hold together. "You ready to go?"

"I'm ready," I said. We got up together, and together looked at the house, which was shut up now and quite blank to our gaze. Not a sound came from it. We made our way back to the company, and it took a long time. We came under the eye of the platoon leader, and he ordered us to the battalion aid station after lecturing us angrily; and at the battalion aid station we were examined and then sent back to the division hospital, for our wounds were considered serious. We were treated like casualties of the war, and the medical people seemed almost glad to have us, for they had been without occupation since the peace.

We kept silence all the way. We were three days at the division hospital, while Willy's nose was re-broken and set, and my ear was sewed back to my head, and we did not speak. Upon our return to the company, Willy perceived that I wanted to see Elfrida, and told me that he would not let me go alone. I then perceived that he too wished to see Elfrida, and so we went together, our silence once again resumed. We looked like wounded soldiers, certainly. Willy had a bandage that boxed the center of his face, like a mask, and I wore a handsome affair that fitted my head like a pirate's bandanna.

We walked furiously, and when we reached our destination, we found an empty house. Naturally we entered at the front door, and encountered the smell of settled dust. We ransacked the house, and even searched the garden; and discovered, of the family we sought, only a wrinkled handkerchief that Willy said was the grandmother's, and Willy's leather slippers on a shelf in a closet.

He broke silence with that. "She decided we'd never come back," he said, "and so she left. The Russians are going to have this city, and she knew it, and knew we were going, too. . . ."

I could not think of anything to say. I could not understand Elfrida's departure: it seemed to me perverse. She had left an established safety for the hazards of the road, and she had left me—and left Willy, I had to grant. We did not enter into the problem of what we ought to do next; instead, we continued seeking Elfrida. Willy knew of another German Army motorcycle, and we went on that, Willy driving, and I on the pillion seat behind him. "Hang on," Willy said. I gripped his sides, and we flew. I felt like the tail on a kite, and naturally I was alarmed, but I welcomed the feeling. "Turn it on!" I said. We circled the western edge of the city, as I grew accustomed to the smell of hot metal beneath me, and then we set about searching the roads that led westward. We tried the *Autobahn* first, and then a lesser road; we traveled some twenty miles on each before nightfall. We did not find our lady, and so we went home sick and discouraged.

The next day we rose early, having made arrangements with the platoon sergeant about being absent from reveille; we set off as before, I embracing Willy as he piloted the fierce little machine, and we found Elfrida not fifteen miles from the city, on a lane running between poplars. This was the second road we had tried. We could not help shouting. "There she is!" Willy said. "There she is—carrying the baby!" I said, and when we got down from the machine we were both smiling.

We must have been a strange image to that family, we who had last appeared to them in ferocious combat. Slowly the family came to us, rallying around the motorcycle. The little girls were solemn; Elfrida looked oddly blank, puzzled, and the older women huddled themselves behind her.

"Hello," Elfrida said. She bowed her head, and she composed an image of mourning. She was sad; her face was almost sullen. "I do not understand why you have come after us," she said.

Things were awkward then. Willy and I stopped smiling and moved apart; neither of us spoke: we looked at each other speculatively. Elfrida spoke to the children and the women, and they all walked away from us, the women touching the children, moving them. Elfrida shifted the baby boy from her right arm to her left, and said: "I cannot understand why you are together now." She looked at each of us in turn, her gaze steady. "Nothing is possible now, of course," she went on. "You will go home to America. I must go back to Köln. We are all . . . quite far apart now."

Her expression changed; now she looked resolute—resolute and tired.

"I wanted to see you!" Willy said, and stopped; for a moment he looked at me, as if I might find him the word he needed. Elfrida gravely turned her eyes upon him, those large violet eyes, and they were not without sympathy. Faintly she nodded; her expression became a little quizzical. "So?" she seemed to say. "After so much living, no more than this to say?"

"We came together because neither of us would let the other go alone," I said.

"Ah, naturally," Elfrida said. "And will you go back together?"

Silence. Willy looked at the backs of his hands. I stared at the ground.

"I am ashamed that I made trouble between you," Elfrida

said. "Between comrades." She held her head high, and clearly she was taking a punishment. "I feel guilty," she said.

Willy stirred the dust with the toe of his boot, his face looking stricken, vague.

"Don't feel that way," I said. "You shouldn't."

"We came because we wanted to see you again," Willy said suddenly. "He—" and he pointed at me—"he loves you too, I guess. God damn him." Willy was taking courage, though he was still staring at the ground. "And I . . . I do, too. I wish it all hadn't happened. We had a good thing, Elfrida! Wasn't it? You were happy with me. Why did you—"

"Ah," she said. "But perhaps I did spoil it. I had reasons! Later, of course . . ." She looked at me, just as Willy had done, for the word that might end her difficulty. "Now I feel sad. I did not want to leave our house. Sad for everything. Sad to lose everything."

"It didn't have to happen," Willy said stubbornly. "Why did it have to happen?" We stood about aimlessly, as if we truly could not understand. I felt my unhappiness expand, and perhaps the others were feeling the same way; and then I said: "It was in the cards, Willy. In the cards." Then I felt better, and I sensed a brightening all around, but there was nothing further to say, and nothing at all to do. Willy could not go to Elfrida and ask forgiveness, for he would not. His nature would not allow it; and he would have to fight his way past me to reach her. I could not renew my suit, for Willy would contest any move I made. Elfrida was, of course, immobilized in the rush of adverse wills, and still had her family to think of.

"I do not quite know my feelings," Elfrida said, after a time. "You both know what I can say. We have . . . come a long way together."

She waited politely for someone to speak; looked at each of us, and then said: "I have loved you both, truly. And I think I will survive. I think I will choose to survive." Then, carefully: "I must go to my duties." She turned away from us, and Willy lifted his right arm as if to stay her.

"Good luck," I said.

"Good luck!" Willy echoed, and lowered his arm gently.

She went to her family, gathered them with a word, and started walking again, toward the west. I noticed that she had the gait of the pregnant woman now, and was beginning to look heavy at the belly. She tilted her torso backward as she walked, balancing herself against the compact, uncertain weight of the future. The effect was stately. She had a noble stride, as all about her the children moved, skipping and bright, and the women somberly marched behind.

When she was perhaps a hundred yards away she turned and waved, and then continued on. Willy's child was going with her, and some sense of that unhappy fact caused him to say: "There goes the best wife a man ever had."

The figure began to lose its accidental qualities, and seemed only the figure of a woman, deep-bosomed and erect. "She's really just what I wanted," Willy said. "I've been in love with her all the time!"

"Well, so have I," I said. "But that's nothing."

The family receded in distance, dwindled from the view, and then vanished in the shade of poplars.

"Anybody would love her," I said. "Anybody that knew her."

A Note about the Author

EDWARD LOOMIS was born in 1924 in Newport News, Virginia, grew up in the Midwest and the West, and was drafted out of a California college (Deep Springs) into the army. After the war he went to college again, first to Western Reserve and then to Stanford University, where he became a Ph.D. He has been a college teacher of English since 1953, first at Stanford, then at the University of Arizona at Tucson, and is presently on the faculty of the University of California (Santa Barbara College). He is married to Ruth Fetzer, whom he has known since childhood; they have two daughters.

July 1960

A Note on the Type

THE TEXT of this book was set on the Linotype in Janson, a recutting made direct from the type cast from matrices long thought to have been made by Anton Janson, a Dutchman who was a practicing type-founder in Leipzig during the years 1668–1687. However, it has been conclusively demonstrated that these types are actually the work of Nicholas Kis (1650–1702), a Hungarian who learned his trade most probably from the master Dutch type-founder Dirk Voskens.

This book was composed, printed, and bound by KINGSPORT PRESS, INC., Kingsport, Tennessee. Paper manufactured by S. D. WARREN CO., Boston. Typography and binding design by VINCENT TORRE.